THE SWEETEST FRUITS

VIKING

ALSO BY MONIQUE TRUONG

The Book of Salt

Bitter in the Mouth

THE SWEETEST FRUITS

Monique Truong

VIKING

VIKING
An imprint of Penguin Random House LLC
penguinrandomhouse.com

Copyright © 2019 by Monique T. D. Truong
Penguin supports copyright. Copyright fuels creativity, encourages diverse voices,
promotes free speech, and creates a vibrant culture. Thank you for buying an authorized
edition of this book and for complying with copyright laws by not reproducing, scanning,
or distributing any part of it in any form without permission. You are supporting writers
and allowing Penguin to continue to publish books for every reader.

ISBN 9780735221017 (hardcover)
ISBN 9780735221031 (ebook)

Printed in Canada
1   3   5   7   9   10   8   6   4   2

Designed by Amanda Dewey

This is a work of fiction based on actual events.

for Damijan

Tell all the truth but tell it slant—

~EMILY DICKINSON

ELIZABETH BISLAND

(1861–1929)

. . . .

NEW YORK, 1906

Lafcadio Hearn was born on the twenty-seventh of June, in the year 1850. He was a native of the Ionian Isles, the place of his birth being the Island of Santa Maura, which is commonly called in modern Greek Levkas, or Lefcada, a corruption of the name of the old Leucadia, which was famous as the place of Sappho's self-destruction. . . . To this day it remains deeply wooded, and scantily populated, with sparse vineyards and olive groves clinging to the steep sides of the mountains overlooking the blue Ionian Sea. . . . This wild, bold background, swimming in the half-tropical blue of Greek sea and sky, against which the boy first discerned the vague outlines of his conscious life, seems to have silhouetted itself behind all his later memories and prepossessions, and through whatever dark or squalid scenes his wanderings led, his heart was always filled by dreams and longings for soaring outlines, and the blue. . . .

~Elizabeth Bisland's *The Life and Letters of Lafcadio Hearn*,
Volumes 1 and 2 (1906)

ROSA ANTONIA CASSIMATI

(1823–1882)

. . . .

IRISH SEA, 1854

Patricio Lafcadio Hearn was born hungry. I could tell by the way that he suckled. From the first time that his mouth found the nipple, he was not wont to let it go, his eyes opened and unblinking, watching and daring me to tug myself from him.

All babies were born with an empty stomach, but not all of them were born with such need in their eyes.

His elder brother, Giorgio, my first blessed one, had to be coaxed and tricked. The tip of my little finger dipped in honey was what he took first into his rosebud mouth. Then, patiently, I would guide him to my breast, where honey and milk would mix. This soothed him, but it was not enough to keep him. Giorgio shared my milk with Patricio for less than two months.

I beg of you do not call them "George" and "Patrick." Those are not their names. Their father's language is not mine.

Even before I was certain that there would be a blessed second, I suffered his appetite, which was growing in me swift and strong. Patricio demanded of me the small things from the sea. Whelks, which no one sold because the people on Santa Maura, same as on Cerigo, the island where I was born, would not buy something that they could gather like pebbles at the shore. In the mornings, I would leave my first with Old Iota, the only woman on our lane with no children of her own, in order to bend over the wet sand until I felt light-headed or until my basket was full. Patricio wanted the whelks boiled, their spiral of flesh removed one by one. He allowed me olive oil and lemon juice with them but never vinegar.

When there was no longer a doubt and whelks became too difficult for me to collect, Patricio insisted on cockles, of which there were sellers because cockles were found on the sandbars far from shore, where the tide came in like the hand of God.

To lose your life for mere cockles is a curse as old as the sea, and may you never hear it spoken.

Like his father, Patricio disliked garlic. He purged me of all foods, even the favored cockles, if they took on its flavor. I would whisper to him that these cloves were the pearls of the land, holding them close to my swollen belly so that he could become accustomed to their scent, but he was not to be convinced. He emptied and emptied me again until I was starving. I soon gave up on the hope of garlic and steamed the cockles open with a sliver of shallot instead. Patricio could not get enough of those briny creatures. It took buckets of them to fill us.

During the last months when we were one, Patricio confined us to sea urchins, their egg-yolk bodies scooped onto chunks of bread. Every day, to make sure that we had enough, Old Iota paid four boys to wade into the shallows at low tides, where these spiny orbs darkened the water like the shadows of gulls flying overhead. Fattened on this fare, day in and day out, I took on such weight that I could take only a few steps around the bed, an animal tied to a stake.

By then Charles—the father of Giorgio, Patricio, and soon, God willing, my blessed third—was already on another island, in waters so far away that I could not understand the distance between us. Before his ship set sail, Charles had told me the exact nautical miles between the islands of Santa Maura and Dominica, but a long string of numbers was as useless to me as the letters of an alphabet.

When I open my mouth, I can choose between two languages, Venetian and Romaic, but on paper I cannot decipher either one. When I was young, I had begged to join my elder brothers in their daily lessons, but my father refused. He said that if I ever left his house, I would enter into the House of God or the house of my husband. In either structure, there would be a man present to tell me what was written and what was important to know.

My father was not thinking about a man named Charles Bush Hearn from the island of Ireland when he told me my fate. My father was not a man of original thoughts. He repeated what came out of the mouths of other men, primarily those of nobility, minor like himself. He taught my two brothers to do the same. They all believed that this echoing made them wise and far wiser than me.

To be a daughter is another curse as old as the sea, and I was born hearing it.

Giorgio was six months in this world, and Patricio was five months in me, when Charles left us in Lefkada town, on Santa Maura Island, in the care of Old Iota. When I first met her, I could see that she was not really old. I recognized her as the woman who lived a few doorways down from mine. She and I had never traded words. If I were to be honest with God, I never traded words with any woman on that lane until my firstborn, Giorgio, had left it shrouded in myrtle leaves. After my saint of a boy, my shadow of a child departed before a full year of life, I wanted to blame God, to curse Him with all the profane words that I had heard my brothers use against Charles and me, but I did not. I needed Him to be there for Patricio.

Giorgio had been denied the Sacrament of Holy Baptism because of my sins. The Orthodox Church did not want his soul when he was born to me, and the Orthodox Church did not want his soul upon his leaving me. There could be no funeral service for Giorgio among the Icons, the censers, and the beeswax candles. No "Holy God, Holy Mighty, Holy Immortal, have mercy on us" intoned three times. No "Blessed are those whose way is blameless," which so rightly described my blessed first. No "With the Saints give rest, O Christ, the soul of your servant where there is no pain, nor sorrow, nor suffering, but life everlasting."

The full weight of what I had done broke me on that morning of sunlight and rain when I could not wake Giorgio from his sleep. I wanted to throw my worthless shards onto the cobblestones and let passersby grind them into dust with the heels of their shoes, but I had to gather them up for Patricio. I could not fail two sons. I did not know then that there would be a blessed third who, God willing, will be another son.

At the graveside, I held on to Patricio's sleeping body so tightly that Old Iota had to pull my arms apart so that he could breathe. There were three of us that afternoon, taking in air. The farmer, who had dug the small basin of dirt among his quince trees for an indecent price because he knew that it was there or the sea, refused to be present, as if hiding in his house meant that God would not see his greed. As sunlight poured down upon us, I knew in my heart that it was not God who had rejected my son. It was men who had rejected him. Perhaps that thought was another of my sins. Perhaps I added to my tally by intoning three times "Holy God, Holy Mighty, Holy Immortal, have mercy on us."

Old Iota sucked in her breath when she heard those words coming from my mouth. We both knew that at the graveside they belonged in the mouth of a priest. But what was I to do in the face of absence and silence? Giorgio was my child and a child of God. I knew both to be true. I listened to my heart that day, and it was a fist pounding with anger. My heart opened my mouth. My mouth pleaded, even if to no avail, for my blessed Giorgio.

Cradled in my arms, Patricio slept. He must have felt my body trembling when the farmer emerged at last from his house to shovel dirt, cleaner than himself, onto my blessed one. Patricio must have heard the summer soil crumbling as it hit the myrtle leaves and then the small wooden box beneath. It was the sound of a sudden downpour, and it made me look up at the sky. The date of Giorgio's passing, August 17, 1850, I have committed to memory, but it was this rain of dirt that marked when my blessed one was taken from me, when the distance separating his body from mine became eternal. Words and numbers could never do the same.

On our lane, the mothers—previously so close-lipped, their eyes hooded in judgment—felt pity toward me. They came to my front door, in twos and threes, with whole walnuts, hazelnuts, and almonds. In Lefkada town, these were offered for the remission of the sins of the recently departed. The custom was familiar to me, but their choice of offerings was not. Every night, I threw the walnuts, hazelnuts, and almonds away with the vegetable scraps. Every morning, Old Iota picked them out, wiped clean their hard shells, and stored them in a clean cloth sack. By the end of the first week, she had enough for months' worth of baking. She was practical in ways that I had yet to learn.

I asked Old Iota if she knew what these mothers—I did not say "mothers," I said "hags"—had said about her when she was not in the room.

Without looking up from the eggplant peelings and the to-mato seeds that her hands were searching through, Old Iota asked whether I knew that the walnuts, hazelnuts, and almonds were not for Giorgio's sins but for mine. "On Santa Maura Island," she said, "the hags bring sugared almonds when a baby passes."

The women had whispered to me—as if Old Iota did not know the details of her own life and might overhear them and learn something new—a story that began with a sixteen-year-old Iona, as she was called then, the only daughter of a widower who married her off to the eldest son of a farming family, a day's mule ride from Lefkada town.

Iona did not meet her husband until the day that they received the Sacrament of Marriage. In a house in the middle of a sea of olive trees, Iona then gave birth to five boys in six years, but none of them had a heart that would beat for more than a month, the last one not even a day.

How many dishes of sugared almonds did Iona discard before she understood that there would be another? The mothers on the nearby farms would continue to offer them, a custom of the Orthodox Church but with roots that were deeper, older, and more practical. These mothers with their work-worn hands were guiding Iona onto her back again, so that she could be one of them again. They told Iona to eat half of the sugared almonds, to let their sweetness spread over her tongue, and then feed the rest to her husband with her fingers. This made Iona blush. "Another baby will soon grace you," said these mothers. They said "grace" to cover up the animal acts that they wanted for her, and Iona did as she was told.

Iona's last born died within moments of opening his eyes and was not baptized before he took his last breath. Iona's husband left her and the body of this baby, who would always be lonely in Purgatory while his four elder brothers had one another's company in the Kingdom of Heaven, at the front door of her father's house. That was when Iona first met the quince farmer with the small graves hidden among his trees.

At the age of twenty-two, Iona had nothing. Upon her return to Lefkada town, her neighbors gave her a new name and a new age. Her cheeks caved. Her breasts sagged. Her hair streaked with white. The black dresses of widows became her habit, and Old Iota became her name.

When Charles hired Old Iota, she was twenty-eight, and I was twenty-six.

It was the sixteen-year-old Iona whom I thought of whenever I found myself staring at her. I searched her forehead, creased like a slept-in bedsheet, her hands knobbed and full of bones, and I wondered if she ever felt graced by her husband, whether sweetness ever spread from Iona's tongue down to the rest of her as well. Whenever I thought about the animal that she once was, I knew that I was missing Charles, not with my heart.

I could not write to my husband of my thoughts for him, so I saved them for Holy Confession at the Church of Santa

Paraskevi, where the Reverend Father would listen to my words until he stifled a moan.

Afterward, I intoned the Prayer of Repentance. Its last line, "Teach me both to desire and to do only what pleases You," was an honest plea. Then I closed my eyes and waited. In the darkness, the body I saw was not Charles's and certainly not the Reverend Father's, whose long beard was a bib for rusk crumbs and droplets of red wine. I saw the Son of God, His limbs gilded, His hair long and woman-like, His wounds displayed and unashamed. I had worshipped at His nailed feet since I was a young girl, and it was His body that I saw first among men. Without the image of the Crucifixion, how would I have known of a man's muscled thighs, his taut abdomen, and the mystery behind the cloth?

Elesa, you hesitated at "abdomen." Did your mother—may she rest in peace—never teach you this word in Venetian? You can write it down in English, if you need. Patricio will know what it means one day. Patricio will read it and not blush. Nor will God. Do you think that He will deny me the Kingdom of Heaven? You have heard only the beginning of my story. God has other reasons to deny me, my dear.

Pick up the pen. We are too far on the Irish Sea for you to change your mind now. An arrangement is an arrangement.

Did you make certain to bring enough nibs and bottles of ink, as I had asked? It is important that you write my every word. Patricio, I know, will want to find me one day, and I want him to know where to begin.

Charles and I received the Sacrament of Marriage within the small, windowless Santa Paraskevi, two months after Giorgio was born. We lit our marriage candles there. The Reverend Father bound our right hands together there. He placed crowns of fresh myrtle leaves upon our heads there. The Reverend Father was a short man of God, and Charles had to get onto his knees to receive his crown. The sight of this made me smile. Our witnesses were the landlord and a butcher.

Lefkada town was blessed with churches. I had hoped for the Church of Agios Spyridon with its high, round windows facing the town's Central Square or the Church of Pantokratoras with the delicate ironworks, like vines, over every window, but Charles chose Santa Paraskevi because the Reverend Father there was the only one who had said yes. The list of objections, which the Reverend Father ignored, included Charles's faith—the Church of Ireland, same as your father's, Elesa—may he rest in peace; Giorgio, who was asleep at home in the arms of Old Iota; and my blessed second, who unbeknownst to me was in the church with us that afternoon. Patricio, you must have been within me, because I was already craving the fruits of the sea.

That Reverend Father must be hard of hearing or blind, I had said to Charles when he told me of the arrangements. Charles replied that the only thing that the Reverend Father was afflicted with was poverty and a love for Holy Communion wine. Charles had sent over a barrel of kephaliako, a red wine that was considered Santa Maura Island's finest because it was not watered down, then another barrel, and another, until the Reverend Father had said yes.

After an early supper—Old Iota, who cooked for us, knew to leave out the usual head of garlic from the stifado, which was heavier than usual with beef, a nuptial gift from the butcher—Charles returned to the officers' quarters as he did every evening. The house was rented only for Giorgio and me. When my blessed one woke later that night, I fed him from the breast, and it ached. I took us into the kitchen, and there I saw the two myrtle crowns, the edges of their green leaves beginning to curl. I placed them both on my head. "I am wedded to myself," I said aloud. My voice startled me. My thought startled me more. I had never heard anyone say this before, but it sounded true to me. For the second time that day, I smiled.

Giorgio had fallen back to sleep, his lips still around the nipple but slacken, as if at the end of a kiss. The ache remained, and that should have meant that my days of blooming roses would soon be upon me again. But it was not to be because, Patricio, you were to be.

"Blooming roses" was a phrase of Old Iota's. I laughed when I first heard her whisper it. One husband, five sons—may her babies all rest in peace—and she still spoke as if she were a virgin.

You look like a plum, Elesa. Are you unwell?

Sit back down, my dear. I would not advise that you go on deck right now. During the first few days of a ship's voyage, you will find yourself slipping on vomit there. Do not make the novice traveler's mistake. "To take the air" on deck is another way of saying "to empty your dinner" on deck. In a while, you may ring for the steward, Elesa. A pot of tea and a plate of shortbread will settle both of our stomachs, but for now we will continue.

The roses first came to me when I was seventeen, I told Old Iota. From the beginning, they were accompanied by a moth trapped inside my skirt, its wings fluttering. When I asked Old Iota if it was the same for her, she hid her face with her hands. I had no mother, so I thought that I was dying. When I continued to live and to bloom, my father's disinterest in me turned into disgust or shame, for what I did not know. Soon that change would darken my life, a cloth over a birdcage.

My father began by forbidding my brothers from gathering their school friends at the house, not even to complete their lessons in the late afternoon shade of the courtyard. He paused, and he drew an even wider border. "Nor do I want them near the entrances of the Villa Cassimati," he declared. A "villa" was what my father insisted on calling the house, and to distinguish it from the neighbors', which were actual villas, he gave it his family name, as though it were another of his sons. My brothers nodded their heads in unison. They did not object because they now had a reason to be elsewhere. Their school friends had been some of the few visitors to the house. I would miss their faces more than I would miss my brothers'.

Next, my father denied me the half-light of the moon and the stars. The shutters to my bedroom windows were to be kept shut, day and night. "Especially at night," he restated. My brothers elbowed each other's ribs. That rough touch was a dagger in mine. It told me that they were privy, yet again, to something that I was not. It told me how alone I was in that house.

My father then forbade me from ever leaving the Villa Cassimati, not even to accompany Kanella, the cook, on her morning walks down to the marketplace in the center of Kapsali town. "But how will Kanella know what to buy?" I pleaded.

"There is nothing new there," my father said. By "there" my

father meant the marketplace, but he could have been speaking about all of Kapsali town or the whole of Cerigo Island. "Kanella will buy what she has always bought. She will cook what she has always cooked. We will eat as we have always eaten," he said, his eyes not once leaving the pages of his book, which even I could tell was always the same one. When my father was not an echo, he spoke in circles, a snake swallowing its tail.

For the next eight years, my father forbade me everything except for the Villa Cassimati and a church in the Fortezza. I could walk there with my eyes closed. Instead, I could walk there only when accompanied by my father or brothers on Sundays, Holy Days, and Pascha.

I would come to despise the house where I was born, even its courtyard with the orange bougainvilleas and the sprawling fig tree whose leaves broke the sunlight into pieces of gold. I resented most of all the birds that flocked to the tree when the figs were ripe. The fruits on the uppermost branches, the ones closest to the sun, were the most plump, but Kanella would not bother with them. "We have enough," she insisted, waving a hand back and forth in front of her face. "Let the birds have them," she said.

Kanella was from the countryside, and they all believed that this setting aside was required. Whether it was fruits of the arbors or of the vines, the peasants, as my father and brothers called them, always left some of the harvest as an offering to the birds. In return, the birds gathered and pecked, cawing their hunger and their gratitude. It never took these creatures long to cover the courtyard with their fallen feathers and their sticky pieces of flesh, which upon second glance were the pink insides of the ripened figs, torn apart by beaks and claws. The birds would then lift, a dark shawl picked up by the wind, and disappear.

I would watch them and cry. After the first year had passed and I understood that the birds were free and I was not, I began to collect their feathers. If I had enough, I could sew them onto my clothes and paste them onto my shoes. I was too stupid and dull at eighteen to dream of flying. I only wanted to wear my dress of drab feathers and lie down and die, a bird that had lost the battle for the sweetest fruits.

I did not know then that all women bled.

Do not write that down, Elesa.

On second thought, please do.

Patricio should know the body that God gave to women.

Kanella knew, but she did not tell me. She gave me the cloths. She had them laundered when they were soaked through. She shooed me into my bedroom whenever the back of my dresses showed their blooms. She gathered chamomiles on her daily walks and dried them for tea for when I bowed to the pain. What Kanella never did for me was what I needed most. She did not tell me that my father's house was not my prison. It was the body that God gave me that was my prison, and within that body there were both the lock and the key. Kanella knew.

On the morning of my twenty-fifth name day, Kanella informed me that from that day forward I could attend a service of the Daily Cycle at the church in the Fortezza. She specified the Third Hour service, which began at nine in the morning, when Pontius Pilate handed down his judgment against Christ.

I was taken aback by what she was saying to me. My father and brothers were never at home in the mornings, which Kanella, of course, knew.

"But who would accompany me?" I asked her.

"You can walk there on your own," Kanella replied. "Your father has given his consent."

I stood before her, my mouth agape at the thought of the front doors of my father's house opening and my body, alone, slipping through.

Kanella looked at me, her face an empty plate.

I understood so little about Kanella then. It had not occurred to me that she understood everything about me. Kanella was not an old woman. With her olive-oil-smooth cheeks, she was not an ugly woman. She cooked everyday dishes that were beautiful on our tongues, especially my father's. I knew these things about her, but I did not know what they, taken together, would mean for me.

As my father told me it would be, I began the journey from his house to His house. So near to each other, via the street of villas, that four bites of an apple would bring me from one set of doors to the other, but what I saw, smelled, and heard during those solitary crossings would free me from the feathers and from a life of waiting for more of them to fall.

At midmorning, the aromas, which hung like damp laundry over the street of villas, were the same as those coming from Kanella's kitchen. Onions and olive oil. The whole island by noon was a pan of sweet onions melting. The midday meals of all Cerigotes began with those two ingredients. When I told this to Old Iota, she said that the onions and oil made Cerigo seem real to her. She often looked at me wide-eyed whenever I would tell her about my island of birth. She looked at me with envy too. Old Iota thought it was brave that I had boarded a ship and sailed away from my family and the rocky soil where their bodies would one day lie. She knew the reason why I had to leave Cerigo. She insisted that I was brave nonetheless. She had never traveled afar. She did not know how easy it could be to leave, how cowards always depart.

The street of villas also gathered all the aromas that followed the onions and the oil. The thyme and laurel of Kanella's kitchen, the tomatoes of Villa Lazaretti, the wine of Villa Venieri. Lamb, fish, or cuts of beef would then follow. No one in those villas of nobles, minor and otherwise, went hungry.

"We trace our bloodlines to the Republic of Venice" was what my father reminded my brothers whenever he heard them "corrupting" their speech with Romaic, the language of the countryside, of the interior lands, and of those who smelled onions and oil and knew that there would be nothing else to add to their pans. "We speak the language of our forefathers," my father commanded, and my brothers followed.

Kanella understood Venetian, but mostly she spoke Romaic. I did not know that they were two separate languages as I learned them both during my first years of life. When they untwined themselves, they became the language of the rich and the language of the poor. I grew up with both because I grew up with Kanella as my caretaker. According to my brothers, the house was full of servants when our mother was alive. These servants were let go, one by one, until Kanella became the only. Except for the cook, his sons, and me, my father rid the Villa Cassimati of all the bodies that reminded him of his young wife and of her once bustling household. Death caused most men to grieve. Death caused my father to feel anger at the one who had departed and the one who had stayed. When my brothers were feeling very cruel, they would tell me that a fever ended our mother's life but that my birth had weakened her first.

When my brothers were still wetting their beds, they sometimes spoke about our mother. They did this in front of me in the same way that they would later read aloud to each other in front of me, boasting and prideful, knowing that I had no way to join them. They said the following about our mother—when they said "our," they meant the two of them. She had long black hair. She was beautiful. She was sad. She often hugged them, but sometimes she would slap them with great force and without cause. She sang the same lullaby to them every night until they fell asleep, but they claimed that they had no memory of its melody or its lyrics. My brothers, for all I know, were telling each other lies.

What I wanted to know was the scent of my mother's hair. I hoped it was lavender water, as it eased my temples when they throbbed. I wanted to know the color of her eyes. I hoped that they were dark brown and ringed with green, like mine. I wanted to hear her voice, the exhale of her breath.

What will my blessed second remember about me?

Patricio, if you are reading this, you must be a bird.

If my blessed third is a boy—please bring him to me, God, not upon the waters of these seas but let him wait until we reach Santa Maura, the island where his brothers were born— he must be a bird as well. For them, I must imagine flight.

During my years inside, I had imagined nothing—I woke, I ate, I slept—and my words began to dull and fade. Once they came back to me again, it was as if I were learning their meanings for the very first time. There was the joy of "sunlight," uninterrupted by leaves and petals. The rays that fell between my father's house and the church in the Fortezza were sharp needles, pushing themselves into the cloth of my dress and the straw of my bonnet. There was the joy of my own "breath," my own "pace," my own "body." There was the joy of the "bells" of the church beginning to toll, joined moments later by those in the center of Kapsali town. The thick walls of my father's house had dampened even them. I could feel their ringing with my whole body again, and it felt as if I were surrounded by a back-and-forth sea.

When I was very young, a pair of hands had dipped my body into the Ionian, let me go, and then pulled me back again. I remember these movements repeated, perhaps many times. I remember that I was left to drift toward the rocks. I remember that I was always just an arm's length away. I was being taught to swim, I tell myself. I was not being given to the sea. In truth, only the pull of the currents and the opposing strength of the hands have stayed with me with any certainty. I believe this to be a memory of my mother. I never shared it with my brothers because they would have taken her away from me. I believe the memory to be true because those hands were stronger than the sea.

Patricio, I wish I could have given you the Ionian. After Giorgio went to God, I had thought about bringing you, my blessed second, down to the shore, but Old Iota had worried. She thought that I was still too weak. "Your grieving arms versus the currents?" she scoffed.

She was right. I was weak. I could barely tug you from the nipple.

I cannot undo what has been done nor can I do what has never been done. The sea that you have never touched will wait for you, as you will wait for it, Patricio.

I sound like my father when I say such things. Perhaps I am the snake swallowing its tail now.

I was twenty-five years old when I was allowed the Third Hour service at the church in the Fortezza, but I was as ignorant as a girl of seventeen, the age when I was first confined.

There is no need to furrow your brow, Elesa. I am aware of your age, but you at seventeen are not ignorant. You can read and you can write. You are blessed, despite your recent circumstances. With your alphabet, you are feathered for flight. Yes, do smile. That thought is deserving of one.

I was ignorant, but I was not unchanged.

My body had burst the seams of my girlish dresses. Their hems were let down, darts and smocking details undone, and scraps of fabric and ribbon were added to lengthen the sleeves and loosen the necklines. These make-do alterations would have continued but for Kanella, who informed me that, also with my father's consent, I would be receiving additions to my wardrobe. Though she did not say it, I understood that I was being dressed for God. Seamstresses came to the Villa Cassimati and measured me for three day dresses and a fourth with pale gray lace around its high neckline for the Holy Days and Pascha. I was also provided with a corset, six petticoats, and five chemises. A straw bonnet was also added to the order.

The first seamstress who came to the house sobbed upon seeing me. Kanella was as surprised as I was by the woman's outburst. "Sióreta Cassimati looks like . . . looks like . . . a twin of her mother," the seamstress managed to say between her gasps and gulps. I heard Kanella shushing her as the woman was being led toward the back door of the house. Kanella returned and found me in the courtyard lying under the fig tree, my body curled around its trunk like a maggot. I had never heard anyone, except for my brothers, speak a word about our mother. I do not even know, to this day, my mother's given name.

Elesa, I can see it in your shoulders, as if someone has pulled them up by a rope. You want to interrupt me, as Old Iota had done, when I told her this story.

"Where was your mother's family?" was what Old Iota had wanted to know. To all of her questions about the maternal side of my family, I had replied "Malta." I knew it to be the name of an island where my mother was born and where her people remained. I did not know much more. I said "Malta" the way other people said "death." Both meant a breach. Whenever Old Iota heard "Malta," she made the sign of the cross three times, as if protecting herself from a curse.

Old Iota then shared with me that, after the passing of each of her sons, she had curled her body around the trees on her husband's farm. The older the olive tree, the more gnarled its trunk, the longer it had survived in such poor soil, the more she wanted to encircle her body, emptied and slight, around it.

We will see Malta before the end of our voyage, Elesa. Once we cross the Irish Sea, we will dock in Liverpool for several days. Then the ship will embark on the long southern crossing for Malta, where we will dock again.

On the voyage out—Patricio, you will not remember that journey because you were only two years old at the time—I learned that we passengers were not the cargo of worth on a Dublin-bound ship. The barrels of red wine and dried currants were. I do not know what goods from Dublin or Liverpool will be making this return journey with us. Rifles, parasols, and saddle soaps, I would think.

After Malta, depending on the prevailing winds, Santa Maura Island will be only a few days away.

Elesa, I know you have no memory of Santa Maura, but you will recognize it the moment you see it on the horizon. Your mother was born there, so you already know it in your blood and bones, its outline clearer to you than any map. When Patricio makes this voyage one day, it will be the same for him when he continues southward. "Cerigo," he will say. "Mother" is what he will mean.

We are still weeks away. You will have time to prepare, Elesa. We both will have plenty of time.

First thing I will do is find Old Iota. She will weep when she sees that Patricio is not with me. She will think that he has gone to God, as his elder brother had. I will show her the calotype of him to assure her that he is alive. She will not understand the image on that piece of paper at first, as I had not when Patricio's grandaunt had given it to me as a departing gift. But Old Iota will learn to see the image for what it is. A little boy, with his father's large round eyes and caterpillar eyebrows and his mother's head of dark waves, who at the age of four is standing sturdy, staring straight ahead, as if to say, "Life, I await you."

I will have no difficulties locating Old Iota. Everyone knows her and her story in Lefkada town. Her grief is her twin wherever she goes. It grips onto her hand. It clings onto her neck and her stooped back. She is, in this way, never alone. Born of grief, loss, tragedy or shame, such companions often follow the bodies of women. Men shrug theirs off by traveling afar, strangling them in foreign fields or drowning them in deeper waters.

On the ship from Cerigo to Santa Maura, Charles taught me the English word "gossip." He told me that in our life together I must ignore gossip and avoid trading in it at all cost. I understood later that by gossip he meant these twins. He said that the inhabitants of my island, and of Santa Maura, indulged in gossip as if they were girls weak for sweets. "They will all sink under the weight of it," he declared in his stilted, often unrecognizable Venetian.

Charles was fond of declaring. Perhaps he too was an echoer. He certainly has become a snake.

When my brothers returned from their university years in Padova, they began calling the British "the Occupiers." They would call Charles, an officer and a surgeon in the British Army, something much worse.

When Old Iota wanted to know more about my father's family, I had told her that it was as small as his heart. It was God's will that his own father and mother were long passed by the time their three grandchildren were born. My father, their only son, inherited the house above Kapsali town, the farmland in the interior of the island, and whatever else kept food on our table and my mother and then Kanella by his side.

By and by, I understood that Kanella was a very good cook but that she was an even better broker of my father's consent. Long before my years inside, Kanella's household duties had been reduced to those of the kitchen. She still walked down to the marketplace every morning, but on the way back a porter was with her. The foodstuffs were not any heavier. Kanella was just no longer a beast of burden. She also had two women who came every morning to sweep, dust, launder, and assume the chores that had once been hers. These women, who only spoke Romaic and only spoke to Kanella, came to the house during the hours when my father was in the belly of Kapsali town conducting the business of owning what he referred to as the Cassimati Estate. I should have known that "estate" was a bloated term, same as "villa," same as "nobility." There were tracts of land, but they were shrinking with each passing year, sold to cover expenses that I dimly understood then. For instance, where was Padova; what was a university; and why had my brothers returned from these locales so changed in clothing and in manners but more like my father than ever before?

After I met Charles, or "Assistant Staff Surgeon Charles Bush Hearn," as he had introduced himself, he answered these questions and many others for me. His knowledge of the everyday mysteries of my own family and my own island impressed me. He offered me unfamiliar words for familiar things. I had never even heard of the "United States of the Ionian Islands" before him. "Where is that?" I asked him. To his credit, he did not laugh or deride me for my ignorance. That would come later.

"Where is *here*, Sióreta Cassimati," he replied, sweeping his arms around him. "You, Sióreta, are an Ionian Islander under the amical protection of the United Kingdom," he added, bowing his head in my direction. He listed these islands for me, slowly, as though he were pausing to consider whether their names befitted them. He began with Cerigo, which he said was a far distance from the others and the farthest one south.

Corfu

Paxos

Cephalonia
Zanté
Ithaca
Santa Maura

Charles could have been naming the distant stars. These islands did not exist for me until that very moment, when he brought them into being with his breath.

Patricio, do you remember how the creatures and the objects of your first years of life came into being once I named them for you? Remember when a boat was not yet a "boat," a bee was not yet a "bee," a cup not a "cup" until I taught you their names? Remember how your eyes opened wide, as if I were the one who created the boat, the bee, the cup? That was how I must have looked at Charles back then. Your father's language has given you other words and names now, but I gave you the first ones. Remember, Patricio, your tongue grew nimble mimicking the sound of my voice.

I was not a young woman when I met Charles Bush Hearn. I was an old maid. At twenty-five years old, the next roof over my head would have been a convent's. I was being dressed not for God but for His Son.

Kanella did not tell me my fate. The two women who worked for her told it to each other, as they scrubbed the tile floors of the Villa Cassimati on their hands and knees.

I should have been at the Third Hour service that morning, but I awoke late to find roses in my bed. I got up to call for Kanella, but when I opened my bedroom door I heard the women's laughter and then their words, both being traded without restraint as they must have thought that the house had no ears but their own. I did not recognize the story they were telling as my own, at first.

"The rich are heartless," a voice, smooth as the tile floor, asserted.

"Well, you know what they say. The poorer you are, the bigger your heart!" a voice, coarse as the bristles of a scrub brush, declared.

Laughter.

"My heart is the size of a honeydew."

"My husband's heart is the size of a watermelon!"

Laughter.

"Her father's heart is an olive pit."

"A lemon pip!"

Laughter.

"They say there have been offers, but he does not want to pay her dowry."

"You mean his cook does not want him to pay!"

Laughter.

"You know what they say about the cook?"

"She cooks best with her clothes off!"

Laughter.

"The cook has it all figured out."

"The cook found the only Bridegroom who does not ask for a dowry!"

Laughter.

"Rich father. Poor daughter."

"Heartless!"

I stood in the doorway waiting. I heard only the scraping of the bristles against the tiles. The sound of their labor, uninterrupted by mirth, told me how pitiful the last line of my story was to them.

I tried to recall what these two women looked like; how old they were; whether I had ever been told their names. I could recall nothing about them except that one was taller than the other. They were faceless to me. How was I not faceless to them?

I went back to my bed of roses and closed my eyes. When Kanella returned from her morning errands, my fate tellers were gone, and the house smelled of lye and thyme. I was dreaming of St. Catherine of Alexandria. She had visions of the Mother of God and the Divine Child, who in His infancy had accepted Catherine as His pure bride. As His betrothed, her faith grew stronger. Her defense of her faith grew stronger as well. The Roman Emperor beheaded Catherine for both crimes. The Angels then took her body up to the Mount, where it was later found, perfumed and invested with miracles.

"You are twenty-five," intoned St. Catherine, as she unlocked the heavy doors of a convent. Inside, there were cages, not of birds but of roses.

"You are twenty-five," repeated the voice, but it was Kanella's, as she lifted up my bedcovers. "You are too old to allow this to happen. Mark out the days and learn to foretell," she scolded. She left the room and returned with a change of bed linens. As she stripped the sheets, I stood by the shuttered windows watching her work. My words had left me again. In their place was the hymn to St. Catherine, "Let us praise the most auspicious bride of Christ. . . ."

Kanella was right. I was too old. I had to learn to foretell.

The following morning, I saw Charles for the first time. I

was certain that God gave him to me, so I loved him upon first sight.

Even at nine in the morning, the church in the Fortezza was full of shadows. Lit by candles that gave off more smoke than light, the air inside was heavy with beeswax and incense. I thought of this weight as the breath of God. I breathed it in, deeper and deeper, until I felt light-headed, until I was a dust mote, floating. I saw miracles that morning that I have not told to another soul. I saw the Icons blinking, first St. John of Chrysostom and then St. Basil. I saw the Theotokos—you know her as the Mother of God, Patricio—nodding off to sleep and waking with a start, jostling the sleepy-eyed Divine Child upon her lap. I witnessed Jesus on the Cross sneezing sound-lessly. This made me weep for him more than the sight of his wounds. I longed to cover his bare shoulders with a shawl and to cup his cold feet in my hands.

Elesa, we will never finish if you continue to lay down your pen. You do not have to believe me in order to write what I say. Believing me is not part of our arrangement. Patricio will be-lieve me. He is the only one who must.

In the Orthodox Church, Patricio, we do not have pews. We stand in the nave for services, the women and girls on the left side and the men and boys on the right. The curls of smoke from the censers were forming lace doves, which hovered near the Holy Altar as they often do, but that morning a dove broke from the flock and flew toward the far right edge of the nave. My eyes followed, and the dove took me to the face of a young man with large round eyes, thick curved brows, and a head of brown curls swept to one side of his forehead. His face was pleasing but so pale that I thought that he was frightened. I

wanted to see the rest of him, but I caught only the red jacket
of his uniform as he turned and departed through the front
doors of the Church. Connected by a thin, strong rope, his
body pulled mine out of those same doors. My legs were certain of what they had to do. They followed Red.

I had never left in midservice before. I had never even considered it as a possible act. Like flight, to leave—Where would
I go?—was beyond the borders of my thoughts. I was breathless
that morning because I knew that I would do it again.

Red was walking toward the center of Kapsali town, his
strides long and purposeful. He was already past the Villa Venieri
when I closed the church doors behind me. I would not be able to
follow him, if he went much farther. I broke into a run, something that I had not done since I was a little girl. The road sloped
downward and I reached him faster than I thought I would. He
stopped and turned toward me. My legs, removed by the Angels,
disappeared, and the rest of my body fell into a heap of flesh and
fabric. A cry came from me, more out of surprise than pain.

"Sióreta, Sióreta?" he inquired, as he knelt down beside me.

I hid my face in my hands. Where are the Angels now? I
wanted to know.

The Angels knew that they were no longer needed. My silence was enough.

Red thought that I was in too much pain to speak. He picked
me up in his arms and began to carry me back toward the
church in the Fortezza. I peeked through my fingers and thought
this would not do. We will be seen. "Please, over there," I said,
my voice barely above a whisper. He leaned his head into mine.
I dropped my hands, and we were face-to-face, his breath on my
cheeks. I pointed him toward a narrow path, which led behind

the Villa Venieri and wound its way along the high walls of the adjacent villa. There the path opened onto a spit of land with a view of the Ionian Sea. Long ago someone had placed a bench, painted a middling blue, facing whatever color the water was that day. The view was unremarkable. Who on this island had not seen the sea? The bench served no purpose, except to prevent someone from walking off the overlook on a moonless night. Unfrequented and shade bare, the bench's only witness was the Ionian. The Angels took my legs, but they had given me foresight.

Cradling me in his arms, Red sat down on the bench.

Keeping my voice low in order to keep his breath on my cheeks, I whispered, "I am hurt."

He asked if I was in pain.

I answered with my given name.

He asked if my ankles had given way.

I told him my family name.

He asked if he could lift the hem of my dress past my low boots.

I told him my age.

He assured me that he was a surgeon.

I told him that I was unmarried.

He undid my bootlaces.

I hid my face. I did not want him to see me smile.

He pressed his fingers gently around my bared ankles.

I sighed into my hands.

He slid me from his lap and placed me next to him on the bench. He asked if I would take my hands from my face. I did and I pressed it into the red of his sleeve instead. He laughed low and said, "Sióreta, Sióreta . . ."

We continued in this manner until the church bells began to chime again. We had repeated ourselves often because his Venetian was a shadow language. I understood the general shape of what he wanted to say but not the finer details.

When I told him that I had to return home, he asked when he could see me again.

"Tomorrow, here, at nine," I answered.

He laughed low again and said, "Sióreta, Sióreta . . ."

Before I left, he kissed my hands, first the left and then the right. I felt the kisses on my ankles, as if his lips had touched me there.

Charles called me "Sióreta Cassimati" until the day he kissed me on the lips. I would say until the day I allowed him to kiss me on the lips, but I do not see the reason to tell an untruth.

Elesa, one day you will hear "kiss" and not suffer that flush of shame on your face. It is all the acts that follow a kiss that you must guard yourself against until matrimony. On Santa Maura I know you will be welcomed into a family of women. Your mother had told me that she was the youngest of eight sisters, but these women will not tell you what I will. Consider this ship your Padova, Elesa.

Put down your pen, my dear. What I will tell you now is for your ears only. Your mother, if she were alive, would want you to know the ways of men. Patricio will not need me to teach him. He will learn all of this in due time.

After the kiss, I was "Cara Rosa, Cara Rosa." Charles always said it twice. He told me that it was the most beautiful couplet he had ever written. I asked him what a "couplet" was.

Our courtship followed a simple routine. We met on that bench every morning, except for Saturdays and Sundays, at the hour of nine. Then we met less often, but at the same hour, near the stables in the Fortezza in a small room where the shelves were lined with saddle soaps, chamois cloths, and brushes. The door to this room had a lock and Charles the key.

The first morning Charles took me to that room it was raining. He had waited by the Villa Venieri and signaled for me to follow him back up the street of villas and into the Fortezza via a side entrance that I had never used before. Our courtship on the bench was only in its second week, but I trusted him entirely. I trusted that to follow him was better than standing in the rain, in the church, or in the courtyard of the Villa Cassimati, staring up at the birds. Charles walked quickly, but I could not. I needed to keep a distance between us. My umbrella hid my face but could not hide that I was a woman.

Once in the Fortezza, we passed an area where there was a group of Cerigote washerwomen. Their manner of dress—loose tunics slipped over their heads and tucked into their full skirts—differed from my own, which, according to the seamstress, was "in the mode of the young ladies of Venice." I could not even feign that I was one of them, if I were to be questioned. The downpour that morning had the washerwomen rushing to and fro, removing the last of the Occupiers' laundry from the lines. They were far too busy to pay me any attention, I thought. I did not care about the British soldiers seeing me. Cerigote eyes and Cerigote mouths were what I knew I had to avoid.

When Charles reached his destination, he turned his head to make certain that I would know where to go. Then he unlocked the door, went inside, and waited. I walked toward that entryway with purpose and certainty but without haste.

Write *that* down, Elesa. Here, let me repeat it.

I walked toward that entryway with purpose and certainty but without haste. That is what fate feels like, Patricio. You cannot stop your movement forward, but your heart is calm, your steps are steady, and your mind is clear of questions and doubts. Fate took me to the man who would become your father, and now fate has taken me away from you, my blessed second. Doors open and doors close, and we must be prepared to enter or leave.

Patricio does not need to know what followed, Elesa.

Before I could knock, the smell of horses and men rushed out of the opening door, and I slipped in. My dress was drenched from the bottom up, the hems of the skirt and petticoats soaked through. Charles lifted me up by the small of my waist, seated me on a wooden table, and repeated an act from our first meeting. He unlaced my boots.

The next morning, the sun shone, and we met again at the bench on the overlook. Charles could not let go of my hands, but he found it difficult to meet my eyes. After a long silence, he asked if I was in pain.

"Yes."

"Cara Rosa, Cara Rosa, do you have regrets?"

"No."

After another long silence, he asked, "Will you meet me *there*, again?"

"When?" I asked him.

I was spare with my words when I was with Charles, as the fewer that I used, the better we understood each other.

Charles, with hand movements and a small sketch of the island, said that he was being sent to the northern tip of Cerigo and would not be able to meet me again for a fortnight. We then agreed to meet at the room near the stables upon his return, rain or shine.

The following week brought with it steady rain. I resumed my mornings at the Third Hour service. I prayed that God had not taken Charles away from me. I looked for signs of his promised return. I looked for lace doves and sleeping saints. I found nothing in the church in the Fortezza except the smell of rising damp and rotten teeth. On either side of me were low-hanging stomachs and descended bosoms. Around me was what I would become. I prayed for rain on our appointed day because rain or rather my umbrella would hide me again. Then the Angels visited me, and I prayed for full sun instead. "The more Cerigote eyes who witness you in the Fortezza, the better," the Angels counseled. "You want to stay in your father's house?" they wondered. "You want to marry the Son of God?" they taunted. "He already has brides all over these islands," they said.

The number of Angels is not important, Elesa. Is that what you have been sitting there wondering about all this time? If you must know, there were three, but I never saw them. I only heard their voices.

My mind was raw and bruised with worry. By the end of the first week, I could not remember Charles's family name. I could not remember his full rank. Did he tell me he was a surgeon? I took out the calling card that he had given me, and I stared at the words, begging them to tell me what they knew. They refused, as always.

God heard my prayers though. All of them.

Charles returned. The sun shone. We met in the room near the stables. We met there again in the weeks to come.

I was soon glowing, my skin stretched with what I thought was happiness. Kanella noticed my appearance and so did Charles. Both of them knew before I did.

I was craving spoon sweets. I ate jars of them. Cherries were my favorite. The whole soft fruits, dripping their dark syrup, made me sigh. Giorgio, already within me, preferred the small fruits of the land.

When I saw Kanella for the last time, she would tell me that she had been counting the days, as she wanted to be absolutely certain before she told my father. She never had the chance. Other Cerigote eyes and mouths had done it for her, just as I had prayed.

Charles had stammered and blushed when he asked about my "menses," which was a word that had no meaning to me. He posed his question a different way by inquiring when I had last worn "guard-napkins." He sounded confused. Did he think that I was a soldier? Perhaps they needed these items in order to eat. I asked if he was feeling feverish. I thought he might have caught an illness during his frequent trips to the north.

As it often happened between us, Charles and I agreed not to understand each other. I shrugged and smiled, and his questions went unanswered, as though he had never asked them. I finished tying the ribbon of my bonnet, and he kissed me good-bye. My departure from the room near the stables was always first and on my own. I opened the door, and I smelled them. Vinegar and the center of bones. That was what their rage smelled like to me.

My brothers pushed me aside and rushed into the room of animal smells, less pungent than their own. They kicked the door closed behind them. They shouted from within. They made the loud sounds of men angered and dishonored. The washerwomen were now gathered by the door. One of them looked directly at me and told the others that I was "the poor daughter." A taller woman next to her repeated the words, as if saying them a second time made them truer. I recognized their voices. They were the floor scrubbers, the fate tellers, the Cerigote eyes and Cerigote mouths that, as the Angels had promised, would free me.

The Angels then feared for my life. They said that men often released their unspent fury upon women. They said my brothers were these kind of men. They told me to run and hide. Red will find you, the Angels promised.

I ran to the overlook and to the bench. I sat there until the sun was directly above me. I heard footsteps, and I heard my name, spoken by a voice as flat as the sea that day. I turned and saw Kanella's face. There was no arched brow of surprise, no outraged fire in her eyes, and certainly no tears. How did she know that I would be here? I asked the Angels.

Kanella has an eye for detail, the Angels replied. The chips of middling blue paint on the back of your dress told her where to find you months ago, they said.

Kanella placed a jug of water and a warm loaf of bread beside me on the bench and said that I should eat in my condition. She dropped a small cloth bag onto my lap and said to save these dried sultanas for my breakfast. "You will be sleeping here tonight," she said. "Your father will not allow me to pack a valise for you. You will need new clothes soon anyway. Your surgeon will come for you tomorrow. He cannot remain at the Fortezza after the din that your brothers caused this morning. They are now telling anyone who will listen in Kapsali town that they stabbed him and that he is fighting for his life in some mountain cave. Those two could not stab a spitted lamb. They cannot hurt a man, but they will kill you, Rosa."

The Angels whispered in my ear, and I repeated their accusation. "You tried to kill me first."

"Ungrateful girl," Kanella replied. She knew exactly what the Angels meant. "You think a convent would not be living? Having no man but God to tell you what to do is not a life? You will see."

You will see.

That is how the old curse the young, Elesa.

Before Kanella walked away, she untied her shawl, the color of ripened wheat with a fringe of carnation pink, and left it on the back of the bench. "It belonged to your mother," she said.

I drank the water that Kanella had brought me. I ate the bread that she had baked for my family that morning. When the sun went down, I draped the shawl over my shoulders, and I slept soundly under the light of the moon and the stars. When I awoke with the sunrise, I could not remember what my father looked like, how old my brothers were, their given names, where the family house was located. My prayers were answered yet again.

I sat up when I heard footsteps and "Cara Rosa" spoken twice.

Charles had not been stabbed. He had no injuries whatsoever. He looked refreshed, as if he had slept in his own bed last night, as if he had begun the day with a full breakfast and a warming cup of tea. Charles slipped English words into his speech whenever he became agitated, and that morning many of his words were in this language. "Fortuitously, the arrangement for my departure had been in the works for months now," he began. I asked him what "fortuitously" meant.

Charles was being transferred to the Fort of Santa Maura, on the northernmost of the Ionian Islands, and he would sail there the following week. I would remain in Kapsali town until he could make the arrangements for me to join him. Sióra Gazi, a special friend of the British commander, would take excellent care of me—Charles lowered his voice at this point as though the sea would overhear him—given my condition.

I pieced together much of this conversation afterward, with the help of Sióra Gazi, who was not a friend but the mistress of the British commander. Before Charles walked me down to her seaside villa, I threw my mother's shawl off the edge of the overlook. It had Kanella's scent all over it. Onions and oil.

What I felt for Charles in those days must have been love because I did not fault him, not even after Sióra Gazi informed me that he had known for many weeks about his transfer to Santa Maura. She said that, given my condition, he should have arranged for my travel prior to the fracas with my brothers. She puffed on a thin cigar and blew out the smoke, which for a moment fogged the star-filled sky above us. We were sitting on her terrace, and the Ionian Sea was spread before us and within it was a bobbing half-moon. As she took another puff, I asked her, "Sióra Gazi, what is my condition?"

Charles did not sail for Santa Maura for another three months, nor did I, as we would depart on the same vessel. The delay, according to the Sióra, was due to a malarial outbreak on that island. The British commander was unwilling to transfer his men there before the all clear was given. By then I was two months from giving birth. Sióra Gazi said that she could tell from the position of my belly.

The months, unexpected and unplanned, that I would live with the Sióra were my Padova, my university, Elesa.

The Sióra spoke a throaty but refined Venetian and had fluency also in the English language, but she claimed that language was unnecessary for women like us. "Men do not look to us for our words," she said. "They look to us for the body that God gave us. You can be fluent with your body, Rosa, and it will serve you equally well." Then she showed me how.

The tip of the tongue, the lick of the lips, the downward-cast eyes, the flicker of the lashes, the tuck of a strand of hair, the breath sharply inhaled, the breath slowly released, the shoulders shrugged, the bosom jutted, the bosom covered by modest hands, the hands trembling, the hands steady, the body walking away, the head turning back, the blush of the cheeks, the blush of the neck, the blush of what he cannot yet see.

Sióra Gazi often laughed when she taught me these wordless confessions and denials. The Angels murmured their approval, as she continued the lessons that they had in haste begun on the morning when God had given me Charles.

I also learned how to laugh out loud, which the Sióra said could be a woman's charm but must be used sparingly. Rein it in, allow it to slip forth at the last moment, like the skin beneath a corset.

She assured me that with these gestures, learned and practiced, my body would be understood by any man.

"Any man?" I repeated. A man other than Charles was a thought that had not entered my head.

"Yes, Rosa, *any* man," the Sióra replied. "Your body is your way out or your way in. For now, your unborn child has made that decision for you, but you must not forget that Charles is but one man. If you believe him to be the one and only—only God is the One and Only, Rosa—then your body belongs to him. If you believe him to be one of any, then your body remains your own.

"A woman's body is God's creation," the Sióra continued. "Men will try to shame you with the story of Eve," she warned, "and tell you that as Eve's daughter you have sinned. These are words spoken by men who are afraid or who covet what they do not possess. There are women who will say these words to you as well, and they do so for the same reasons, Rosa."

I could not write down the Sióra's words as you could, Elesa. I committed them to memory instead. No man had to teach me that skill nor could he keep it from me. Memory belongs to us all, man or woman. We are all the children of God, the Sióra said. We are all beloved in His eyes, she assured me.

When Charles and I arrived in Lefkada town, he reported to the Fort of Santa Maura, and I stayed in a rented room above a butcher shop near the Central Square. The butcher and the butcher's wife were the first Lefkadans whom I would meet. He spoke Venetian, albeit in a form that was a bit unusual to my ears, and Romaic, and she only the latter. We understood one another. I understood them so well that I soon despised them both. The room came with two meals a day, brought up by the wife. She smelled of flowers that had sat in a vase for too long or rather she smelled of the murky water that these flowers sat in. Her husband carried with him the odor of unwashed feet and rising yeast. Each of their five children had their own scent as well. I had not met them, but I could smell them whenever they came into their father's shop. There was Horse Dung, Warm Milk, Fish Guts, Burnt Olive Wood, and Geranium Leaves.

My blessed first did that to me. Patricio, you in turn would do the same. My blessed third, within me now, has cursed me of late with the opposite, a nose that cannot even smell the sea that surrounds us.

When you and I first met, Elesa, your mourning dress had carried with it your mother's scent. I knew that the garment must have belonged to her. I wondered whether the lavender water that clung to it soothed you as much as it soothed me.

But now I can no longer locate the scent of her on you, Elesa.

I can see you, and in you I can see her. But in grief and in loss, I have found that the eyes are not enough. They can see cloth. They can see skin. They cannot bring a body back to you the way that a scent can.

In the room above the butcher shop, I closed the windows to keep out the odors of Lefkada town. The blood smells of the butcher shop I could not keep out. They seeped up from below. I tied a handkerchief moistened with lavender water around my neck, like a bib, in order to lessen the stench.

My blessed first had brought with him other changes as well. My ankles were lost in a stocking of fat and skin. My nose was a plump shallot bulb. My earlobes lengthened. My fingers and toes thickened. My hair fell out in clumps. I had discarded my corset months ago. In Lefkada town, I was covering my swollen bosom and rounded belly with a shawl that Sióra Gazi had given me as a farewell gift. She chose one that was also the color of ripened wheat but with a fringe of midnight black. When the butcher's wife delivered my meals, she made it a point to ask if I was warm enough. With all the windows shut, the room was stifling and hot, and she knew it.

The wife's evening meals were forgettable and included surprisingly little meat, but worst were the breakfasts, which every day were exactly the same. A dish of yogurt, two rusks, and a small bowl of quince spoon sweets. I was already missing the cherries of Cerigo. Soon enough, the butcher's wife caught the dissatisfaction on my face and asked if the breakfast was not to my liking. "Perhaps you will need an egg," she said, as she stared at my belly, barely covered by the drape of my shawl. Then she repeated what Kanella had said to me on the overlook, "You should eat in your condition."

The wife must have complained to her butcher husband, because by the end of that week Charles had moved me into my own house, which soon came with it the company of Old Iota and then my blessed Giorgio. My first night in that house I could not sleep. I lay in bed and swirled my hands around the full moon inside of me. I thought about the Theotokos, and whether She had touched Herself in the same way, Her body a mystery to Her. She was the only Mother I had ever known. In my condition, I felt closer to Her. I prayed for Her forgiveness. I prayed that She would welcome my blessed one into Her arms. As dawn showed itself in the windows, I heard the Angels of Cerigo, but their voices were low. I could not tell whether they were whispering words of assurances to me or taunts.

Back in Kapsali town, my brothers had made certain that no church would perform the Sacrament of Marriage for Charles and me. They ensured that my blessed one would never be an heir to Eternal Life. They went from parish to parish exposing my shame, which was also theirs, and that fact increased their hatred for the child within me. Like their father, they were heartless. One night when they had far too much to drink, they came to the front doors of Sióra Gazi's villa. Slurring their words, they shouted from the street for their "whore of a sister," exposing again the details of their own shame.

Sióra Gazi and I had finished our supper and were spending the remainder of the evening on the terrace, as was her custom. All of the lamps in the house were extinguished so that the Sióra could better see the stars. She smoked thin cigars, one after the other, and sipped a small glass of fortified wine. It was a moonless night, and her face was barely visible except for the smoke that billowed from her mouth. When she was informed about the commotion at her front doors, she asked her male servant to bring her a pen, ink, paper, and some candlelight. She wrote a brief note—her handwriting tall and slanting with its loops narrow and slim—and handed it to him. I went inside to watch from an upstairs window as my brothers ripped the note from the servant's hands. Vinegar and the center of bones were rising from my brothers' bodies as they read it. I felt my evening meal returning to my throat. My brothers looked at each other and without exchanging a word they ran into the night, as if dogs were after them. The Sióra never shared with me what she wrote. "Your brothers," she said, "are never coming back." True to her words, the night ate them whole.

By the time that we were on Santa Maura Island, the undeniable state of my condition meant that the Sacrament of Marriage had to be delayed until after the birth of my blessed one. I cried and begged when Charles told this to me, but he calmly repeated himself, as though I had not heard him the first time. Charles said that once we were in Dublin, he would arrange for our child to be baptized. No one will know of our circumstances there, he said. He thought that this promise would ease my mind. It did until I understood that the Church of Ireland was not my religion, and Ireland was not my island.

When Giorgio was six months in the world and my blessed second was five months within me, the promise of Dublin disappeared. Charles received his orders to sail for Dominica, and there was no set date for a return to Santa Maura.

"George will miss his father," I said to my husband, making sure to use the English name that he had given to my blessed one. "Who will buy George his first toy soldiers?" I asked.

Sióra Gazi had told me that a boy child is a blessing to his mother. We did not need to discuss what a girl child would mean for me, as we both knew. The Sióra said that in times of strife or before a physical separation with the father, place the boy in front of the man. Make the father see his son. Remind the father that his blood runs through the boy's veins. "Your body will fade, Rosa, but this being who was once a part of you will always keep his father's attention," advised the Sióra. "Unless the father is a snake," she warned. "God does not give many advantages to women, but He does give us boys, Rosa."

"George will need new clothes soon. He is growing so big

and strong," I cooed. "George has such an appetite. Soon he will eat only beef, like his father," I sang.

George was at the center of all that I said to Charles during his last week on Santa Maura.

Elesa, you should write down the following. Patricio will want to know how he came into his names.

I told Charles that my blessed second would be a boy.

"How do you know, Cara Rosa, Cara Rosa?" he asked.

"I know because I am his mother," I replied.

"Name him Patrick then," Charles instructed, knowing that he would not be present for the birth or the Baptism.

I heard "Patrick" with its ugly clipped ending, a branch that has suddenly snapped, and I was already changing it to "Patricio," which would leave the mouth opened and rounded, a cherry freed of its stone.

"He will be a fine lad of Ireland with that name," Charles declared.

When you were baptized, Patricio, I added "Lafcadio." That was the name of Iona's fifth and last son. Old Iota wept as she stood by our sides.

Santa Maura became my island, Patricio. I was a married woman and the mother of two sons there, though these acts did not occur in the order that I would have preferred.

In the early mornings, I walked along the bay when the air smelled of drying fish and fennel fronds. In the hours before noon, I visited the merchants on the Central Square and bought trinkets and little charms to keep Giorgio safe, as he was not protected by God. On days when the sun baked the flat streets of Lefkada town, I asked Old Iota to hire for us a horse and cart and a driver who would take us to the nearby hillside, where the breezes fanned the leaves of the olive trees and the scent of ginestra soothed Giorgio's crying.

Old Iota disappeared during these excursions. Even in her widow's weeds, I could see that it was Iona who cradled you in her arms. Do you remember the ginestra, Patricio? The hills were golden, as if lit by a second sun when they were in bloom. A handful of thyme crushed in your hands, a butter cake, and a spoonful of light honey. Wherever you are now, my blessed second, if you can find these things, gather them together and that will be the scent of ginestra. Breathe in, Patricio, and you will remember your mother when she was at her happiest, your brother at his most hale, and the twins Old Iota and Iona who held you for the first two years of your life, as if you were their blessed own. Your father, you will not remember, because he was already afar.

Prior to his departure, Charles had entrusted a sum of money not to me or to Old Iota but to a butcher, the one who had the room above his shop, the one who had witnessed the Sacrament of Marriage, his sour yeast and unwashed feet stench in my nostrils. This man, round and soft with the flesh of the animals that he sold, was to be the holder of my purse strings because he could read and write. "You do not even know your numbers, Rosa. Old Iota is no better," Charles had said, his eyebrows lifted in disbelief that I would object to the arrangement that he had made on my behalf. "You and Old Iota know what? One to ten, courtesy of your fingers?" he added. "That is not enough for such matters. That is enough for buying fish and garlic."

I did not correct my husband, but he was wrong. I knew the number of name days that had passed. Twenty-seven by then, more than enough for buying fish, garlic, and more.

The butcher, Charles informed me, would pay the monthly rent on the house and Old Iota her wages. Every week, the butcher would dole out to me an allowance for foodstuffs and sundry expenses. If I needed to send news to Charles, the butcher would write to him on my behalf. The butcher, in turn, would read to me any letters that arrived from Charles. It was a gentlemen's agreement between two men who knew more than fish and garlic.

Elesa, there is no need to write down what happened next— What good can come from Patricio knowing the ways of women?—but you, my dear, should know that it was an agreement that would work in my favor as soon as I understood that the butcher was not a gentleman.

In the absence of Charles, Old Iota never cooked beef. She preferred rabbit or chicken, the smaller animals of the land. The butcher's youngest son, Geranium Leaves, made these deliveries to our front door. About a month after the birth of my blessed second, the butcher began to deliver Old Iota's orders. He arrived in the early mornings with his hair combed and still wet, and he would ask if the Sióra was home. If told no, he would reluctantly leave the order plus a gift for me in Old Iota's hands. He delighted in purchasing for me pastries and confections. Boxes full of kourabiedes, their little half-moons dusted with icing sugar; amygdalota, shaped like tiny pears, each studded with a clove for its stem; and pasteli, chewy and thick with sesame seeds. If I agreed to see him, then Old Iota would take Giorgio and Patricio out for a stroll.

Elesa, your eyes are betraying you. You must learn to hide their disgust, as the Sióra would tell you. Dear girl, do you think that I *gave* myself to this man of meats? I was not a fool, and I was not blind. Also, I could still smell him before he even turned onto my lane.

Reminding myself of his odor has soured my stomach. Pour me a glass of water, Elesa. Pour one for yourself too, if you would like. Or, perhaps, we should stop for that pot of tea now?

You would prefer to continue? Ah, I thought so. You are a very bright girl, Elesa.

Tip a bit of whiskey into that water glass. The flask is underneath the bed pillows. Then I will tell you what to do when life gives you a butcher.

Sióra Gazi said that whatever their profession—military commander, surgeon, landowner—when it comes to matters of the heart—the Sióra did not say "heart," she said "flesh"—either a man is a butcher or he is not.

I laughed out loud when my butcher was an actual butcher.

You are polite to him. You look somewhat disappointed whenever he departs your company. You note where his eyes linger when he offers you his goodbyes. My butcher's eyes were on my waist, which was not surprising, because his wife, like him, was barrel-shaped, her waistline lost long ago to her five children.

My blessed third is heavy within me now, so I know it is difficult to imagine me as I once was. My waist, corseted, same as yours, Elesa, could be encircled by a pair of male hands.

At the butcher's next visit, you call attention to his region of interest by wearing a bright ribbon around it or pinning a fresh flower there. You touch the place often, smoothing the fabric of your dress or brushing away fanciful lint or crumbs. You may even spill a drop of coffee there, which requires you to rub the area with a handkerchief dipped in water, leaving a coin-sized stain behind, a little circle of wetness for him to think about later, once he is alone with his hanging carcasses. Then you wait. You wait until you know what you truly want from your butcher.

After the birth of Patricio, my body was my own again. With Charles on Dominica, I knew that it would remain that way, its figure slimmed again, its waist cinched, its roses in full bloom. I wanted to clothe it, for the first time in my life, with choices that I alone would make. I wanted new dresses measured and fitted, all with much more than a touch of pale gray lace. I wanted a parasol, a pair of ivory-colored ankle boots, matching gloves, a shawl that was not the color of ripened wheat, and two bonnets.

When I went to Sióra Gazi's villa with nothing more than a cloth bag of dried sultanas, Charles had to purchase for me a makeshift wardrobe. He found for me secondhand dresses, all ill fitting—their sleeves too long, their ample necklines requiring the addition of a shawl for modesty—along with a set of petticoats and chemises and four white linen nightdresses embroidered with white silk-thread bees. Sióra Gazi disapproved and fumed over the carelessness of these items, except for the nightdresses, which she declared were exquisite. She showed me how the bees were there not for the eyes to enjoy but for the fingertips, which was ideal for a nighttime garment. The shop owner had told Charles that the pieces were part of a trousseau belonging to a British bride-to-be, but the garments were never worn because the young lady died of malaria upon her arrival on Cerigo. I asked Charles what a "trousseau" was.

It was not Charles but Sióra Gazi who explained to me the meaning of a trousseau, and I had wanted one of my own ever

since, even if it were after the fact. A trousseau was what I
wanted from my butcher, and I wanted him to pay for it with
my absent husband's money.

I untied the pink strings wrapped around the box of kourabiedes, the third box that week from the butcher. I peeked inside. Butchers are simple creatures, the Sióra had told me. The
quantity of their gifts is indicative of their desire. He brought
for me four layers' worth, enough for his own family of seven.

Kanella's kourabiedes were far better than those sold in
Lefkada town's best bakeries. Hers crumbled the moment I bit
into them, their almond pieces toasted and chopped fine as
sand, their icing sugar freshly dusted and never caked.

Who is Kanella? the butcher would have asked, if I had
shared with him my thoughts.

She is my family's cook and the woman who wore my mother's clothes and now mine, as if I too were dead, I would have
had to answer.

So instead I smiled and thanked him. I set the box aside, and
I sat down next to him on the settee.

The Angels of Cerigo returned to me, though now they all
had the throaty voice of Sióra Gazi. They told me to grab on to
the meat man's hands and place them around my waist. I did.
Now, jump up as if you have changed your mind and are ashamed.
I did. Turn your back to him. I did. Tell him to leave you
and pause before adding "for now." I did.

The butcher was back early the next morning, without Old
Iota having placed an order. He arrived with a chunk of lamb
shoulder and a large box of pasteli, my favorite of the confections. The Angels were adamant that I should blush when I see

him, so I rubbed my cheeks with my fingertips before he was shown into the house.

That was all it took, Elesa.

The butcher's hands around my waist a few more times, and I began assembling the pieces of my trousseau. When the silks for my dresses were more costly than I had anticipated, the butcher wrote to Charles to say that the landlord had raised the rent on the house. When a linen bonnet was more to my taste than a straw one, the butcher said that he would write again for additional funds. When Charles did not arrange for the requested amount to be delivered, the butcher made up the difference with his own meat money.

God gives, and God takes.

My trousseau was just completed, when Giorgio went to Him.

Elesa, you may begin to write again. Patricio should know what happened after my blessed one left this world.

I took apart one of my linen nightdresses to swaddle Giorgio's body for burial. In the eternal darkness, he could touch the white silk-thread bees and know that beauty surrounds him still.

When the butcher wrote to Charles of Giorgio's passing, Charles wrote back to inquire about Patricio's health. He did not ask about mine. The household funds, nearly depleted by the quince-orchard burial, were not replenished, as the butcher had requested.

Geranium Leaves made the deliveries to the house again. The butcher added a sum of his own money to my weekly allotment from Charles. I would like to believe that the butcher did so out of compassion for the loss of my blessed one.

Desire is a moth, Sióra Gazi had said to me. Its life is frantic and short, and then it dies.

I am thirty years old, and my life with Charles, though mostly without him, as his truer companion is the British Army, has come to an end. During the past two years in Dublin, Charles was more often elsewhere with his regiment, first on Dominica and now in Crimea. I do not know where Crimea is. I know that it is not an island. The few months when we did live together under one roof as husband, wife, and son, I could not breathe, as if my husband brought with him into every room a swarm of gnats, clogging my mouth and throat. The only interest he took in me was at night, which, given the alternatives, I preferred, as no words were needed then.

Please leave that out, Elesa. Write this instead.

In Dublin, Charles's Venetian was far worse than it had been on Cerigo and on Santa Maura. Even when I loved him, I had never loved this language coming from his mouth. It sounded stingy to me. There was a lack of fullness to his words. At the end of them, he never lingered. Every one of them was a dry peck on the cheek.

"This Ireland cannot be an island! You lied to me. You promised me an island," I had shouted at Charles when he told me that he would be leaving for Crimea.

"Ignorant woman," he said, as though he were observing that the Dublin sky was gray again that morning. He did not even look up from the newspaper. He took a sip of his tea and ate a bite of his toasted bread, but in his mouth, the whole of his body, there was nothing but the frigid waters of the Irish Sea. Charles never raised his voice to me. I wished that he had. I wanted to know that he felt the stabs of rage in his eyes that I felt in mine, that his heart was a fist breaking through his chest, that the Angels were howling in his ears. I threw my teacup against the wall, and it broke into pieces, leaving a stain of milky tea on the wallpaper.

"Wasteful woman," Charles said.

I knew what my husband's departure would mean for Patricio and me. We would have to reside again with Mrs. Brenane, Charles's maternal aunt. While I did prefer the outskirts of Dublin to the city itself, I did not prefer Mrs. Brenane's household in Rathmines to my own. Widows, especially those without children, had only their grief for company, so they nourished and indulged it, like a lapdog or a parrot. Mrs. Brenane's grief inhabited all the rooms of her manor house and made it seem much smaller than it was. Her live-in servants took up room as well, the entire top floor, though I doubted any of them ever slept soundly up there, given what she expected of them during their waking hours.

I had never seen dust treated like a disease before. Each book in her library had to be taken off the shelf every day and caressed with a cloth, like the forehead of a dying man. I had never seen people treated like they were diseased either. Her servants all wore a white cotton cloth tied over their mouths. Every day, their clothing, right down to their undergarments, had to be hung up outside and beaten as if they were odd-shaped rugs. That sound—multiple sails whipping against a strong headwind—and the chirping of the birds signaled the break of dawn in Rathmines.

Patricio, when you and I first came to your grandaunt's manor house, I thought that we also would be made to wear a cloth. We came to Mrs. Brenane's because she came to us first.

We had been in Dublin for about a month—a city so shrouded in fog upon our arrival that I knew it at first only by its sounds—and were staying on Lower Gardiner Street at the town house belonging to your grandmother Hearn, Mrs. Brenane's sister. I never learned which one was the elder of the two. Both wore the same facial expressions—the disgust that comes with the taste of a spoiled oyster—and had sallow, papery skin that would have cracked, if they smiled. I did not need their language to understand that there was no love lost between the sisters and that they had chosen you and me as a site for their duel, but without their language I had no way of understanding the nature of their feud until we were already living within Mrs. Brenane's home.

As a young woman, Mrs. Brenane had left the Church of Ireland to marry a man of the Catholic faith, and her sister never forgave her for the religious conversion or for the unusual wealth that came with that Catholic husband. Mrs. Brenane, in turn, never forgave her sister for never forgiving her. Mrs. Brenane gloated when she heard that her nephew Charles had married a foreigner, reported to be a dark-haired Gypsy by the servants, and sired a swarthy son on a malarial island. Mrs. Brenane made it a point to visit us so that her sister would know that she knew.

Patricio, your grandmother Hearn despised me from the moment she learned about me, which was only days before you and I came to Dublin. That was when your father's letter from Dominica had arrived at his family's town house. Charles had not written to his mother about me or either of his sons before then. She, to this day, does not know about your brother, Giorgio, and his brief life on Santa Maura. When you first peeked your face around my skirt, she stared at you, as if you would pounce and attack her ankles. When you did not, she reached out and felt the small gold rings that you wore in your earlobes then. Her hands pulled back without even patting your head of curls or brushing your soft pink cheeks. Charles had instructed his mother to come to the wharf to meet us, and for me to hold a sheet of paper with "Hearn" written on it by the ship's purser. From Dominica, Charles had sent the travel arrangements including the arrival instructions, via his letters to the butcher. I had asked the butcher to inquire about Old Iota. Charles wrote back that Old Iota would not be traveling with us. This was not a pleasure trip, he wanted the butcher to remind me. Charles was correct. There was no pleasure in the journey and certainly none at our destination.

Patricio, touch your earlobes. Can you still feel the little dips in them? Old Iota had pierced your lobes, as she did Giorgio's, when you were just days old. It was the custom of my island and of hers. It was not the custom of your father's island. Your grandmother made me take the gold rings out of your lobes while we were still inside of the carriage taking us from the wharf to her house. I pretended not to know what the woman wanted, but the carriage ride was too long for me to resist her fingers as they reached out again and again for your ears. I took the earrings out myself. I kissed them and crossed myself three times before I handed them to her. I knew she was cursing us. The holes in your lobes have closed, but the dimples that took their place, are they still there, my blessed second?

Upon stepping inside your grandmother's house, she forbade me to speak to you in Venetian or Romaic. To her, they were one language, which she referred to as "foreign." English was the tongue that she insisted that we both learn. She assigned to us a girl of about fifteen, who looked like a colorless creature from the depths of the sea washed ashore after a storm, to be your nanny. Soon it became clear that she was there also to be my monitor, reporting back to your grandmother every time I uttered a word to you that she, the deep-sea dweller, could not understand. Your grandmother Hearn took your earrings, and she took our languages. I had been a mute in my father's house. I would not be one again. So when Mrs. Brenane sent her carriage for us, I did not hesitate. I left with you and never returned.

Elesa, it was at Mrs. Brenane's where I met your mother. She was waiting there for me, an Angel of flesh and bones. You must not cry, my dear. She is with God now. We cannot begrudge her for leaving us to be with Him.

Mrs. Brenane had made a great exception when she hired your mother. Patricio's grandaunt insisted that everyone in her employ share her chosen faith. She wanted only Catholics, but she did not want the diseases that came with them, which went by two names in Ireland, "typhus" and "famine," your mother would later tell me. The former was the reason for the cloths and the daily airing of the servants' clothing, your mother explained. As she was not a live-in servant, she was exempted from wearing a mouth cloth. She would be the only one within that household whom typhus would take.

Your mother addressed me as "Sióra" when we met. She wore the scent of lavender water in her hair, dark and full of waves like my own. I wanted to kiss her for both. Instead, I sat next to her and held on to her hands, as a dear friend would or, perhaps, a sister. A woman on that grim island with whom I could speak Venetian, and I could not find one word to say to her. Instead, I wept, while Patricio napped, his head upon my lap. Your mother promised me that she would return the following morning, and she did.

The first thing I asked your mother was how Mrs. Brenane had managed to find her. It had not occurred to me that Charles was not the only man within his regiment who had found a wife on one of the Ionian Islands and brought her north with him. Her husband, your mother told me, had also been garrisoned at the Fort of Santa Maura but had been returned to Dublin years prior due to his poor health. When Mrs. Brenane asked for a Venetian and English speaker among the wives of the men within that regiment, she heard about your mother and decided upon her as our interpreter.

Every weekday, as the breakfast table was being cleared, your mother arrived at the manor house in Rathmines, her wings folded and tucked away so that I alone could see them. Mrs. Brenane and I had saved our questions for each other, and your mother would patiently ask and answer them on our behalf. Mrs. Brenane then left for the midday prayers. That was when the truth was spoken in her manor house.

The Hearn family, like her own husband's family, are Anglo-Irish, your mother began. The Anglo-Irish worship in the Church of Ireland. They are few in numbers but hold most of the island's land and wealth. Like the Lazaretti, Venieri, and Cassimati of Cerigo Island, I understood at once. The Anglo-Irish speak English, the language of the island's conquerors, your mother said. This was also a familiar story to me. The nobilities of Cerigo, as my father had taught my brothers, spoke Venetian because the Republic of Venice had centuries ago conquered and bestowed upon us their bloodline and their language.

The other inhabitants of Ireland, your mother explained, are known as the Irish. They worship in the Catholic Church and speak a language of their own, which was thought to be a lesser language by those who owned the land. Same as Romaic, I understood at once.

Your mother, at Mrs. Brenane's request, then told me about the disease known as "famine" that had afflicted the Irish and about the desperate years of hunger, prior to Patricio's and my arrival on their island. She told me how the Anglo-Irish had continued to feast on butter and beef while the Irish became walking skeletons, which death then mercifully took.

"Why does Mrs. Brenane want me to know this?" I asked.

"She wants Patricio to be raised a Catholic," your mother replied, looking quickly over her shoulder, forgetting for a moment that no one else in that household could understand Venetian.

"Patricio already has a God," I said.

"Mrs. Brenane wants your son to have *her* God, and if I were you I would consider it carefully before denying her," your mother advised.

"Because the Catholic God is a *better* God?" I asked.

"No, Sióra," your mother answered, crossing herself three times. "Mrs. Brenane," she said, "wants an heir. Why do you think that she has welcomed you and Patricio into this house?"

"To spite her sister," I answered.

"What better way to spite the family than to graft another Catholic onto the family tree?" she said.

"Patricio has a God," I repeated.

"Sióra, your son and you will need more than one God, if your husband does not return from Crimea."

Elesa, your mother was right, but she did not know that I was not to be a branch of the tree.

Only you, Patricio.

After Charles departed for Crimea and it became clear that I would have a blessed third, Mrs. Brenane made her offer to me: Leave Ireland and leave Patrick. Mrs. Brenane needed an heir but had no need for me. She offered me first-class fare back to Santa Maura, as she thought that it was my island of birth. She even offered to find a traveling companion for me in case I gave birth during the journey. Your mother was deeply angered by Mrs. Brenane's demands, but I was not.

The Angels told me that it was for the best, Patricio.

If your grandaunt is still alive, do not allow her to read this, Patricio. But if she has gone to her Catholic God, then you, my blessed second, are the heir to a great fortune, as she promised me you would be.

When Mrs. Brenane called you "Patrick" or "Little Man," I had squeezed your hand tightly in my own, but, Patricio, you would squirm until I let you go. You would then toddle toward your grandaunt in recognition of your other names. When I was alone with you, I would slap you whenever you tried to form your new words with me. Your eyes would open wide, and there was a startled moment of silence before you began to cry.

It is that silence that rings now in my ears. Forgive me, Patricio. I know you did not understand, but I had to make you remember that Venetian and Romaic were our languages, and English was theirs.

I know that Charles, upon learning of my departure from Dublin, will fold up the letter from his aunt and let out a sigh of relief. He may even slap his knees and let out a whoop of joy. Mrs. Brenane would have written that Patrick was safe in Dublin and under her guardianship. She promised me that she would not write to Charles about my condition. I promised her that once my blessed third is born I would find someone to write to her, especially if the baby was a boy.

Elesa, thank God, your father was wise enough to make your travel to Santa Maura Island known to Mrs. Brenane before typhus took him. He joined your mother so soon after her passing. That is love, I remembered thinking when I saw their shared gravestone.

Dublin has taken your family from you, Elesa, but Lefkada town will give you one again. Though I wish the reasons for it were different, I am pleased that Mrs. Brenane has arranged for your company on this journey, my dear girl. My blessed third will be grateful for your company as well, if God wills a birth upon these waters.

Our own arrangement pleases me too, Elesa. It is a practical one, as all arrangements should be. You will have something in addition to your youth to contribute to your mother's family in Lefkada town, and I will have a story for Patricio to read one day. He will want to know who brought him into this world and who took him from his island of birth. These pages will tell him, and he will come and find me, unless I am already with God.

It is my hope, Patricio, that you will forgive me. I will not say for my sins. To love is not a sin. Remember this, my son. The Catholic Church that you now worship within and the Orthodox Church that is my own will tell you differently. I, your mother, cannot love you more, my blessed second. I cannot love you more than to leave you.

God takes, and God gives.

When Old Iota understands the reasons for my return to Lefkada town, her practical nature will take over, and she will hurry off to find the butcher. He will locate a house for me and my blessed third. I will pay for it from the sum that Mrs. Brenane gave me, once I had placed my X on the paper that promised you to her, Patricio.

God willing, I will give birth to another boy, in a house in Lefkada town with Old Iota by my side, as I had done twice before. I will then ask you, Elesa, to write to Mrs. Brenane, who will call Patricio to her side.

She will say, "Patrick, your mother, who loves you, is safe, and she has given you a brother." Your grandaunt, Patricio, will say this to you in English, the language that had already separated you, my blessed second, from me long before the waters of this Irish Sea.

ELIZABETH BISLAND

(1861–1929)

. . . .

NEW YORK, 1906

A strange mingling of events and of race-forces had brought the boy into being.

It was in the late '40's, when England still held the Ionian Isles, that the 76th Foot was ordered to Greece, and Surgeon-Major [Charles Bush] Hearn accompanied his regiment to do garrison duty on the island of Cerigo. Apparently not long after his arrival he made the acquaintance of Rosa Cerigote, whose family is said to have been of old and honourable Greek descent. Photographs of the young surgeon represent him as a handsome man, with the flowing side-whiskers so valued at that period, and with a bold profile and delicate waist. A passionate love affair ensued . . . , but the connection was violently opposed by the girl's brothers, the native bitterness toward the English garrison being as intense as was the sentiment in the South against the Northern army of occupation immediately after the American Civil War. The legend goes that the Cerigote men——there was hot blood in the family veins——waylaid and stabbed the Irishman, leaving him for dead. The girl, it is said, with the aid of a servant, concealed him in a barn and nursed him back to life, and after his recovery eloped with her grateful lover and married him by the Greek rites in Santa Maura. The first child died immediately after birth, and the boy, Lafcadio, was the second child; taking his name from the Greek name of the island, Lefcada. Another son, James, . . . was [also] the fruit of this marriage, so romantically begun and destined to end so tragically. . . .

It was inevitable, no doubt, that the young wife, who had never mastered the English tongue, though she spoke . . . Italian and Romaic, should have regretted the change from her sunlit island to the dripping Irish skies and grey streets of Dublin, nor can it be wondered at that, an exile among aliens in race, speech, and faith, there should have soon grown up misunderstandings and disputes. The unhappy details have died into silence with the passage of time, but the wife seems to have believed herself repudiated and betrayed, and the marriage being eventually annulled. . . .

A boy of less sensitive fibre might in time have forgotten these shocks, but the eldest son of Charles Hearn and Rosa Cerigote was destined to suffer always because of the violent rending of their ties. From this period seems to have dated his strange distrusts, his unconquerable terror of the potentialities which he suspected as lurking beneath the frankest exterior, and his constant, morbid dread of betrayal and abandonment by even his closest friends.

Whatever of fault there may have been on his mother's part, his vague memories of her were always tender and full of yearning affection.

To [James] the brother he never saw he wrote, when he was a man, "And you do not remember that dark and beautiful face—with large, brown eyes like a wild deer's—that used to bend above your cradle? You do not remember the voice which told you each night to cross your fingers after the old Greek orthodox fashion, and utter the words— . . . 'In the names of the Father, and of the Son, and of the Holy Ghost'? She made, or had made, three little wounds upon you when a baby— to place you, according to her childish faith, under the protection of those three powers, but especially that of Him. . . . We were all very dark as children, very passionate, very odd-looking, and wore gold rings in our ears. . . .

"Whatever there is of good in me came from that dark race-soul of which we know so little. My love of right, my hate of wrong;—my admiration for what is beautiful or true;—my capacity for faith in man or woman;—my sensitiveness to artistic things which gives me whatever little success I have,—even that language-power whose physical sign is in the large eyes of both of us,—came from Her. . . . [ellipsis in the original] It is the mother who makes us,—makes at least all that makes the nobler man: not his strength or powers of calculation, but his heart and power to love. And I would rather have her portrait than a fortune."

Mrs. Brenane, into whose hands the child [Lafcadio Hearn] thus passed, was the widow of a wealthy Irishman, by whom she had been converted to Romanism, and like all converts she was "more loyal than the King." The divorce and remarriage of her nephew [Charles Hearn] incurred her bitterest resentment; she not only insisted upon a complete separation from the child, but did not hesitate to speak her mind fully to the boy, who always retained the impressions thus early instilled. . . .

Of the next twelve years of Lafcadio Hearn's life there exists but meagre record. The little dark-eyed, dark-faced, passionate boy with the wound in his heart and the gold rings in his ears—speaking English but stammeringly, mingled with Italian and Romaic—seems to have been removed at about his seventh year to Wales, and from this time to have visited Ireland but occasionally. Of his surroundings during the most impressionable period of his life it is impossible to reconstruct other than shadowy outlines. Mrs. Brenane was old; was wealthy; and lived surrounded by eager priests and passionate converts.

. . . .

*Of the course and character of his education but little is known. He is
said to have spent two years in a Jesuit college in the north of France,
where he probably acquired his intimate and accurate knowledge of the
French tongue. He was also for a time at Ushaw, the Roman Catholic
college at Durham, and here occurred one of the greatest misfortunes
of his life. In playing the game known as "The Giant's Stride" he was
accidentally blinded in one eye by the knotted end of a rope suddenly
released from the hand of one of his companions. In consequence of this
the work thrown upon the other eye by the enormous labours of his
later years kept him in constant terror of complete loss of sight. In
writing and reading he used a glass so large and heavy as to oblige him
to have it mounted in a handle and hold it to his eye like a lorgnette,
and for distant observation he carried a small folding telescope.*

*The slight disfigurement, too,—it was never great,—was a source
of perpetual distress. He imagined that others, more particularly
women, found him disgusting and repugnant in consequence of the
film that clouded the iris.*

*This accident seems to have ended his career at Ushaw. . . . [Later
in life] in a letter written . . . to one of his pupils . . . , he says:— . . .*

*"When I was a boy of sixteen, although my blood relations were—
some of them—very rich, no one would pay anything to help me finish
my education. I had to become what you never have had to become—
a servant. I partly lost my sight. I had two years of sickness in bed. I
had no one to help me. And I had to educate myself in spite of all
difficulties. Yet I was brought up in a rich home, surrounded with every luxury of Western life. . . ."*

*The rupture with his grand-aunt was complete. . . . Her property,
which he had been encouraged to look upon as his inheritance, was*

dribbling away in the hands of those whose only claim to business ability was their religious convictions, and a few years after their separation her death put an end to any efforts at reconciliation. . . . Some provision was made for him in her will, but he put forward no claims, and the property was found practically to have vanished.

To what straits the boy was driven at this time in his friendlessness there is no means of knowing.

. . . .

Sometime during the year 1869—the exact date cannot be ascertained—Lafcadio Hearn, nineteen years old, penniless, delicate, half-blind, and without a friend, found himself in the streets of New York.

. . . .

What drove him . . . to endeavour to reach Cincinnati, Ohio, is not clear. . . . [H]e made the journey in an emigrant train and had not money for food upon the way.

~Elizabeth Bisland's *The Life and Letters of Lafcadio Hearn,*
Volumes 1 and 2 (1906)

ALETHEA FOLEY

(1853–1913)

. . . .

CINCINNATI, 1906

Pat wasn't from here.

That was my first thought when I saw him at Mrs. Haslam's boardinghouse. I didn't know his name right then, but that hunch would prove to be more than true.

While I was in the kitchen, Mrs. Haslam's was always full. If you were the kind who were only passing through, you might not give much thought to the supper table, but if you were a stayer—the spinsters and the widowers—then a fruit pie every other night and a roast on Sunday were sought-after fare.

Faces like Pat's were the ones that I'd learned not to get attached to. I didn't even bother with their names. Same as horses on a farm, the color of their hair was enough to identify them. Chestnut, bay, blond, or black as coal in Pat's case. If they were male and young, they were soon headed elsewhere. Out West, down South, back East, wherever the trains and steamboats could take them.

Before the Civil War, when we heard "Cincinnati," we thought of the Promised Land, the Ohio our River Jordan. Who knew that the Promised Land would be full of young white men itching to go elsewhere?

Mr. Bean, the printing-house man with the gray hair and gray fingernails, was introducing Pat to the other boarders seated at the table, and I was placing a tureen down on the sideboard. It was the middle of summer, but Mrs. Haslam always had me prepare a soup because she said it filled people up, and they would eat less of the pies and the roasts, which were more costly for her to provide. Mr. Bean liked a nip of gin before and after supper, so I thought that he was already slurring his words when he said, "This young fellow is named Laf-ca-di-o Hearn."

My ears couldn't recognize "Lafcadio" as a man's name back then. I'd never met another.

Miss Caroline, who was hard of hearing when it suited her to be, asked Mr. Bean to repeat the new one's name. Mr. Bean stood up again, cleared his throat, and said it twice in full. Pat kept his eyes on the tablecloth the entire time.

I took a moment from serving to study the new boarder's profile. I liked it. His nose cut a strong, sharp line with a slight bump near the bridge, and he had a mustache but a clean-shaven chin. He looked like he had spent time out in the sun though. His coloring was almost the same as mine. I must have been looking at the right side of his face because I didn't see anything else out of place.

Then Pat himself stood up and offered the table his name. I could hear from his lilt that he was an Irishman, but not a Cincinnati one. He was soft-spoken, and his words weren't half-swallowed.

Miss Caroline was again the first to say something. She commanded him to speak up. I was setting her soup down in front of her—I'd made green pea with egg dumplings that night—and I almost spilled it because her voice was so demanding and loud.

Pat looked over at her. He covered his left eye with his left hand, and looked at her some more.

The other boarders weren't sure what to do or whether they could begin eating. Soup, in summer or not, wasn't half as nice if it was lukewarm.

Pat cleared his throat and said in a voice loud enough for Miss Caroline to hear, "I also answer to Patrick Hearn."

The table erupted with welcomes and greetings for "Patrick Hearn." Mr. Bean said that the young man would soon be joining his place of employment as a proofreader. Young Mr. Hearn is now the private secretary to the city's head librarian, Mr. Bean added, in a tone that said that Patrick Hearn was worth a second glance.

The younger men at Mrs. Haslam's would call him "Pat." That was what I called him too, when we became acquainted.

Mr. Wheeler, who wasn't at all young and who worked as a clerk at a tobacco warehouse—he smelled of cigars though he never smoked—greeted Pat the next morning at the breakfast table as "Paddy." Pat refused to acknowledge the man, as if he hadn't heard a word of what Mr. Wheeler was saying to him. Mr. Wheeler didn't seem to notice and kept on talking. In between bites of his coddled eggs, Mr. Wheeler said that he was barely out of the cradle when "your people"—Mr. Wheeler meant the Irish, but Pat didn't look up from the newspaper that he was reading—started coming in droves to Cincinnati. They were a sorry lot back then, Paddy. Their children roamed the streets like strays, Mr. Wheeler continued. Not a one of them in school. The Civil War changed them for the better. Every last man and boy fought for Ohio's Tenth, along with us native-borns. That war gave them discipline, Paddy. It taught them hard work. That is what I say, whenever I hear people speaking ill about the Irish; that they are taking over the city's police force and fire brigade and such. Who better suited than their kind for these jobs is what I say, Paddy.

Every time Mr. Wheeler said "Paddy," Pat would turn a page of the newspaper, rustling it like a dried cornstalk.

Miss Caroline was also at the breakfast table, and I saw the crumbs around her lips formed into a half smile. She took her coffee with three spoonfuls of sugar, and she always drank two cups with breakfast. Mrs. Haslam used to say that spinsters had the biggest sweet tooth, followed by widows and children. Mrs. Haslam complained that she had to buy an extra pound every month just for Miss Caroline and Miss Beryl. Miss Beryl, a spinster too, had already left the boardinghouse by the time I'd started, but Mrs. Haslam always brought her name up whenever she complained about Miss Caroline, as if there were still two.

Pat and Miss Caroline, in spite of their shouty beginning, became friends. Both didn't abide chatter, especially in the mornings. She was devoted to the pages of the *Cincinnati Commercial* but also read the *Cincinnati Enquirer* when Pat began to write for it. They traded newspapers at the end of each day, and the next morning at breakfast Miss Caroline would silently point to the stories that he'd written. I didn't understand that this was a game they played until Pat told me that the *Enquirer* printed his stories without his name. He had a term for it.

Yes, that's right, Miss. A byline.

Listen, Miss Caroline may not be as important in the world as Pat, but it's because you don't know her story yet. She, as with most spinsters I've known, was of independent ways. Miss Caroline and Pat had that in common. They also didn't have a lot of money by the standards of white people, but the money they had they spent on books and on their underthings.

You're taking notes now, Miss?

Well, I can tell you how I met Pat—I know that he made a name for himself as "Lafcadio Hearn" but that wasn't the man I knew—and what he wore underneath his clothes, those two stories don't have much to do with each other. Why I left him, now *that* had to do with the state of his underthings.

Charlotte had tried her best to warn me, but I didn't hear her like I should have. Charlotte did the laundry at Mrs. Haslam's back then. She took over the work from another gal, around the same time that Pat came to stay. Charlotte—Mrs. Haslam and the boarders called her "Lottie"—was from Kentucky, like me. We didn't look much alike—different as a buckeye and a peanut—but Charlotte was a sister to me from the moment that we met. I liked hearing her stories even more than Pat would like hearing mine. Charlotte and I, we grew up with stories that were brambly, full of leaves, and with branches going every which way. When you reached the middle was when you were rewarded with the juicy berries, the sweetest fruits.

Charlotte's stories always took awhile to tell because her words were slowed and spent by the late afternoon when we would see each other, as her day had started as early as mine. I would be out on the back steps, which led from Mrs. Haslam's kitchen door down to the backyard, peeling potatoes or topping and tailing runner beans, when Charlotte would come by to deliver her bundles, each one wrapped in butcher paper. Charlotte rued that the paper was more costly than the laundry soap, but there was no way for her to skimp on the packaging.

She said that if you pay to get your laundry done, then you want to believe that your garments have never touched anyone else's.

"Same washtub," she said.

"Same washtub," I repeated, laughing low right along with her.

When I first knocked on Mrs. Haslam's kitchen door, I knew that her house, despite needing a new coat of paint, was aiming for a better class of boarders. There were no laundry lines or poles in the backyard. That meant the boarders would have to send their laundry out, which was an added expense for them. I'd worked at houses where the boarders took their turns at the backyard pump and washtub and, worse, at houses where the boarders never did. You can tell a lot about a person once you've seen their laundry hanging out to dry. Moth holes, careless mends, cotton, flannel, or wool, they all tell you what a person chooses to keep closest to them. Most of the time, it's what they *have* to keep closest to them because their choices in life are spent up or spent elsewhere.

Charlotte knew her numbers—one to ten, like I did—but she never learned her letters. None of us could, back then. So she drew a little picture for each of her customers at Mrs. Haslam's and the other boardinghouses where she found work. The tag on Miss Caroline's bundle had a snowflake drawn on it. Charlotte smiled when she showed it to me, and then she explained why. I'd been at Mrs. Haslam's for about two years by then, and Miss Caroline had been there from the start. Still, I would have never guessed.

"Miss Caroline's underthings are bedecked with lace," Charlotte whispered. She claimed it was French lace, but I wasn't certain how she would know. The lace didn't speak to her, did it? Charlotte had never met a Frenchwoman or a Frenchman for that matter, but lace from France she insisted she knew because the finer trimming shops in the city displayed them in their windows. She never thought that she would see some at Mrs. Haslam's. Lace as delicate as just-fallen snowflakes was how Charlotte went on to describe it. After spending the better part of her time waxing about that French lace, she added at the very end, like an extra yolk in a cake batter, that Miss Caroline's underthings, every single smock and drawer, were sewn from heavy China silk. Charlotte then left me, slack-jawed, to finish her rounds for the day.

When I saw Charlotte again, I had to promise to bake her a cobbler—it was high summer, so she asked for blackberries, as any gal from Kentucky would—if she would unwrap the snowflake bundle so that I could see and touch.

I shivered.

Charlotte, right alongside me, shivered too.

Then we both laughed because it was only cloth, but it made us feel joy.

On Tabb Plantation where I was born, we young ones would bathe in a shallow stream that ran along its border. It must have been the property line because we were told never to wade to the other side. There was a time in the year, right after the crab-apple blossoms had dropped, when the water felt like that to me. Silk on my skin, and when we were young, our skin was also silk. That was how I would describe that stream to Pat. It was in the first story that I would tell him. Looking back now, it was an odd place to begin.

"Silk?" Pat asked.

"Silk," I said again, nodding my head.

Pat closed his eyes when he listened to my stories. I thought at first that I'd lulled him to sleep, so I stopped talking. His eyes opened, and his good one had a look in it, as if I'd denied him something good to eat. He explained that he listened best in the dark, and I believed him.

"I've longed for that stream," I told him. "Never longed for Tabb or for what it meant to be born there," I told him too.

That's right, Miss. My last name isn't Tabb.

My mother was hired out to Foley Plantation before I was born, and Mr. Foley purchased me when I was young. He gave me to his daughter and her new husband, who owned Salee Plantation between Dover and Augusta, if you know that part of Kentucky. I was their wedding gift.

When I told Pat how I came to be at Salee, his good eye blinked and blinked. He said that my condition then was full of sadness. I told him it wasn't sadness that I remembered about those days. It was toil and no pay—

I haven't told you how Pat and I became acquainted yet? Is that so, Miss?

I didn't know you were in a hurry. Are you talking to some-one else this morning about Patrick Hearn?

I didn't think so, Miss.

No one else in Cincinnati can tell you about the man I knew.

If I were you, I'd help myself to a cup of coffee, have a listen, and take some more notes. Pat always had pages of them. You haven't been writing that much down, Miss.

Mr. Anderson tells me that you're with the *Enquirer*. Now, if that paper didn't give Pat a byline, you probably don't have one either. Pat was always on the lookout for a story that no one else had too. He said that's how reporters make a name for themselves. Isn't that right, Miss?

To be forthright with you, I didn't know that young white ladies did newspaper work.

Times have changed? I'm sure you're right to say so, Miss.

Mr. Anderson says that I was ten and eight when Pat and I met. He says the year was 1872.

Mr. Anderson has had to figure it all out—my birth year, my age, my comings and goings, and Pat's as well—because Mr. Anderson says that the Probate Court will want to know once we put forward my claim.

Mr. Anderson says that Pat was five tens and four when he passed. May he rest in peace.

I know his passing was two years ago, Miss. But the letter from his book publisher didn't come to me then. It got here less than a month ago. Without it, Mr. Anderson and I would have never known that Pat had left me nothing. That was why Mr. Anderson went to your paper, Miss. We're both glad to know that the *Enquirer* is taking an interest.

His full name is William I. Anderson, Miss.

Yes, you could say that we're related. We're all God's children.

Everyone these days, they know their date of birth—year, month, even down to the day—and their age. Before the war, we were "young," which meant we weren't being put to work yet, or we were "grown," which meant we were working. Then we were "old," which meant we were headed to the Hereafter soon. No numbers needed.

Folks now, they know their numbers well past ten, and some,

like Mr. Anderson, even know their letters. But I tell them we're still in the same washtub. Mr. Anderson doesn't like it when I say such things.

He's like you. He says that times have changed. He says he's an oculist.

He's an optimist? I'm sure you're right, Miss.

Mr. Anderson tells me that I'm five tens and three or, as he says it, "fifty-three" this year.

I asked him to show me what fifty-three looks like in tally marks. He did. I felt every one of those lines and slashes, each one a heavy coat worn on top of the other. Even on the hottest Cincinnati days, when the Ohio looks like it's steaming, I can't take those coats off, not a one. If that's what fifty-three means, then he's right. I'm fifty-three this year.

Look around you. This is what I've to show for all those years. A two-room cottage at the back of someone else's house. At least it's rent-free, I tell myself. Mr. Anderson owns the main house. He's done well enough for himself. He doesn't need to collect an old lady's rent.

Pat was two tens and two when we met, Mr. Anderson says.

I would have said that Pat was the younger one. His heart wasn't fully grown back then, and it made him shy or not enjoy the company of people. I couldn't tell which at first.

From the start, Pat didn't lounge on the front porch with the other boarders and Mrs. Haslam, taking in the breeze or the moonlight. After supper, he would smoke his pipe on the back steps instead. It being summer, I kept the door to the kitchen wide open, and Pat would look in and nod. When some white men nodded, they meant they might need something from me at any moment, so I better be prepared. Pat nodded like he wanted to say, *Good evening, Miss Alethea, it's a fine night, and the stars are beginning to glow. Why don't you come out and sit awhile with me?*

After a week or so of nods, Pat introduced himself to my back, as I stood at the sink, my arms elbow-deep in grease and water. I turned my face toward him and politely replied that I already knew his name. I addressed him as "Mr. Hearn," and he shook his head, as if I'd given him the wrong answer to a question. I'd seen his cloudy eye by then, and it didn't bother me one bit. His right eye was dark brown and lively, with lashes as long as my own, and I learned early on to look only at it. He agreed to be called "Mr. Patrick" that evening, but soon he was Pat to me. If Mrs. Haslam ever heard me calling a male boarder by his given name, I would have been let go faster than you could say "Pat." That's why I made sure to say his name soft, under my breath, like a secret or a prayer.

Pat soon called me "Mattie," which he said was short for "Mattie de Maysville." He was fond of giving names to people and places, though they already had them. "The Virgin Mother Hen" was what he called Mrs. Haslam, though he knew that she was a widow and childless. She did have a way of moving her head up and down, like a well-fed yardbird pecking at grain, when she spoke. He called Miss Caroline "Miss Silk Purse," which he said was short for "Miss Silk Purse from a Sow's Ear," after I'd told him about her snowflake bundles. It was too good of a story to keep to myself. He wasn't taken aback as I'd been. Miss Caroline was from Boston, he said, and her family had long been in the China trade, which explained the silk. The French lace he couldn't explain.

Pat's thick glasses—he never wore them in public—were his "eye can't see!" He pointed at his left eye and then slapped his knees when he told me that one.

As for Mattie de Maysville, Pat said that *de* followed by the name of a place was how French noble people told the world where they were from. I stored that away to share with Charlotte. "You might know lace, but I know French," I remember teasing her.

Maysville, Kentucky, was where I'd gone first, after Freedom. If you weren't young or old, you were on the move back then. Most of us were walking north, east, or west. Those who headed south were searching for kin.

I was grown. I'd been helping Molly, Mr. Salee's cook, for about five years. My hot water cornbread was almost as good as hers. My stack cake wasn't, but that's because she kept her back to me whenever she added the spices to the stewed dried-apple filling. Molly, as with most cooks, wasn't always forthright. She showed me only what helped her, and the rest she kept to herself.

But this is your home, Mr. Foley's daughter had said to me when I told her that I was leaving. Then she warned me that if I changed my mind I wouldn't be taken back in. I thought it over for about the length of a blue jay's song, and I left. I traveled light because Mr. Foley's daughter said that my clothes were still the property of Mr. Salee. The homespun skirt and blouse and the hand-me-down work boots that I had on that morning belonged to him too, but I could consider them as gifts, Mr. Foley's daughter said.

Molly stayed. She said that she was too old to wander the roads and turnpikes of Kentucky, but she really wasn't. At most, Molly was ten years older than I was. She would head back to the mountains and find her siblings, if she were to go anywhere, she figured. Before we parted, Molly gave me a knitted shawl the dark green of pine needles that I'd never seen her wear, and she said into my ear, "One small spoonful and two blades." I knew right away what she meant. It was the amount of cinnamon and mace that she added to the stewed dried apples, when her back was turned to me. It was her way of wishing me good luck and Godspeed. I repeated it back to her—one small spoonful and two blades—to let her know that I'd heard her and to wish her the same.

I soon met folks who knew where Maysville was, and I walked with them. We followed the banks of the Ohio River, heading eastward. We were still on the Kentucky side of it, but that mighty river, in their minds, had already become a shallow stream. Some of them opined that the Ohio no longer seemed so wide nor its currents so fast. They took turns challenging the river. *We could cross you now!* they were saying, each in their own way. I listened as they talked and laughed at that river.

I told Pat that it was their laughter that made me feel free. I wasn't sure that he took in the fullness of my meaning, but he blinked and blinked and that was a sign that he was trying.

Mr. Anderson figures that I was ten or ten and one at the time, Miss.

Pat said that Maysville was where I was born again as a free person. He said that I'd chosen Maysville, and the first place where you choose to live was where you are truly from. I asked him if his name was "Pat de Cincinnati." He shook his head no.

I didn't have the cold heart to correct him. I didn't choose Maysville. I returned to it. Tabb Plantation was nearby, and I went there to look for my mother. I didn't find her. The old folks who were still there didn't know of her whereabouts because I couldn't remember her name or what she looked like. An old woman looked me over for a good long while and said, "Your face is your father's." I asked her what she knew about him, and she told me.

Later, when it was time to register a name with the government men, I kept Alethea because I believed that my mother had given it to me, and Foley because I wanted her to be able to find me again. I stayed in Maysville for the same reason. I thought that one day I would see her and she would see me, and we wouldn't even need to trade our names to know. But once we did, we would have proof.

I didn't know how to find paying work in Maysville at first. Who did back then? Work was something that found you. So I did what came easiest to me. I talked. I would tell whoever was listening that I was a cook and list all the dishes that Molly had taught me. I talked until the person walked away. After a couple of days of doing this, I met a very old woman—she looked like a sweet potato left too long in the hot ashes—who told me that I wasn't a cook, that she was a cook, and that the family called her Sweetie. I called her "Aunt Sweetie" because no one so old should be called something so young. She needed a helper because hers had just left for Cincinnati, in broad daylight with a little skip in her step, like she were headed to a picnic.

"Can you picture that?" asked the old cook.

"Yes, I can, Aunt Sweetie," I replied, though I knew it wasn't really a question.

I worked for food in my stomach and a roof over my head, and that wasn't that different from my life at Salee, as Pat would later say to me. I told him it wasn't the same. I could leave and find a new roof, and I did. I worked in two other houses in and around Maysville before I too headed for Cincinnati. I wasn't in any condition to be skipping though, by the time I left.

The first thing I remembered buying, once I had a few coins in my pockets, was a length of ribbon, the blue of borage flowers. It looked nice in my hair, which was more reddish brown in those days. The color of my hair was what Pat said he'd noticed first about me.

Yes, I said the color of my hair, Miss.

Pat wasn't from here, like I said. His eye was drawn to different things.

The last house in Maysville where I'd worked belonged to the Anderson family. I was the head cook by then and I—

No, no relation to the Mr. Anderson who's helping me with my court case, Miss.

The Maysville Mr. Anderson came over from Scotland before the war.

My Mr. Anderson was born in Cincinnati, after the war. He's light-complected, but he's a colored man. He owns a printing house on Eighth Street, if you want to write that down. He also owns this house.

I've mentioned that already? Well, I suppose it bears repeating then, Miss.

Before you leave this morning, maybe Mr. Anderson's wife can show you the main house. Mrs. Anderson has fine taste, and he does as well, now. He has an entire room only for his books. It's larger than my kitchen here. I should move my pots and pans into there, I've told him.

No, Miss, I wouldn't begin to know how old I was when Mr. Anderson was born.

I know how old I was when I came to Cincinnati, if you want to write that down. Mr. Anderson says that I must have been ten and four.

Pat's name for me should have been "Mattie de Cincinnati." But once his mind was set on something, it was better just to accept it or walk away. His heart was young, but his mind was an old man. I never liked being called Mattie. There was nothing wrong with my given name, and if he wanted to shorten it, I'd told him that some people call me "Thea." Pat wasn't some people though. I never understood why he chose Mattie over anything else—

It was what, Miss? Alliterative. I don't remember Pat saying that word, but it sounds like one of his.

When Pat was courting me, I enjoyed hearing his stories. They were queer, like the bell jars that Mrs. Haslam displayed in her parlor. I could look inside their glass domes full of dried flowers, curly twigs, pinned butterflies, and stuffed birds, but I didn't always know what I was supposed to be seeing. It was the same with Pat's stories. I heard his words, but I wasn't always sure what I was meant to understand. I would nod my head at this and that, but more often I would ask questions because Pat's stories were full of holes.

No, not like his underthings, Miss. His drawers and under vests were never in such a sorry state, I can tell you that for certain.

The holes, as I was saying, were in Pat's stories and often in the places where he had been. When I asked Pat where he was born, for instance, he said it was a place that no longer existed. For a lightning-strike moment, I thought he meant a plantation, which would account for the color of his skin—lighter than mine but far from Irish white, like Mr. Foley or his daughter. Pat could be putting on a lilt. So many of us were starting new after the war. Why not as a "Patrick Hearn"?

Lifting my chin, I prompted Pat to continue. As he began to tell his story, he lowered his head. That was his habit. He spoke to his lap. He spoke to the floor. He spoke to my back. If I looked at him, even when his eye was downcast, he would redden and stammer.

No, I can't describe his left eye for you in detail, Miss. As I said, I didn't see it.

No, Pat's right eye didn't bulge like a bullfrog's. I can't speak to what happened to it after he left Cincinnati.

No, Pat didn't have a hunched back or a raised shoulder. He was hale of body when I knew him. Again, I can't speak to what happened to him after Cincinnati.

No, Pat wasn't a dwarf, Miss.

We were the same height, unless I had on my tan button boots with the heels, which I never did while I was at Mrs. Haslam's because I didn't own them then. He was surprised and not pleased when I wore them for the first time, which was on the day we married. That night, he found the boots and hid them from me. As if I wouldn't notice that my first pair of fabric boots—I bought them secondhand, but Charlotte described them as "angel-worn" because their soles were barely scuffed— had gone missing? That foolishness didn't last long. How Pat and I laughed and laughed when I found them inside his traveling case with a note tucked inside one of them. He'd drawn a dove flying high above a blackbird—he said it was a raven— and the dove had on a pair of button boots. The raven had a teardrop falling from its right eye.

You're right, Miss. Pat did behave like a child. Most grown men do.

You haven't finished your coffee, Miss. I brewed that pot right before you got here. You're not used to the taste? There's toasted cornmeal mixed with the coffee grounds, like how Molly made it during the blockade. No one does that anymore, especially not on this side of the Ohio, but I still have a taste for it. A tad sweet without even adding sugar, don't you find?

"Tastes like war," Charlotte would say whenever I'd offer her some.

"Tastes like Freedom brewing," I'd say right back, which always made Charlotte take another sip.

"War-coffee" was what Pat called it when we were keeping house. He wasn't fond of the coffee that I'd served him back at Mrs. Haslam's either. "Cincinnati-coffee" was what he called that or, sometimes, just "brown water." He preferred a sludge-like brew or a strong cup of tea. Like I said, Pat wasn't from here.

His place of birth, he told me, was an island in the Ionian Sea, but beyond that he had no memory of it. When he was born, it was called Santa Maura, and the island answered now to Lefkada.

"They named the island after you?" I asked, recalling Pat's first evening at Mrs. Haslam's and the odd sounds that Mr. Bean had offered to the boarders.

Pat smiled, raising his head so that our eyes met—that was when I first saw the ring of moss in the dark brown of his eye—and he replied that he was named after the island.

"Then your island didn't go anywhere. You carry it with you," I said.

Pat insisted upon his version of the story.

The island did go somewhere. It went from the United Kingdom, whose hands it was in when he was born, into the hands of a country called Greece, Pat said. He was ten and four when the name changed, and it had left him feeling lost.

"But you have no memory of the island," I reminded him.

The island of his birth had disappeared from the maps of the world, he said. He was only two when he left its shores with his mother. How could he ever go back now? he asked of his shoes, his voice low and hoarse.

I could hear that he was in mourning. It made me wonder about his mother and whether she was still alive, but I spoke of other things for a while because his eye was becoming a spider-web of red.

"Tell me about the sea," I said. "I've only seen rivers and streams."

Pat had me close my eyes and think of the sound of the wind as it sweeps through a field of tall summer corn. I did. He had me sway my shoulders from side to side, as if I were in midsong. I did. Now, imagine the bluest sky, Mattie, but it is above you *and* underneath you. I did.

With my eyes still closed, I asked him to tell me the scent of the sea.

Raw oysters, he replied.

And there I was. No longer in the dark but in the Ionian.

Pat reached for my hands. I didn't pull them away because he had taken me to the sea. That was as far from Cincinnati as I'd ever been.

Oysters, milk, and butter were the main ingredients for Mrs. Haslam's favorite dish. I could make an oyster stew now in my sleep, but when I first came to her boardinghouse, I had no idea what an oyster was. Molly had never made a stew or anything else with an oyster, at least not while I was afoot. Nor had Aunt Sweetie, who would have called them the Devil's rocks, if she'd ever seen their fleshy gray centers. So when Mrs. Haslam first ordered an oyster stew for Saturday's supper, I spent Friday night in tears. My eyes, the next morning, were so puffed and threaded through with red that Miss Caroline waved me over to her side and whispered—the hard of hearing don't whisper, so that was when I first knew that her hearing was fine—"Are you brokenhearted, Alethea?"

Startled by the spinster's question, I blurted out, "Oysters," which in turn startled her.

Miss Caroline's jaw dropped and a piece of half-chewed biscuit fell onto her plate, followed by a belly laugh that was more a stevedore's than a spinster's. She was lucky that none of the other boarders were at the breakfast table yet, as they would have thought that she was having a fit. I didn't know why Miss Caroline was finding such joy in oysters, but I liked her for it and I liked her from that moment on.

When Miss Caroline calmed herself, I told her all that I didn't know about oysters. I didn't have to tell her that I would be let go, if I couldn't serve forth an oyster stew that evening. I was sure that she'd seen her fair share of cooks come and go at Mrs. Haslam's. There were a lot of us in Cincinnati. Every day brought with it another gal from Kentucky, claiming her hot water cornbread was the best, boasting more years in a kitchen than her years on this earth, and every one of them was starving, as I'd been, for Cincinnati.

Miss Caroline went up to her rooms—she was the only

boarder with two, ever since Miss Beryl had left the adjoining one empty and Miss Caroline took it over—and returned with a small sketchbook and a tin box of water paints and brushes. With a few fast strokes, she handed to me what turned out to be two very fine pictures of an oyster, one with its shell closed and the other with it opened wide. She wrote down the number of oysters I would need for a stew for seven boarders and one Mrs. Haslam, in numbers and also in tally marks.

Take this with you and make sure to ask the sellers to teach you how to "shuck" the oysters, Miss Caroline instructed. Oysters—crates of them, rock-like, sitting atop their beds of ice and salt—arrive in Cincinnati daily, she said, via the trains from New York and Boston and, depending on the month, via the steamboats from New Orleans. Whoever packed them will throw in a tangle of long dark seaweeds, which the sellers will use to festoon their stalls and to announce, without having to say a word, that those creatures are not from here.

Do not worry, Alethea, I will show you how to prepare the stew, which is misnamed, as it is more of a lively simmer, Miss Caroline assured me. I remember that dish well from my youth, and you know it must be downright simple if even I can prepare it. She gave my free hand a sharp squeeze, as I poured her another cup of coffee with the other. Miss Caroline never once called me anything but "Alethea." I liked her for that too.

Years later, when I was leaving Mrs. Haslam's boardinghouse, I prepared for their last supper an oyster stew in lieu of a soup, not in Mrs. Haslam's honor but in Miss Caroline's. Miss Caroline had seconds, which was her way of honoring me. For dessert, I made a stack cake, seven layers thick. Miss Caroline had thirds.

City fare and country fare, I told Pat, was how I wanted to begin and end that meal—

I had been at Mrs. Haslam's for four years, Miss, with Pat under the same roof for much of the last two.

As I was saying, in all that time, I'd never baked a stack cake for the boarders before, thinking it not fancy enough for city dwellers. Stack cakes were Mr. Salee's favorite, but he was from the mountains of Kentucky, as was Molly. When I worked with Aunt Sweetie, she baked all kinds of cakes—white cake, pound cake, fruit cake, Robert Lee jelly cake, plum cake—but she claimed that she'd never heard of a stack cake, which told me it wasn't fit for company.

The only person in Cincinnati I'd been baking stack cakes for was Charlotte. The only thing that I'd asked in return was her honest opinion. Three layers weren't nearly enough, she'd informed me. Five layers were about right, she opined. Seven were for weddings and special occasions, she and I agreed. One day of curing the cake layers with the stewed dried-apple filling wasn't enough. You ended up with a mouthful of dry cake and mushy apples, she complained, while what you wanted was something in between. Two days were better to mellow and marry the two, we concluded. To Molly's mix of cinnamon and mace—one small spoonful and two blades—I added a pea-sized knob of powdered ginger, which made the stewed apples brighter and a bit sharp on the tongue. I added a dribble of dark rum, and those strong drops woke up the sorghum already in the batter. Together they made that cake hum.

You're not writing this down, Miss? Maybe, that's for the best. No need to give away all my secrets, as Molly would say.

Mrs. Haslam could hardly breathe as she watched Miss Caroline take bite after bite. Pat couldn't contain his joy, slapping his knees all the while, when I told him about the sweat beads on Mrs. Haslam's face, her white-sausage fingers wrapped around the handle of her fork, her grip tighter each time Miss Caroline asked for another serving. Pat was sorry not to have witnessed it all for himself.

That's right, Miss. He wasn't at the table that evening.

Pat had already left Mrs. Haslam's and was in a cheaper boardinghouse in order to save money for us. As soon as we married, he wanted to rent a house. He was set on an entire house. He said that he didn't want to share even one wall with another stranger.

Pat couldn't wait for me to give notice at Mrs. Haslam's, but I'd told him that we both couldn't leave there at the same time, as eyebrows would raise. He said that he did not care about eyebrows or any other part of the Virgin Mother Hen raising. We would marry and housekeep like any other couple. Her approval was not required. The only kitchen you will be in, Mattie, is your own, Pat promised.

Yes, I believed him, Miss.

But I stayed at Mrs. Haslam's for a while longer because I had to care about eyebrows raising. I couldn't afford to lose a good reference.

Believing a man doesn't mean making a fool of yourself. That was Aunt Sweetie talking. Molly taught me my kitchen skills, but Aunt Sweetie taught me—or she tried to—what I would need to know in the other rooms of the house. She never married, and she told me that made her wiser than most.

Pat and I, we lived as man and wife, first on Longworth Street, next to where the Adams stables used to be, and then at the corner of Chestnut and John streets.

The one who didn't believe him was Charlotte.

From the start, the drawing that she'd made for Pat's laundry bundle was of a scrawny blackbird with its head lowered and its beak opened, midsquawk. I laughed when she first showed it to me, and I asked her how she knew.

Charlotte had no idea what I meant.

As soon as I began to call him Pat, he began to leave little folded notes for me, hidden under his coffee cup, tucked into the dip of its saucer. Because I wouldn't meet his eye when any of the other boarders were at the table, not even when it was Miss Caroline, that was his way of saying *Good morning, Mattie!* He drew himself as a raven atop a tree branch and I was a dove flying overhead. In the dove's beak, he placed a crab-apple blossom, a length of fancy lace, a scrap of borage blue ribbon, and other notions that were in my stories. That was how I knew that he'd listened, even with his eye closed.

"That Irishman"—that was what Charlotte called him then—"he's a blackbird," Charlotte said. "Birds fly away, Alethea. That's what they're born to do."

"Not a sparrow?" I asked. "Or an owl?" I teased.

"A blackbird," Charlotte repeated.

My cheeks grew warm. I knew what she and the boarders at Mrs. Haslam's saw when they looked at Patrick Hearn. They saw his black suit. He owned two, and they were the same in every way—rubbed thin at the elbows and with pant legs that barely met the tops of his shoes. It was easy for Charlotte to see why. The pants had been brought up to hide their worn-through hems.

But if it weren't for the state of those suits, shabby but always clean, I would have gone on washing the dishes. I wouldn't have paid That Irishman any mind. Just another male boarder with intentions, I would have thought.

Charlotte must have seen the color rising in my cheeks because she added, sudden as winter, "That Irishman has high taste in underthings."

"Silk?" I asked, laughing low.

"Henrietta cloth," Charlotte replied. "Mrs. Haslam has a dress made of it. Wool," she continued, "but whisper light and soft as silk, with a sheen to it."

"The pale gray dress?"

"Yes, but that cloth isn't gray, Alethea. It's a black-and-white weave. Only from a distance does it look gray."

"His underthings are gray, Charlotte?"

"White as snow, Alethea! Henrietta cloth with a white-on-white weave. I've never seen a man's under vests and drawers sewn from something so fine."

My cheeks must have reddened even more.

"I'd be careful, Alethea. That blackbird is a fussy one," she warned, as the kitchen door closed behind her.

That was how Charlotte liked to end her stories, with a question that begged to be asked. But for once, I wasn't tempted to bribe her with a cobbler or a stack cake or anything else to see the inside of the blackbird's bundle. I wouldn't think again about what "fussy" could mean, until I was already the blackbird's wife.

The question that was on my mind that afternoon was for Pat. I wanted to know his mother's given name.

"Rosa," Pat answered that evening, and then he repeated it, his voice dipping and then falling silent. When he began again, the story of his mother opened with an Irishman who was on an island very far from his own when he met Rosa. She then went very far from her island to be with the Irishman on yet another island. The Irishman passed away when Pat was ten and six. The same year he lost his eye, he said.

"That's a sign," I told him. "Which went first?"

"The eye," Pat replied, adding that he missed it more. He lifted his head so that the eye that remained could meet mine. The ring of green was full of fireflies when he looked at me in those days.

"Is your mother still far from her island?" I asked.

Rosa's story, Pat admitted, was not his to tell because he did not know it or her.

"But you know her name," I reminded him.

Pat nodded his head. He lowered it again and said that Rosa returned to her island when he was four. He woke up one morning and her scent was no longer in the rooms that they shared. Lavender, he added, as if he were saying Amen. He was left in the care of an Old Lady, who smelled of camphor and whose face was as cold as her manor house. Rosa's story ended there, as Pat had not heard from his mother since. Maybe she too has departed from this world, he said.

"Your mother is still here," I told him because I knew it to be true.

When I heard the name "Rosa," a feather had swept up my spine. Aunt Sweetie had taught me that a feather meant that the missing one was still alive. If I'd felt a cold hand on my back, then the missing one had passed. While I couldn't put this knowledge to use, as I'd no name for my own mother, it comforted me to know that she—if she were still a feather—could.

Whenever my mother said "Alethea," I would be a feather along the length of her spine.

"Rosa, on her island, could do the same," I explained to Pat.

No, Rosa is a cold hand now, Miss.

After Pat proposed, Charlotte said that I had to learn more about That Irishman's father. She said that men were more their father's story than their mother's. Charlotte was engaged to be married, so she said that she knew a thing or two about men.

"You better not let Mr. Cleneay hear that," I teased.

"Alethea Foley, you know what I mean to say! Mr. Cleneay's father butchered hogs back in Kentucky, and he taught Mr. Cleneay and his younger brothers to do the same. Those boys were the best for miles. Every one of them hired out to other plantations during hog-killing season. Since Freedom, they've been working and saving, and soon they'll own their own butcher shop in Bucktown. Not a stall. A shop, Alethea. With sawdust on the floor, glass-fronted cases, and a brass bell for the front counter. No matter what happens, I know I'll be eating well," Charlotte said, sniffing the air. "I want the same for you, Alethea."

"You want me to ask Pat if his father was a butcher?" I asked, smiling.

Charlotte stared at me hard and then declared what was in her heart all along. "That Irishman of yours—forgive me for saying—doesn't know where he's living. He thinks he's above the law? And you, Alethea Foley, you think that foreigner is going to take you away from here? To an island? To the sea? Between the two of you, I don't know who's blinder."

Charlotte and I didn't speak again until the week before Pat and I married.

When Pat showed me the piece of paper that he said was our marriage license, I looked at it and saw it as proof that Charlotte was wrong. Pat did know where he was living, and he must know something about the laws of Ohio that she didn't.

I don't know where Pat got the license, Miss. Where anyone else in Cincinnati would.

I had proof that Charlotte was wrong, so I forgave her. I headed over to her husband's shop to politely tell her so. Charlotte found me waiting for her by the locked front door of Cleneay Brothers, as dawn was breaking over the low roofs of Bucktown. She hugged me without saying a word. I'd missed her too. My bones had ached with the missing. It had been months since we last spoke, and her life had changed. She was Mrs. Cleneay now. I'd missed that too. Her wedding I hadn't attended because I'd locked the kitchen door when she came to Mrs. Haslam's to invite me. The day after their wedding dinner, Charlotte had brought over a piece of their cake and left it on the back steps. She wrapped it in butcher paper so that I would know. She was telling me, without having to say a word, that I should have been that cake's baker, all seven layers of it. She was right.

Charlotte was still not believing in Pat though.

She asked me whether Mr. Cleneay could take a look at the marriage license.

"That's not needed," I said. "Everything was in order." I repeated to her what Pat had said to me. "Reverend King has seen the license, and he'll be performing the ceremony."

His full name is Reverend John King, if you want to write that down, Miss.

Yes, he's a Negro reverend, Miss.

"Why not Reverend Webb?" Charlotte asked. "Aren't you having the ceremony at your church, Alethea?"

I'd asked Pat the same questions.

Your Reverend Webb will only perform the ceremony if it is in his church, Pat had told me. I am not stepping inside another house of worship, Mattie. I have been clear about that from the start. As soon as we find a place, the Reverend King will marry us there.

Charlotte shook her head. Pat was odd in his ways, but he was steady in his thinking.

Religion, Pat had said to me and then I had repeated to Charlotte, was for people who needed to believe that death was better than life. I was afraid to tell her what else Pat had said, but I did. Heaven is a good story, Mattie, and good stories get retold. Charlotte and I were silent after the words came out of my mouth. I was uncertain as to what she was thinking, but I, for one, felt lonely. Heaven was where I would see my mother, Aunt Sweetie, and even Molly again. Heaven was a good story because it was a true story, I told myself.

Charlotte unlocked the door to the butcher shop and asked if I would watch the front while she asked Mr. Cleneay, who was already at work with his brothers in the shop's yard, a question. I could hear their cleavers, hitting the soft flesh, the dense bones, and the hardwood of the butcher's block. The shop's cases were already half filled. I peered inside their glass fronts—just like Charlotte said there would be—and admired the thick pink chops, the washboard ribs, and the snowy slabs of fatback. I could see why Charlotte's face had filled out since becoming Mrs. Cleneay. When she returned, she, sweet as a sister, offered their parlor for the wedding. I'm not one to cry, but I wept that morning, as the first customers of the day came into Cleneay Brothers. I'd wanted to marry in a church, but to marry with Charlotte by my side would also be a blessing.

Charlotte was one of our witnesses. The other was Mrs. Mary Field, Charlotte's nearest neighbor. Pat's witness hadn't shown, so Mrs. Field was called upon at the last moment. Their Xs were on the marriage certificate, if you want to write that down, Miss.

Mr. Anderson says the year was 1874. I can tell you that it was summertime and I wore a cornflower-blue dress, which Charlotte borrowed for me—cotton lawn, she said—and my tan button boots. Pat wore one of his black suits, freshly laundered, ironed, and scented with lavender—that was Charlotte's gift to us.

Mr. Cleneay's gift was a sugar-cured ham, which I prepared for our wedding dinner at their home.

Though I hadn't told Charlotte, I had followed her advice. Before we married, I'd asked Pat for the story of his father, and it was almost as short as Rosa's.

Charles was an army officer, Pat began, and a surgeon. He must have strongly disliked Ireland, his island of birth, as he chose to live far from it for most of his life. Before Charles reached the fifth decade of life, he died of malaria in a country called India, far from his home and far from his second family, Pat said.

"Did he have a side woman?" I whispered.

Charlotte, I knew, wouldn't like the sound of a second family.

Pat repeated "side woman" slowly, as if he'd never heard of such a thing. Then he explained something to me that was far worse. He said that in his father's religion a marriage could be made to never exist in the eyes of God.

"Your father's religion made Rosa disappear?"

As a wife, yes, replied my husband-to-be.

Charlotte would have walked away at that point and never looked back. I didn't because I believed that Pat wasn't Charles and I wasn't Rosa.

Pat's father married anew and with his wife, who was not Rosa, he had three daughters.

"You've three half sisters, Pat? You're not alone then," I said, echoing one of his oft-repeated complaints, which came forward, one after the other, once he had a sip or two of whiskey. The missing island, the missing mother, the missing eye, the missing father, the missing byline, and soon enough there was just Pat, alone in Cincinnati.

No, I never took whiskey or strong drink, Miss, with Pat or without him.

I've seen what drink can do to a person. It made them happier or it made them sadder. Either way, it soon made them poorer, and I didn't need any help with that.

Pat must have had no whiskey in his glass that night because he declared that he was not alone. He had a younger brother too, he said.

I'd asked Pat for the story of his father, and he gave me three half sisters and a little brother. I scolded him for hiding them until now. Pat was a terrible storyteller, and I told him so.

Pat looked up, his eye aglow. On the contrary, he said. He was a very good storyteller, as the listener clearly wanted to know more, which was the point of storytelling.

Pat lowered his head and said that when he was young, still playing with toy soldiers, a younger boy was brought into the manor house of the Old Lady—the one who smelled of camphor—and was introduced to him as his little brother, James Daniel Hearn. The Old Lady said that James Daniel and his nanny, Elesa, had just come to Dublin.

A return voyage for me—for us both, in a way—Mrs. Brenane, the nanny corrected the Old Lady. I was Dublin born, and Danielo came into this world at the border of the Irish and Celtic seas. He was too eager to see the world, weren't you, Danielo? It was a long voyage back to Ireland and the seas were rougher this time, but he was such a good soldier, the nanny cooed. She gave the little boy a kiss, one on each of his ruddy cheeks.

Pat remembered kisses on both cheeks. Pat heard "the seas" and felt envy about that as well. His father was a "good soldier," and he went on many a "long voyage."

Pat regarded the little boy with new interest and saw that he had tiny gold rings in his earlobes. Pat reached up and felt the dimples in his own lobes and remembered that he had worn them too. He then turned his attention toward the nanny Elesa. Pat, for a brief blissful moment, thought it was his mother. Her large dark eyes, ripe damson plums; her hair full of waves, a night sea without a moon, Pat said. He took in a deep hopeful breath, but there was not a trace of lavender in the room, and he knew.

The little boy began to whimper and cling to the nanny's skirt. The nanny bent down and whispered something encouraging—possibly even loving, Pat suspected—into Danielo's ear, and the little boy toddled over and sat down on the rug next to Pat. The little boy soon picked up one of Pat's toy soldiers—precious to Pat, as they were the few toys that his father had given him—and ran off with it. Pat chased after the little thief.

The nanny Elesa and the Old Lady, who were seated and conversing nearby, must have thought that the Hearn brothers were at play, and they ignored the sudden movements and the waving of limbs.

The boys circled each other until the little thief unwisely headed toward the landing of the grand staircase, which ran through the center of the manor house, like a spine broken and twisted. Pat tried to push the little thief down the polished steps. The little thief dropped the toy soldier and clung onto a banister with both hands, while letting out the high-pitched shriek of a small animal before slaughter. The nanny came running, and the little thief let go of the banister and clung to her skirt instead. The Old Lady, unused to the din, ordered the nanny to take James Daniel away. The Boy is unfit to have company this morning, the Old Lady declared.

The nanny Elesa had brought with her gifts for Pat, a box of sticky, odd-tasting sweetmeats made of sesame seeds and a cloth bag full of seashells of varying shapes and sizes. At the bottom of the bag of shells were a handful of sand and a thick envelope, the latter the Old Lady took from him when he, in his boyish excitement, had dumped the bag's entire contents all over the nursery's floor.

Pat had not seen his little brother since. He missed not seeing the nanny Elesa more, he admitted.

Pat's stories were often like Aunt Sweetie's. Both were full of ghost-people. They were there but not really there. They were seen once or twice and then gone from sight but not from mind. They appeared again with little notice. Aunt Sweetie's people were dead, which explained their actions. Pat's were often still alive, and yet he never had a good reason for why they acted as they did.

When Pat was ten and six, the Old Lady informed him of his father's passing. She began her letter *Charles left you nothing*. The Old Lady was his father's aunt and Pat's grandaunt and guardian. He always referred to her as the "Old Lady," and she always called him "The Boy." She must have had a heart because it stopped beating when she passed, but there was no proof of its existence when she was alive, Pat claimed. He didn't shed a tear for his father or for her when she went to her God. Pat was in Cincinnati when he received this letter, and it began with a similar declaration, he said.

"Was the Old Lady meant to leave you something, Pat?" I asked.

Charlotte would have turned back at this point to hear more, I knew.

Pat answered my question with a question.

"Of course it matters, Pat!" I answered.

Charlotte may be right, I remembered thinking. Pat doesn't know where he's living. Money matters here. Clothes matter here. The color of his skin matters here. The color of mine matters. Each of these thoughts was a finger that I wanted to jab into his chest. I didn't, but Pat must have seen on my face the will that it took for me not to do so.

Mattie, it was unlikely that the Old Lady had any money left when she died, Pat said. Or, perhaps, she had never intended to keep her word in the first place.

Pat then listed for me what the Old Lady did give him. Camphor, which he said was the smell of death waiting for you; the Catholic religion, which was not the faith of his father or of his mother; and boarding schools, which taught him the language of French and of violence.

"Violence isn't a language, Pat," I objected.

Mattie, a language requires only that you understand it and, in the case of violence, that you obey it. Which is easier to understand, Pat asked, the whip or a man's voice?

"It depends on the man," I replied.

Exactly, Mattie. But the whip is always a whip. To use it is to wound. Pain is its only purpose.

"How do you know this?" I asked. What I meant was *Who whipped you, Patrick Hearn?* Charlotte and I, we've seen white bodies holding whips but never on the blood-raising ends of them.

The Old Lady, Pat replied without a pause. She did not have the stomach or the strength for corporal punishment, but she sent me to a school where the teachers and the boys did it for her, all in the name of her God, all in the name of obeying His will. The whole of St. Cuthbert's smelled of fear and on Fridays of fish, Pat said.

St. Cuthbert's was where Pat lost his eye, Miss. It wasn't an accident is what he wouldn't want you to know. Someone took it from him is what I want you to know.

Pat's vision was poorly from the time he was young. He could not recognize faces until they were near. He could not see a ball aimed at him. He could not see words on a page or a blackboard unless he was close enough to kiss them, he said. When he was ten and six, one morning before Mass, he heard a friendly voice calling to him from behind the college chapel, and he walked toward it. The voice punched him in the face until he could no longer see the gray wool of the English sky. Lying on his back in the grass, Pat heard the voice laughing in the dark. When he could see the wool again, it was only with his right eye.

I can hear Pat's voice, as if he were here with us. Maybe he is. Even as a ghost-person, I know he would sound the same.

What would I say to him? That's an easy question, Miss.

Pat, you weren't alone in Cincinnati. You had Bill and me. You should have remembered us in the end.

I hadn't mentioned Bill before? Is that so, Miss?

I cared for Bill from when he was a baby until he was grown. When I'd left Maysville for Cincinnati, Aunt Sweetie had asked me to do him the kindness of raising him as a mother would. I did.

You could say that Bill and Aunt Sweetie are kin, Miss. We're all God's children, like I said.

Pat met Bill at Mrs. Haslam's. It must have been in the late fall or wintertime because Pat was seated by the kitchen's work table and smoking his pipe, while I did the washing up. Before Pat left that evening, he bent down and asked for "the young gentleman's name."

Bill's voice piped up from underneath the table, "I'm not a gentleman, and my name is Bill."

Pat chuckled and said, "I stand corrected, Not a Gentleman Bill."

"But you're sitting!" Bill objected, his freckled face peeping out and up at Pat's.

Pat got up from his chair and said again, "I *stand* corrected, Not a Gentleman Bill."

"Now you sure are!" Bill agreed.

Pat shook Bill's little hand, sticky with the fried apple pies that I'd made for him from that day's scraps of dough.

The gal, who looked after Bill along with her brood of four, was in bed with a fever in the hours before dawn, and I knew that Charlotte was planning to spend a rare day off with Mr. Cleneay, her husband-to-be. So I'd no other choice but to bring Bill with me to Mrs. Haslam's.

I handed Pat a clean dish towel to wipe off his hand, now sticky as well.

Yes, Bill was underneath that table for a reason, Miss.

Mrs. Haslam would have fainted. *A Negro child and Mr. Hearn!* She would have grabbed her waist and raised her voice, as if I wouldn't have seen for myself whom I had gathered in her kitchen. My saving grace—that evening and every evening there—was that Mrs. Haslam hated the sight of the kitchen, especially after the supper service. The slop and the mess of cooking, she'd told me when she hired me, didn't interest her. She talked about the kitchen as if it were a pigsty. The slop and the mess? Molly's kitchen, Aunt Sweetie's, and none of mine have ever suffered from slop or mess. What Mrs. Haslam meant was that if I did my job ably, she wouldn't surprise or shadow me like other employers would.

I gave Bill another fried pie, and Pat eyed the golden half-moon as it traveled from my hand to Bill's. So I gave Pat one too, and he sat down again. Bill settled cross-legged by Pat's chair, his little body half under the work table and half out.

I returned to the last of the dishes. At the sink, with my back to them, I could hear them enjoying their treats. Bill with his mouse-like nibbles because he was trying to make the sweetness last, and Pat with his wide-jawed bites—two and the fried pie would be gone—so that no one could come along and take it from him. There was hunger in both of their bodies. One I could feed, and the other I couldn't.

When Pat didn't see Bill in the kitchen the next evening, he asked after him, and then he asked for his story.

I told Pat the same one I've told you, Miss.

Yes, he believed me.

Pat asked how old Bill was, and I replied that he was almost five. Pat blinked and blinked. He didn't mention Bill's name again in the days that followed, and I thought that he'd forgotten about the boy, as men often forget about children, even when they are their own. Then, one evening, Pat placed a toy soldier with a brightly painted red coat and white britches on the kitchen's work table and said that it was for Not a Gentleman Bill. Over the course of that next week, the soldiers and then their horses kept on appearing, in twos and threes, until Bill had a full set.

I didn't know right then that Pat and I would be man and wife, but I knew that if he asked I would say yes. Charlotte had told me that she knew that she and Mr. Cleneay were meant for each other when she got a lump in her throat *and* she couldn't stop singing. When Pat gave me the sea, my heart was in my throat, and now that he had made Bill's hazel eyes shine, my throat was full of songs. To this day, Bill still has those little men, chipped and faded, in a cigar box tucked among his books.

No, Miss, Pat was never a father to Bill. Pat couldn't be what he had never known.

I suppose you're right, Miss. I couldn't have been a mother to Bill either then.

But for three years, we were a family in the ways that we

knew how. We shared a roof and the walls of a tidy house. We ate our meals around the same table with three matching chairs with a fourth should there be a guest. After a good night's sleep, we woke to find one another still there. Until one day, we didn't.

No, Miss, Pat didn't leave me for another Negress.

Is that what you've been sitting here thinking? That Pat had a—What do white people call it?—a civility toward my kind—

A proclivity. Yes, that's the word, Miss.

Truth be told, I thought it too, at first.

When Pat and I were first trading stories, I'd found it strange that he knew the names of the streets in Bucktown— even the one where Bill and I were rooming at the time. Pat also knew his way around the Levee and its alleys where the stevedores and longshoremen drank away their wages. Pat said that his work had brought him to these colored neighborhoods, but I wasn't sure how. A secretary to a librarian and a printing-house proofreader, neither had any business being in those neighborhoods. The white men whom we do see there, day or night, had a taste for strong drink and for the lowest of women.

I was too ashamed to tell Charlotte. I didn't want her to think poorly of Pat. I didn't want to either, but I did. I stopped talking to him altogether. I would acknowledge his greetings same as before but then continue with my evening chores. He continued to smoke his pipe on the back steps, despite seeing nothing but my back.

Penniless and friendless was how Pat decided to explain himself to me. When he first came to Cincinnati, he only had the name and address of one man, he said.

"The man was a kin of yours, Pat?" I asked.

He was someone's kin but not mine, Mattie. He took one look at my face, read the letter that I had brought to him, looked me over once more, and then sent me on my way. He shooed me out of his house as if I were a cur. I stood outside his front door, my hat still in my hand, because I had nowhere else to go and no idea what to do next. In my travel case, I had books and no clean clothing left, and in my suit pocket a single coin.

Pat must have been a pitiful sight, because the man's wife, probably defying her husband's orders, opened their front door—Pat remembered the aroma of a meaty dinner wafting out—and handed him two crumpled bills from her apron pocket. He said her gesture of kindness woke him from his stupor, but it also made him understand that he was a mere beggar to this woman and man.

Pat, the beggar, slept on a park bench his first night in Cincinnati and many nights thereafter. When the air turned cold, he traded a day's work at a stable for a night's sleep with the horses and the hay. If the stablemen were Irish, they might share with Pat a corner of bread, a bit of cheese, an apple, and whatever else someone, who was their kin, had wrapped in a clean cloth for them that morning. When Pat couldn't find work—he shoveled coal, he shoveled horse dung, he shoveled salt, he shoveled sand—he would walk the city's streets with his travel case in hand, as if he were just arrived or headed elsewhere soon.

Bucktown and the Levee were the neighborhoods where it was easiest to be without, especially at nightfall, Pat said. Food was cheapest there, and so was drink. For the price of a glass, he could come out of the cold. Those whiskey-shops never closed, and if they did, few of them cared if you stayed. They would lock you in with the bottles and charge you in the morning for what you had drunk overnight.

I stared hard at Pat when he told me about his early days here, not because I didn't believe him but because I did. You don't live with the streets as your home and not leave a part of yourself there. The soft parts were what you left behind, or sold, or lost like a rotted-out tooth—in its place, a gap, a soreness, and the taste of blood.

The Patrick Hearn who came to Mrs. Haslam's didn't look to me as if he had parts of him missing except for the sight in one eye. He was a young white man of books, papers, and ink. His hands showed no sign of hard labor. His fingernails were trimmed and had no careless lines of grime. He was gentle of voice and of body. His hair was neatly cut, but the barber always missed a tuft above the right ear. Pat must have not noticed or, if he did, he kept returning to the barber out of habit or out of loyalty. I hoped that it was loyalty, which was a good trait in a man, but I couldn't decide.

It was Aunt Sweetie who made up my mind. As Pat blew his pipe smoke into the kitchen doorway to let me know that he was again there, I heard her voice. Aunt Sweetie had told me, back when I was preparing to leave her kitchen for another, that I needed to listen to a white man's footfall in order to judge his character. If his steps were taken with care, that's a good sign. If he walks with heavy steps, announcing himself even before he enters a room, you best find yourself a new kitchen, Alethea.

Pat's footfalls were almost silent. It was rare that I would hear him. It was the smell of his pipe tobacco that told me that he was near.

Aunt Sweetie said that she was wiser than most, so I decided, then and there, that I would trade stories with Pat again.

I'm glad that I did because he also knew the Cincinnati that I didn't, and he shared that city with me. The West End, Over-the-Rhine, Downtown, the neighborhoods on the Seven Hills.

I had few days to myself when I worked at Mrs. Haslam's, so our "Cincinnati journeys," as Pat called them, had to wait until we married. For our first, Pat and I took the streetcar to Walnut Hills, where he showed me the white-columned house where Mrs. Harriet Beecher Stowe had lived when she was young.

Yes, I knew who Mrs. Stowe was, Miss.

If you don't mind me saying, you must think I'm the one who's not from here. You're right. I couldn't have read Mrs. Stowe's book, but I knew of it. I've never seen the sea either, but I knew of it, Miss.

For our next journey, Pat and I took the incline from Main Street up to Mount Auburn—when white people live on a hill, they'll call it a mountain, was what I learned that day—where the grand houses belonged to the leading families of Cincinnati, Pat told me. Their houses were like roosters with their chest feathers puffed, I told him. In Mount Auburn, I enjoyed the animals in the zoo more. There were elks, buffaloes, elephants, monkeys, hungry-looking dogs that Pat called hyenas—

You're not writing this down either, Miss?

Truth be told, Pat never fancied the zoo either. He said that if he wanted to see caged animals, he could take the incline right back down to Main Street.

"These animals don't have to work for their keep and cage, Pat," I said, stopping in midstride. I could have added that the zoo's brick buildings were sturdier than any in Bucktown or the Levee, but I didn't.

Pat blinked and blinked, and he ceased his complaining about the zoo and its ticket price.

No, he wasn't a stingy man, Miss.

Pat didn't like feeling duped, and the zoo, he said, was not about the animals but about the humans who flocked there to be on display. He thought it foolish to have to pay money for such a common sight.

Pat spent the bulk of what he earned freely, on books mostly. After rent and food that is.

Yes, Miss, also on his underthings.

A few months after we married, Pat asked if I ever dusted his books. I hadn't. I'd never lived surrounded by so many books. Some were new but most were secondhand, he said. I didn't think of them as things—a vase or a table—that I would sweep a feather duster or a soft rag over. I didn't think that they were alive—a house cat or a pet bird—but maybe they were something in between. I'd never seen anyone carry a vase from room to room, onto the streetcars, or take it to bed with them the way that Pat did with a book. He even talked to some of them. He cursed at them too, slamming their covers shut.

Pat also spent his money on pipes, fountain pens, and whiskey. He spent on clothes for me and for Bill, whenever I would ask. He never begrudged me a single item, but my shoes and boots had to be griddle-cake flat. He gladly spent on school fees for Bill and foolishly on his playthings.

Pat couldn't understand why we could never take Bill with us on our Cincinnati journeys. Pat asked if we could make an exception for the zoo. I told him no.

The white people of this city, I told Pat, were far too busy to see a colored person, particularly if we were light-complected enough—Bill is lighter than I am. His father is a Scotsman; I don't know much about his mother's people, Miss—but if there were two or more of us, they would spot us without fail. Then, without fail, there would be trouble, if we weren't working for them or on our way to work for someone like them.

Pat didn't believe me.

I don't need you to believe me was what I thought. I might have also said it aloud because Pat stayed at the *Enquirer* that night and the nights that followed, coming back home only for a change of clothing and not saying a word to me.

I'd never been good with drawing pictures, so I asked Charlotte to do it for me. I left the note unfolded on the entryway table so that Pat would see the raven and the dove sitting on a tree branch, side by side. He must have seen it because he came home for supper that evening and brought with him a new hoop and stick for Bill.

No, the note wasn't an apology, Miss.

I wasn't wrong about needing to leave Bill at home. I wasn't wrong not to trot that boy through the streets of Mount Auburn or Mount Adams. If the three of us were questioned, I could claim to be his mother, but what good would that do him? No one in those neighborhoods would take Pat to be his father. The three of us were far from a family in those people's eyes. Here stands Patrick Hearn, a white man. Here stands a Negress and her fatherless child. Between us, there was no marriage, no house, no bond except for labor or something sordid. There was no need to have white strangers saying things to

Bill's face that he would hear soon enough. I knew what could come out of their mouths. Pat didn't.

That note was a reminder. Pat and I were on the same branch now was what I wanted him to know.

I know you've been wanting to ask, and the answer is no, Miss.

White passersby didn't take notice of Pat and me when we were together in your parts of the city. My hair was pinned up, and I would wear my best dress and hat. You would be surprised what a well-trimmed hat can do for a face like mine. If accosted, Pat was prepared to say that I was a Spaniard. I'd told him that we had to have a story. You can't be too careful, I insisted. He scoffed, but then he couldn't pass up the chance to spin a tale. He renamed me "Adelina" and said that I was an opera singer touring the Midwest. He had me memorize "coloratura soprano." He practiced as well, for he would say that he was my husband and manager. On the streets of Cincinnati, Pat was of the mind that we could be anyone we wanted to be. To Pat's disappointment, we were never called upon to play our parts.

Pat playacted in other ways. He could flatten his Irish lilt at will or he could take on a heavier brogue. In Mount Adams, where the policemen and firemen had their own tidy houses, Pat sounded like them. These men, out of uniform and in their day-to-day, would stop to greet him. They would tip their hats to me. I would nod back. Pat couldn't see their faces until they were right in front of him, but if they called out "Paddy" or "O'Hearn," he would answer them with an open smile because he said that they, like him, were the sons and grandsons of Ireland. If they called out "Herr Hearn" or "Hearnmann," he would know that they were the sons and grandsons of Germany. They would all laugh at his ready quips and slap him on the back. Often they would pull him aside and say something into his ear, and he would pump their hand by way of thanks.

These men have the best stories in Cincinnati, Pat boasted.

"You mean the lowest stories," I objected.

I mean the stories that sell the most newspapers, Pat objected right back.

He was right. Their stories fed us. Charlotte had pork. I had the city's muck and crime. Pat was doing very well at the *Enquirer* by the time we married, and these men were the reasons why. He said that they were his eyes and ears.

That's right, Miss. Pat began working at your paper while he was still a boarder at Mrs. Haslam's.

Proofreading at a printing house, for a man with his poor eyesight, wasn't going to benefit him or his employer. Pat's heart also wasn't in it. He wanted to write the stories, not rid them of their mistakes, he complained to me. Pat kept long hours at the *Enquirer* because he said that the best stories in Cincinnati happened in the dark, right before dawn. He told them to me first.

The news stories, Miss.

Yes, I said the news stories.

I heard about the doctors who kept stillborn babies like pickles in jars; the roustabouts who fought each other in Thurber Alley because it staved their boredom; the girls from the countryside who were maltreated by the men of the city; the unclaimed bodies of the poor that were bound for Potter's Field but ended up at the city's medical schools, butchered like hogs instead. Pat told them all to me first.

I made certain that Bill was in his bed and sleeping soundly before we would begin. Pat would light his pipe, and instead of Mrs. Haslam's kitchen we were now in our own. Instead of washing up for eight, there were the wares for three. Instead of stories of Rosa, Charles, and the sea, Pat now told me stories of Cincinnati. I didn't know that so many people in this city murdered and maimed, their floorboards dark with dried blood, their flocked wallpaper marred with bullets and bits of brain, their breath rotten with gin and sin—

No, I didn't enjoy those stories, Miss. The readers of the *Enquirer* did.

I had to listen to them twice. The first telling was Pat's way of hearing the whole story again, before he wrote it down. He would sometimes miss the heart of the story, which I could hear.

Pat, for instance, once told me about a mob that had surrounded a young loafer who had been arrested and was being hauled through Rat Row by three policemen. The mob, Pat said, was intent on teaching the wretch a lesson with their fists and their boots. Drunk and mean, that young wretch had hit an old man bloody for no good reason—not to rob him or settle a grudge—and mob justice decided that he should be ripped apart, like an alley cat onto a mouse.

"What were the policemen doing, Pat?" I asked.

The officers shielded that wretch with their own bodies, Pat said.

"Three policemen protecting a common criminal from blows? Had you ever seen such a sight, Pat?"

Pat hadn't. His readers, I knew, hadn't either.

"What was the criminal's name, Pat?"

Pat lifted his notebook up to his right eye and answered with a name that sounded German to my ears. Cincinnati taught that to me. Who knew that the Promised Land was full of Germans, I'd thought when I first got here.

"Captain Eichelberger was one of the officers, Pat?"

No, it wasn't a blind guess, Miss. It was a name that I'd often heard coming from Pat's mouth.

The captain, I'd figured, was more of Pat's eyes than any of the other policemen. If Captain Eichelberger was present, then Pat's notebook would be chock-full. The young man that night was missing a side tooth, and the rest of them were tobacco-stained. His shirt, soaked with sweat and dirt and speckled with the other man's blood, had been carefully mended, and someone had even embroidered the young man's initials at a corner of the shirttail. Pat couldn't have seen these details with his own eye, but when he was offered them, he included every last one because they made the readers feel as if they had lost the tooth or were wearing the shirt, he said.

"The captain knew the young man's family from Over-the-Rhine or Mount Adams, Pat?" I asked.

Pat lifted his notebook up to his eye again.

It was all there. He just hadn't seen it yet.

A loafer to the mob, a wretch to Pat, and a young man to Captain Eichelberger, the criminal had been blessed that night with three Angels in blue. That was the heart of the story, not the mob. The young man might have reminded the captain of a wayward nephew or cousin who had a mother waiting at home, a brood of sisters and brothers too. When the captain showed toward the young man the first sign of mercy—a blue arm extended, the palm of a hand like a shield—the other two police officers followed his lead. Pat had said that violence was a language. Mercy was a language too, I told him.

For the second telling, Pat would read the story to me once it had appeared in the pages of the *Enquirer*. I teased him that he liked hearing the sound of his own voice. He did, but that wasn't why he did this. I was his witness. Pat needed to know that he had worked and that he had worked well. So this wasn't the moment for asking any more questions. Instead, I would say "What a story!" or "Such an odd turn of events!" and that's how he knew that I'd listened. He would look up from the *Enquirer* and take a long puff on his pipe.

I didn't always understand Pat's stories once they had reached the pages of your newspaper, Miss. As with his lilt, Pat could change his words at will. I preferred the plainer ones that he used when he told his stories to me. The readers of your newspaper preferred the ones bedecked with lace, as Charlotte would say. Maybe the readers wanted the lace because they had to pay money for the stories. I got them for free.

Well, not free. In exchange for being Pat's cook, maid, and washerwoman.

"You mean for being his wife," Charlotte had said, when I'd gone to her to air my complaints.

I'd never been anyone's wife before, and Molly and Aunt Sweetie weren't anyone's wives either. We all cooked for other women's husbands. Cooking for your own husband turned out to be more of a chore. Pat never complained to me about the fare at Mrs. Haslam's, except for the Cincinnati-coffee. Not that I could have done anything about it, if he had. I wasn't to take a menu request from a boarder unless it came through Mrs. Haslam first. She called it the Michigan rule.

When I began working at her house, there was a new boarder who wouldn't eat animal fat or flesh. He was from the state of Michigan and belonged to a faith with a number in its name that I'd never heard of before.

Yes, that was it, Miss. Seventh-day Adventist.

Mrs. Haslam said that I was to serve him only vegetables and grains. I told her that the vegetables on her table were cooked with bacon or lard and so were the grains. She shrugged her shoulders and told me to use only lard from now on, as the new boarder would see the bacon pieces. If he never had lard before, how will he know what it tastes like, she reasoned. I followed her orders, and it turned out that he had grown up eating, as we all had, lard. After relishing what had been served to him for the first week or so, he ate a forkful of succotash one night and loudly complained to Mrs. Haslam, in front of her other boarders, that she hadn't respected his wishes or his faith. She told him, her head bobbing up and down, that he was in the wrong boardinghouse and in the wrong city. "Cincinnati is Porkopolis, sir!" she declared, her voice shaking. That was the first time, since I'd started working there, that I'd seen Miss Caroline smile.

Mrs. Haslam refused to rent rooms to Michiganders for years after that, and the Michigan rule came into being. Later, when I told this story to Pat, he began calling her "Mrs. Porkopolis," before settling upon his other name for her.

The point of this story, Miss? I thought it was plain.

The point was that for two years, Pat, the boarder, had eaten my cooking and found it *not* to his liking. Now Pat, the husband, was set on improving what came out of my kitchen.

First, he declared that my hot water cornbread was fine for breakfast, but not for supper.

"You want biscuits instead?" I asked him.

Biscuits weren't fine either, he replied. For breakfast, yes, but for the supper table, the only proper bread is a yeasted one, Mattie.

I'd never heard of such a thing. I ignored the yeast rule for as long as I could. Pat took to buying round loaves of bread with a hard crust—he told me that their bakers were from Germany—and adding them to our supper table to make his point.

"Your husband didn't grow up in Kentucky or in Ohio, so why do you want to cook for him as if he had?" Charlotte asked, when I'd gone over to Cleneay Brothers to ask for her advice. "You're being stubborn, Alethea. Bread, like anything else, is a matter of taste, and everyone has a right to their own tastes," she said.

Charlotte was with child, but she wasn't showing yet, so Mr. Cleneay thought it was still respectable to have her helping behind the counter. Some women, when they were in the family way, spoke plainly and only with an ear for the truth. Charlotte was one of them.

I bought some baker's yeast that morning, and the following evening we had a fresh white loaf for supper. I'd split the top of the risen dough, the way that Molly did, and poured melted butter into the gully that opened up, before placing the pan in the oven. No bakers from Germany did that, I wanted to say to Pat.

Pat had other ideas about the supper table. I suppose I should have been grateful that he didn't share them with me all at once.

Days before our first Christmas as man and wife, Pat asked what would be on the table.

"A ham," I answered, "with a brown sugar glaze."

Pat didn't say a thing.

A baked ham was what I'd made at Mrs. Haslam's every Christmas. It was also what I'd made for our wedding dinner. "The crab-apple jelly that Charlotte gave me back in the fall would make a nice glaze," I added, thinking that brown sugar sounded too plain to Pat for Christmas fare.

Pat, again, didn't say a thing.

I waited. I knew that the silence meant that Pat was picking and choosing his words. He had something to say, all right. He asked for less pork and more beef at our supper table, not only on Christmas but also on the other days of the year.

I didn't say it out loud, but I heard Mrs. Haslam's *Cincinnati is Porkopolis, sir!* ringing in my head. I did say to Pat that pork was cheaper around these parts, and he assured me that we could afford the extra expense of beef. That was how I knew that he'd received a raise at the *Enquirer.*

By the time Charlotte was about to give birth, she had a gal named Lucy who was helping her with the cooking and household chores. Cleneay Brothers, as Mr. Cleneay had promised her, was doing well, and the shop certainly wouldn't miss my orders, but still I wanted Charlotte to know.

"Pat likes beef better than pork," I said.

Charlotte rocked gently in her chair, her belly rounded and full. Now that she didn't have to wash and iron her own or anyone else's clothing, Charlotte only wore white, the color that had bedeviled her as a washerwoman. Shirtfronts spotted with jam or greasy gravy, sweat-yellowed underarms, blood on her husband's aprons, these were all someone else's troubles now. Charlotte, an angel, looked at me and said, "If he doesn't relish what's on your table, he'll dine elsewhere, Alethea."

That was all that Charlotte had to say on the matter, and it made my blood run cold. I knew what she meant. I knew that she wasn't warning me about someone else's cooking.

At the center of our first Christmas table was a roasted joint of beef. The crab-apple jelly I'd stirred into the pan drippings to give it sweetness and a pleasing gloss. Mashed turnips, sweet potatoes, a pickle plate—there were green peaches, watermelon rinds, and onions with mustard seeds—yeasted rolls, eggnog, apple custard, and gingerbread men for Bill.

Of course I can still bring to mind what was on that table, Miss. If I cooked it, then it's worth remembering. Any cook worth her salt will tell you that, Miss.

More beef roasts followed, as did beef stews—Pat liked his with carrots and parsnips but not potatoes—and beefsteaks. Porterhouse and tenderloins were the cuts that he preferred.

For a man who never went into the kitchen except to tell me a story, Pat had very particular ideas about how foodstuff should be prepared. If the stew meat wasn't as tender as he'd like, he would remind me that I should never add raw meat to a pot of hot broth or water. Always best to start the meat in cold liquids, Mattie. This is true whether the meat is fresh or dried, smoked or salted, he added.

I'd never heard of such a thing. Have you, Miss?

Well, you've that in common with Pat then. He didn't know much about cooking either.

I heard Charlotte's warning in my head whenever Pat would offer up another of his cooking remarks. They weren't cooking advice because you can't give advice about a skill that you don't have.

I disagree, Miss. I never did the same to Pat.

My "advice," if that's what you want to call it, wasn't about his writing. They were about his storytelling. I can tell stories too, Miss. Writing was what Pat did for a living, and I never presumed to tell him how to make his living.

Pat had kept his promises to me. I was his wife. I was no longer working in someone else's kitchen. I was taking care of Bill, as I'd promised Aunt Sweetie that I would. In exchange, I listened to Pat's remarks.

About soup making—I, who made a tureen of soup for a table of eight every night for over four years.

About how I needed to garnish the dishes I served to him with lemon slices, parsley sprigs, or mint leaves—a plate of food isn't a hat, I'd wanted to say to him.

About when to add sugar to the eggs in a cake batter—before the eggs are beaten, he said.

"Is that so?" I'd say. Or "Now, why didn't Molly teach me that?" Or "I'll do that next time, Pat."

I confided to Charlotte, then the mother of a baby crawling on his chubby limbs, that my spirits were low. Pat and I had been man and wife for about a year, and the southern Ohio heat arriving too early that summer was making me lose patience.

"I don't care if he dines elsewhere, Charlotte," I said. "It would be a relief," I admitted.

"Where would you go, Alethea?" asked Charlotte. She was already in the family way again—the second one would also be a boy. She spoke plain and with an ear for the truth more than ever before. Being with her made me want to do the same. She didn't have to ask where Bill would go because she knew that, no matter what happened, he would be with me.

"Where would I go?" I repeated.

The question that I heard was *Where would Pat go?*

Mr. Anderson tells me that I was two tens and one that year. Pat was two tens and five. Pat's heart still wasn't fully grown, but it would be by that summer's end.

When the days were still long and the windows were opened wide to lure in the breeze, I heard a knock at the front door as I was setting the supper table. I found Pat slumped against a corner of the porch. He was snoring quietly, and I could smell whiskey on his breath. I called him by his name, tugged on his sleeves, and then I dragged him inside the house.

No, I'd never seen him that way before, Miss.

I couldn't bring him up the stairs on my own, so I brought down a pillow for his head and left him in the entryway to sleep it off. When Bill came home, I told him that Mr. Pat was feeling under the weather. Best not to wake him, I said.

Pat woke up on his own.

Deplorable moral habits, Pat said to me. He repeated the words, the second time slower, and he explained what "deplorable" meant. Worse than terrible, Mattie.

I knew the meaning of "moral" and "habit," but I couldn't understand what these words could mean when spoken together.

"Start from the beginning, Pat," I said, sweeping his hair, which he was wearing longer in those days, off his forehead.

The beginning, he said, was when one Patrick Lafcadio Hearn met one Alethea "Mattie" Foley. He professed his love for her, and she agreed to be his wife.

"Pat, please. Start from the beginning of *this* day."

The beginning of this day, he said, was when his editor marched over to his desk in the newsroom and told him to leave the premises immediately. When asked why, the editor replied that it had come to the *Enquirer*'s attention that young Mr. Hearn here—the editor was addressing the other report-ers who were now gathered around—has been cohabitating with a woman of color. We cannot have a man of deplorable moral habits employed here, Mr. Hearn.

Pat laughed out loud. He thought it was a queer joke being played on him by his fellow reporters. He looked around at the stance of their bodies—you and I would have looked at their faces, Miss, but Pat would have seen only smudges there—and he understood that these men, with their arms crossed and their legs planted wide, no longer meant him well. Pat claimed that at that moment his ears failed him. The editor continued with his speech, his mouth opening and closing, but Pat heard none of his words.

"As if someone has swaddled a scarf around your head," I said.

Pat nodded, saying that what he did next—collecting his notebooks, his files, his half-written articles, his pipes, his pens—were all acts that were done as if by another being.

"You saw yourself, as if you were floating above your body."

Pat nodded.

"You felt small and made of something weak, weaker than flesh."

Pat nodded, adding that he left the newsroom without say-ing a word.

"Because your mouth was full of sawdust."

Pat nodded.

He headed to a whiskey-shop. The drink made him angry, he said.

"At yourself."

Pat nodded.

I should have told them to go straight to Hell, Mattie. I should have said that there is nothing about you or me that is deplorable. I should have told them your name, your precious name that means truth in the language of the Greek gods. I should have told them that you are a natural beauty. I should have said that you are a born storyteller, and all of them were amateurs compared to you. How dare they call you a woman of color, Mattie—

"That's what I am, Pat."

He looked up at me, his eye swollen with sleep and tears. I said nothing, Mattie. Nothing, Pat repeated.

At the whiskey-shop, he drank until he felt emptied of anger, until he couldn't remember how he got home, until he knocked on his own front door because he couldn't find his key, until he tried to sit down and passed out instead.

"Where are all your things, Pat?"

He couldn't remember. Then he said that he must have left his belongings at the whiskey-shop to cover his tab.

"You'll go get everything tomorrow, Pat. Here, take the week's food money and use what you need. We'll make do. We've lived on less before."

Pat then wanted to know how I knew. The muffled hearing, the view from above, the weaker than flesh, the dry mouth, he said.

"They came with my condition, Pat. Charlotte has felt the

same. So have Mr. Cleneay and his brothers. Molly, Aunt Sweetie, every colored person you've seen and not seen on the streets of Cincinnati, Pat."

He blinked and blinked.

"The first time is hardest."

You become accustomed to it, Mattie?

"No, Pat. It's hardest because the first time happened when we were young."

Tell me, Mattie, he said, closing his eye.

"When I took my first breath, my first meal from my mother's breast, I couldn't have known that I was a slave. I couldn't have known what a free person was either, as I suckled and waved my tiny fists, grabbing on to air, as if it were all that I had on this earth. When I began to crawl and play with the other young ones who were born in the shacks nearby, we couldn't have known that we didn't belong to our mothers, that their love and their bodies couldn't protect our own. But one day, we, every one of us, learned that we were lesser—worse, that our mothers were lesser—than the white people, lesser than their children, who lived at the edges of our lives."

Charlotte remembered seeing her mother whipped by a white man who had the face of a boy—wasn't even grown enough to have a full beard, she remembered. Her mother locked eyes with Charlotte and told her, clear as if she'd spoken the words aloud, to stay where she was. *Don't move toward me, my child. This will pass.* Charlotte stayed where she was, but she lost the use of her ears for the first time. The whip hitting her mother's back and cutting through became a mute. Her mother's lips continued to move, but Charlotte heard something akin to silence. Charlotte floated above herself and her mother, but she didn't know at such a young age that she should float away, head northward, into the gathering clouds. After the whip left, her mother hugged her but told Charlotte to keep her arms to her sides. *Don't touch my back, my child. This too shall pass.*

Mattie, was this Charlotte's mother or was it yours, Pat wanted to know.

"Charlotte's," I replied, "but to the whip, she was no one's mother, Pat."

Charlotte learned her first lesson of lesser when she was five. Pat learned his lesson at two tens and five.

Yes, the dismissal from the *Enquirer* was a surprise to Pat. It wasn't to me, but you didn't ask that, Miss.

Pat slept all of the following day. I brought him his meals, though he claimed no hunger pangs. The next day he did the same and the next. On the fourth day, I went to the whiskey-shop myself to pay off his tab and to collect his belongings. I didn't want Pat's pens and pipes ending up in a pawnshop.

I knew where to go, Miss, because Pat was, in many ways, a very good storyteller. Pat's stories were as good as maps. The ones about his first days in Cincinnati were often set in a whiskey-shop at the border of the Levee and Sausage Row.

I knew to look for some trees in the front that Pat had described as looking half-starved, a sagging porch—but that could have been any of the buildings there—*and* a barkeep who kept a crow by his side that sounded like a colored man laughing.

The amount that the barkeep and the crow wanted sounded higher to me than the tab for one man, even if Pat had made a full day's effort at drinking. The barkeep called him "Mr. Lafcadio" and claimed that Mr. Lafcadio had also bought rounds for others that day.

Yes, he was a Negro barkeep, Miss. His crow was colored too, if you want to write that down.

The barkeep asked, "Are you Pat's new woman?"

"I'm his wife," I replied.

The crow at the barkeep's side laughed, and he hushed it by lightly touching the top of its sleek head.

The barkeep's face still wore a pinched look, but the hard gleam in his eyes had gone away. "Mr. Lafcadio's tab is high," he explained, "because there are drinks from the past month on it too. Mr. Lafcadio, he comes in and sometimes he has money and sometimes he doesn't. I serve him no matter what because he's been coming in here for years."

I paid Pat's tab with the food money for the week, all of it.

The barkeep counted out the money for me, Miss.

You're right. He could have cheated me, and he could have lied to me about Pat's comings and goings too.

Cheaters and liars looked away when doing their business is what I've learned. He looked me in the eyes. Better still, he looked me in the eyes like I reminded him of someone he knew. So I believed him. If I hadn't, I would have asked Charlotte to send over Mr. Cleneay and his brothers to settle the sum for me.

There's more than one way to arrive at the truth, Miss.

I gave the barkeep my promise that I would return the next day with the rest of what Mr. Lafcadio owed him. He then handed over Pat's belongings, and the crow laughed as I walked out into the midday light.

Pat didn't even look at his belongings when I placed them by the bedside. He opened his eye for a moment when I'd entered the room, and then he closed it again.

The whole of Pat was a closed eye for days to come.

Then one morning I awoke and he was already dressed, shaved, and hungry for his breakfast. Riffling through his papers and notebooks that had sat unmoved for weeks, he asked whether I had brought everything home.

"What are you looking for, Pat?"

The notebook with the article ideas, he replied, and then he found it lying on top of the pile.

With a cup of tea and four griddle cakes in him, Pat left the house that morning with the notebook in hand. He didn't say where he was going, and I worried that he was returning to the *Enquirer* to try to get his job back. Fool's errand, I would have told him. Another lesson of lesser was that there were no second chances.

But Pat wasn't a lesser. He was only married to one.

Pat came home that evening with a job, not with the *Enquirer* but with the *Commercial*, Miss Caroline's newspaper of choice. He'd even received his first week's pay in advance, which he handed over to me. I don't know if it was all of it, but it was more than ever before. Pat hadn't asked how I'd made do, but he must have known that there couldn't have been any fresh meat, milk, eggs, or butter for Bill and me while he was away. "Away" was what he called the weeks that he had remained in bed. I've never been away, because no matter what happened— no matter what lessons I'd learned—I would have to be up again before dawn.

When you've been taught that you are lesser, there was another way to empty yourself of anger, the stubborn kind, the kind closer to shame. It was cheaper than drink, but it cost those around you more. I didn't tell Pat about this other way. He came to it on his own.

Pat from the start kept an even longer workday at the *Commercial*. He was proving his worth to his new master, I told myself.

Yes, Miss, I meant his new employer. I misspoke.

Pat began by taking his notebook of ideas and writing them all up for the *Commercial*. He even wrote a story about me.

Can you imagine that, Miss?

Cobbling together the stories that Aunt Sweetie had told me and that I had told him, Pat wrote that a reporter—at the *Commercial* Pat didn't have a byline either, at first—sat on the kitchen stairs of a boardinghouse while its cook—a healthy, well-built country girl, good-looking, robust, and ruddy—shared with him ghost-people stories.

Pat didn't mention me by name or Mrs. Haslam's, but if you read that story now you would know, Miss.

Salee Plantation was in there too, but Pat didn't mention its name either, only that it was between Augusta and Dover. He called it a farm instead of a plantation, which I didn't tell him was wrong when he read the story aloud to me. He included its apple orchard, elder-brushes, and the owls that lived in its beech and sugar trees, but what he described as its farmhouse he took from another story, one that was set in the place where Aunt Sweetie had lived when she was young. Pat said that Aunt Sweetie's farmhouse was more aspic.

Yes, that sounds more like Pat's word, Miss. The farmhouse was more atmospheric.

Pat even wrote Mr. Bean into the story. Well, only his name. I hadn't been able to recall the true name of the queer old man who Aunt Sweetie said had invited his neighbors over for a fancy supper and served them a giant black snake, prepared as if it were a poached fish. Like I said, Pat took from this story and borrowed from that one, until even I couldn't remember where anything had once belonged. Pat assured me that if the story made their skin crawl, then the readers wouldn't care one bit whether the old man's name was really "Mr. Bean" or not. Pat didn't venture whether Mr. Bean himself would care.

"Are you saying the snake is the heart, Pat?" I asked.

The way that the snake can creep underneath the readers' skin, Mattie, is the heart, he replied.

Once Pat began at the *Commercial*, my own workday also had to change. Pat now came home for dinner and returned to the newsroom again, until the early hours of the following day. Serving Pat a noonday meal meant setting the bread dough to rise the morning before. Yeasted bread, he told me, was also required at the dinner table. It meant an early walk to the beef butcher instead of a morning visit with Charlotte at her house. It meant—

But you didn't come to hear about my day, did you, Miss? Well, maybe you'll want to write *this* down.

Pat was becoming another man. The change began with his stomach. He was hungry, but he couldn't tell me what for. His words left him when he sat down at our table. Pat would survey what was on his plate and then pick up his knife and fork, as if they were too heavy in his hands.

Each meal that he ate in this way was a stab in my side.

I asked Charlotte if she knew of other ways of preparing beef.

"Yes. Add some pork to it," she teased, and then she called her gal Lucy out of the kitchen—Lucy was from the state of Indiana—to see if they prepared beef any differently there. They didn't.

When Pat found his words again, I wished that he hadn't.

It wasn't the beef that displeased him. It was the onions. He complained that I didn't use enough of them in my cooking. Then it was the lard. He said that I used too much of it, and all he could taste was the animal and not the summer squash, the lima beans, or the turnip greens. Then it was the wine. When Pat said "wine," he meant grape and not blackberry or strawberry wine. He claimed that the people of France used it in their cooking and that it made their dishes romantic. No, he said it made their dishes aromatic.

I'd no idea where to buy grape wine, and I told Pat so. He looked at me as if he were seeing right through me. Later that afternoon, a delivery boy came to the house with a bottle, and I stared at it, an oyster that I didn't know how to shuck. I brought the bottle over to Charlotte, and she said that Mr. Cleneay would open it for me when he got home that evening or if I couldn't wait, then I would have to go see him at his shop. I went over to Cleneay Brothers, and Mr. Cleneay broke the wax seal and slid the thin edge of a small carving knife around the stopper, jiggling it up and out.

"Are you planning to drink this entire bottle of claret on your own, Alethea?" the butcher asked with a wink.

"I'm going to cook with it, Mr. Cleneay," I replied.

"You don't have to be so formal around me, Alethea," the butcher said.

"I believe I do, Mr. Cleneay. Your wife would think so too."

"You know her better than I do, Alethea," the butcher said.

"Mr. Cleneay?"

"Yes, Alethea."

"What am I to do with this grape wine?"

"You said that you're going to cook with it, Alethea."

"I don't know how," I confessed. I hadn't intended to, but the way that he kept on saying my name made me feel as if I could.

"This is a strong red wine, Alethea. You'll have to get a cut of beef," the butcher advised.

"I was going to, Mr. Cleneay."

"I'm not a cook, Alethea."

"I know that, Mr. Cleneay."

"I would add it to the cooking liquids, Alethea."

"You mean instead of stock?"

"I'm not certain, Alethea."

"Thank you, Mr. Cleneay."

"I'm happy to be at your service, Alethea. I've missed seeing you in the shop," the butcher said. "Your face brightens the day," he added.

"Mr. Hearn prefers beef," I explained.

"There's no accounting for taste," said the butcher, with another wink.

Mr. Cleneay was right. He wasn't a cook. Otherwise, he would have told me not to use the entire bottle.

The stew smelled like a drunk and tasted like vinegar. After one bite, Pat took his plate into the kitchen and scraped its contents into the bin. I'd even placed a sprig of parsley, wilting on the edge of that plate, and it landed on top of the heap, like a curly green bow. Pat left the house without saying a word to me.

I sat in the kitchen for a long while, after hearing the front door opened and shut. I watched the sunlight coming through the yellow-and-white gingham curtains that I'd sewn for the kitchen windows. I watched that light touch the tin kettle, the cast-iron pot and frying skillet, the wooden rolling pin and long-handled spoons, the knives, the blue-and-white dishes and bowls, their matching cups and saucers—I'd asked Pat for four of each, in case he invited someone over for supper, which he never did—and the serving platter with two pink cabbage roses at its center. I'd thought of them as belonging to me, but they all belonged to Pat now. He'd taken away my kitchen. He'd been doing it for months and months with his remarks. He completed the task that day. The slop in the bin was proof that I was no longer a cook. If I wasn't a cook, I was no one.

Pat had figured it out on his own.

If you make the one dearest to you feel lesser than you, then the anger empties out of you, like pus and blood. You think it will make you heal, make you whole again, but it won't. I'd seen it tried before. Molly had as well. So had Aunt Sweetie, Charlotte, Mr. Cleneay, his brothers. Bill would see it too.

I need a witness.

It startled me. It made me look around the kitchen to find the other woman, the one who must have thought it.

I need a witness.

It wouldn't go away. It stayed in the house with me and Bill, and days later when Pat came home it shouted at me.

I need a witness.

No, I don't know where Pat had spent those nights, Miss.

I didn't stop hearing it until we were on the train headed to Indianapolis.

Bill and I, we were the ones who left first, Miss. But we were also the ones who came back. Pat was the one who would leave and never return.

No, I didn't hear voices, Miss.

They'll have me put away, if you write that. If I were you, I wouldn't put that in the *Enquirer*. A reporter is only as believable as her source, isn't that right, Miss?

Yes, Pat did teach me *that*, Miss.

Should I go on? Or do you have more questions about how I hear voices?

As I was saying, Bill and I, we went to Indianapolis. Charlotte's gal, Lucy, had kin there. Her aunt and uncle had a room to let, and the room wasn't in Kentucky was all that I needed to hear. I would never take Bill into that state. Charlotte lent me the money for the train fare, and Mr. Cleneay gave me spending money, more bills than I'd ever seen at one time, wrapped in a bit of butcher paper, when he saw Bill and me off at the station. Charlotte hadn't accompanied us because she was with child again, her third, and for the first time she was suffering from the morning sickness. She rued that it must be a girl this time.

"Girls are trouble waiting to be born," Charlotte had said, laughing low. "Come back to Cincinnati and meet her, Alethea," she added with a smile that said she couldn't wait to meet her daughter.

At the train station, Mr. Cleneay also asked me to come back.

"I intend to," I replied. "I never had plans to be anywhere else but right here, Mr. Cleneay."

What I didn't say was why I had to go away.

Pat wasn't himself these days, and I wasn't myself either.

Well, that's not all true.

Before Bill and I left, Pat was so rarely at home that I went back to cooking how I'd always cooked. Bill and I, we ate biscuits and hot water cornbread with whatever meal we wanted. We ate pork again too, as often as possible, making up for lost meals. I saw Mr. Cleneay nearly every day then. He would set aside two chops for Bill and me or, my favorite, a heap of neck bones.

"Mr. Hearn changed his mind about the pig?" the butcher had asked, his face aglow, when I started coming in again.

"No, Mr. Cleneay. Mr. Hearn doesn't change his mind," I replied.

"There must be a reason that brings you back in, Alethea. I'm guessing it's Bill. He's a growing boy, and growing boys need pork on their plate," the butcher said.

"I'm sure you're right, Mr. Cleneay."

"It's sure good to see you smile again, Alethea."

It was true that Bill at eight was growing tall and smart as a dandy—

Yes, I know the common saying is "smart as a whip," Miss.

Bill was learning his letters at school, and he took to Pat's books like a bee to honey.

See, Miss? That's a common saying too. I'm from here, Miss.

The books were what Bill would miss the most. He could only read some of the words then, and the rest he skipped, like a stone over water. He never lost a taste for reading. He had Mr. Pat to thank for it, Bill would later say.

When we were packing for Indianapolis, I told Bill that we would be traveling light. He asked whether he could bring along some of Mr. Pat's books. I said he could choose one. He chose the thickest one he could find. Bill was sharp as a dandy, as I said.

I asked him what the book was about, and he read the title to me, *The Complete Myths of Ancient Greece.*

"Greece is where Mr. Pat was born," I told him, though I knew that wasn't the full story of Pat's island.

Bill's eyes opened wide. He carried that book to Indianapolis and back, that's for sure. He still has it too.

A drawing wasn't going to tell Pat what I needed him to know, so I asked Mr. Cleneay to write some words on my behalf.

"Please give Mr. Hearn the address of Lucy's people in Indianapolis," I said.

"Are you certain, Alethea?" the butcher asked.

"He's my husband, Mr. Cleneay. He should know where he can find me."

"Is that all, Alethea?"

"Yes, that's all, Mr. Cleneay."

That wasn't all, but that was all that I could say in front of Mr. Cleneay.

Pat was a writer, so I thought he would write to me. That an envelope would arrive and within it a dove and a raven, their heads bending toward each other. Pat had the means, so I thought that he would buy a train ticket to Indianapolis and knock on Lucy's aunt and uncle's door, his traveling case left behind in Cincinnati, because he was there just to escort me and Bill back home. Pat was still my husband, so I thought that I was still his wife.

Nothing and no one came for us in Indianapolis. Bill and I made our way back to Cincinnati on our own.

No, we weren't away for long, Miss.

Bill was wanting to go to school again, and I was wanting to be at home again.

From the outside, the house looked untouched. The dried

leaves hadn't been swept from the front porch, but that was to be expected—I couldn't see Pat picking up a broom. I opened the door, and the smell of his pipe tobacco was faint—it was already faint by the time Bill and I had left. The furniture was unmoved, but the shelves were missing their books. Not a single one remained. I could see Bill's mouth hanging open as he took in the loss. I told him to go to the kitchen and get himself a cup of water. I went upstairs and found the bed unmade, a nest of rumpled sheets and pillows, as if he'd just risen and was in the washroom shaving. I looked underneath the bed frame for his traveling case, felt for its worn leather, its corners blistered with use.

That case could hold an armful of his books, his handheld glass that made ant-sized words look like cockroaches to my eyes, his comb, shaving cup, razor, a black suit, two pairs of socks—both with the same stubborn hole at their big toe, three white shirts and their spare collars and cuffs, two handkerchiefs, and atop of it all a neatly folded stack of his underthings—every under vests and drawers scrubbed until they were white as the finest sugar and ironed until they were writing-paper smooth. Charlotte could have told me about the years that they would take from me, if I'd only listened.

On his frame, he wore the cleaner of his black suits, shirt, collar and cuffs, cravat, socks that left the same big toe out in the cold, overcoat, shoes—his only pair, always in need of a good polish—and his wide-brim hat, the color of a drab country hare, with a crown like a fallen cake. Underneath it all, hidden and closest to him, his Henrietta cloth, never white enough, never ironed enough, never free enough of their stubborn creases that had plagued Charlotte and then me.

All his things were as good as ghosts now—

No, Miss, there's nothing more I can tell you about his underthings.

Would the *Enquirer* readers want to know more about *that*, Miss? The state of a man's underthings? It shouldn't surprise me that they would be drawn to something so common, but if you don't mind me saying, that isn't the heart of this story. If that's what you came here for, you haven't heard it yet, Miss.

The kitchen was just as I'd left it. I'd made certain not to leave any foodstuff behind that would spoil. I knew Pat, left on his own, wouldn't step foot in there. But he must have, because I didn't see the serving platter with the two cabbage roses. My guess was that it broke, and he threw away the pieces. I couldn't see him tucking it into his traveling case on his way out.

Pat left a note for me in the kitchen. Bill saw it first.

A raven perched on a gravestone, its head turned to one side, the eye looking up at a pumpkin-wedge moon. There were letters written on the gravestone, and I asked Bill to read them to me. He said it wasn't a word.

Here, Miss. Mr. Anderson thought that you should see the note. The Probate Court will want to see it as well, he said.

Yes, I know what the letters say now, Miss.

"M de M." At least, Pat had the courtesy not to use my true name when he buried me.

Mr. Anderson says that Pat was two tens and seven, and I was two tens and three, Miss.

If Pat and I were to marry now, we would have a photograph taken. Mr. Anderson did on his wedding day. He stood proud with his young wife. She wore all white, as brides prefer to do these days. Nothing secondhand on that gal, I can tell you. She wouldn't think of it. Charlotte and Mr. Cleneay wouldn't think of it either, only the finer things for their Alma, their third child and only daughter. Three more boys followed her. Five brothers Alma has in all. Males do run in the Cleneay family. The first half of her name was a nod to my own. The second half was for Mary, Charlotte's mother, who didn't survive the state of Kentucky.

Even without a photograph, I would have a marriage license and a certificate of marriage as proof, Mr. Anderson told me. I've seen the certificate once, I told him, when Charlotte and Mrs. Field placed their Xs on it. As for that marriage license, Mr. Pat showed it to me before we married and that was the only time that I had laid eyes on it. Maybe Mr. Pat stuffed those papers in his traveling case, along with that rose platter, I said to Mr. Anderson. I could tell from the set of his jaw that Mr. Anderson didn't find any humor in—

No, Miss, Mr. Anderson didn't call him "Mr. Pat." How could he, when the two of them had never met?

I misspoke. It's been a long morning. When you're at my time in life, names do come and go, Miss.

Mr. Anderson says that a copy of that license would be on file at the city courthouse, but that there was a fire there and my marriage papers, as well as a whole lot of other people's, were all lost to the flames. Mr. Anderson says that once my story is told on the pages of the *Enquirer*, we will go to the Probate Court, show it to the chief clerk, and ask that the record of my marriage to Mr. Pat be "restored." If a license was the only proof of a marriage, then a whole lot of people in Cincinnati should know that they've been living in sin is what I say.

You should write that down, Miss.

For now, that note in your hand is my proof. So are these.

Here, I've five coffee tins full of them. I've kept every note that Pat's ever drawn for me. You can see that the early ones from Mrs. Haslam's were stained with coffee rings.

To see these bits of paper with their doves and their ravens for what they are, you would have to know my story. Isn't that right, Miss?

Mr. Anderson says that the readers of the *Enquirer*—the city's paper of record, he says—should know that I was Lafcadio Hearn's lawful wife, not that woman in Japan.

Yes, Mr. Anderson did tell me her name, Miss.

Yes, I know about their children.

Three boys and a girl, Mr. Anderson said. I've tried to picture them in my mind, but I can't see them. I've never seen any Irish-Greek-Japanese people in Cincinnati. Don't know if they would be welcome here, truth be told. Pat always did claim that he was of mixed blood, the child of Rosa of the Orient and Charles of the Accident.

Occident, Miss? I'm sure you're right.

I don't begrudge the Japanese woman for the years that she had with Pat or for the children he gave her. She shouldn't begrudge me for being his rightful heir. I told Mr. Anderson not to ask the court for all of Mr. Pat's money, only what's rightfully mine.

What would I want her to know, Miss? You think they read the *Enquirer* in Japan, Miss?

Well, I would be honest. I would say to her that there were side women before her. Some of them were probably right here in Cincinnati. He had them down in New Orleans too, I've no doubt. But their stories are their stories, and her stories are hers. I'm not here to take away the man that she or anyone else had in their lives. I'm here to claim the man who was mine.

Yes, Miss, I knew that Pat had gone off to New Orleans.

I didn't know right away because, as you can see, there was no other writing on his last note but what was on the gravestone.

About half a year after Pat had gone away, he sent a man to the house to give me the address of where to find him.

Yes, I was still living in the same house then, Miss.

Pat had paid a full year's rent for Bill and me, before he left. It must have emptied his savings, if he had any. Like I said, he wasn't a stingy man.

"Generous and stupid" was what Charlotte called him, when I'd told her. So is your Mr. Cleneay, I'd wanted to say.

"Glad to have a roof over my head," I said instead.

"What are you going to do now, Alethea?" she asked.

"I'm a cook," I reminded her. "People still pay for that skill, don't they? I'll be giving you back the train fare as soon I find paying work again, Charlotte."

"I didn't mean to offend, Alethea. I don't care one bit about the money. I want to make sure that you and Bill are taken care—"

Miss, did your pen run out of ink? You haven't written a thing down since I mentioned Charlotte again. Forgive me for saying, but you can't understand only one man's story. Those around him have things to say too.

Yes, I know you're the reporter, Miss.

The man Pat sent over? His name is Mr. Watkin. His full name is Henry Watkin.

I'd never heard of Mr. Watkin until that evening when he

was waiting for me on the front porch and introduced himself as a longtime friend of Lafcadio Hearn.

No, Miss, Mr. Watkin isn't a Negro.

Last time I heard, he's living at the Old Men's Home in Walnut Hills. He's full of stories too, but his aren't the same as mine.

Gave young Lafcadio his first real job here in Cincinnati, Mr. Watkin would tell me. Met him on a bench at Eden Park of all places. Lafcadio was, of course, reading a book. He was the worst apprentice typesetter I ever had. He had the eyesight of a day-old pup. Got ink over everything except for the type. Had to find him another job just to get him out of my shop. He was sleeping there at the time, and the wife didn't like the sight of that. Lafcadio was well read, so I thought the library would suit him better and it did. But that librarian was a skinflint. Paid him so little that Lafcadio was still sleeping on the floor of my shop. So I found him another job, a proofreader at a larger printing house. Also bought him a better pair of reading glasses. Loaned him a bit of money too, so that he could pay for room and board at Mrs. Haslam's. I'm glad I did. Meeting you suited him best. He couldn't stop talking about the color of your hair. Cinnamon, Lafcadio said it was.

I'd hear these stories later, when Mr. Watkin and I became acquainted.

The evening we met, Mr. Watkin was all briskness and worry. If he could find someone to watch his shop, he planned to take the train to Memphis the very next day and from there catch a steamboat down to New Orleans, he said. Breakbone fever is the thanks that Lafcadio gets for reporting in that part of the country, Mrs. Hearn. Mosquitoes and Rebs are what Louisiana has in spades, I'd warned him. But you know how Lafcadio can be. When his mind is set on something, it's impossible to dissuade him.

I received a letter from Lafcadio today, Mr. Watkin said. Lafcadio wanted me to give you the address of the hospital where he's confined. He said that your boy Bill could help you with the address. Here, I hope Bill can read my handwriting. Printers, we don't have the best penmanship, Mrs. Hearn.

No, Lafcadio didn't say what he wanted from you, Mrs. Hearn.

I would think for you—and Bill—to send him a letter. Illness can make even the proudest man lonesome, Mrs. Hearn.

I'll ask something of you, Mrs. Hearn, if it's not too forward. If Lafcadio left any of his clothing here, would you send them to him? Better yet, I could take the garments from you tonight and bring them down to New Orleans with me. Lafcadio wouldn't want you to know, but I see no reason not to tell you. He has pawned his clothing, probably everything but what was on his back and on his head. He's as poor in New Orleans as the day he arrived here in Cincinnati, poorer considering that he doesn't even have his health now.

"He left nothing here," I heard my voice saying. My heart was in my throat. My heart was breaking with songs.

Then I best be going, Mr. Watkin said. Showing up unannounced on your front porch wasn't how I thought we would meet, Mrs. Hearn. I hope to see you again when I've better news or, if I don't, I'll send a letter to you and Bill from New Orleans, Mrs. Hearn.

Mr. Watkin turned to leave.

I hadn't invited him in, although the night had been spitting rain at us.

Then, sudden as winter, he turned back around.

Did Lafcadio tell you that I was to be a witness? he asked. At your marriage, Mrs. Hearn. I was all set to come that day, but then the wife thought—well, it doesn't matter now. I know Lafcadio was disappointed. He said a neighbor woman did it in my stead. I apologize, Mrs. Hearn, for not being there for him and for you. He's like a son to me, Mrs. Hearn.

Could you say that again, Miss?

Excuse me for saying, but given your question I don't think you've heard a word that I've been saying.

I'll make it plain. I didn't mention Mr. Watkin to you before, Miss, because I'm the one who'll have to go to court to be included in Pat's life. There's no one who's denying Mr. Watkin's claim to friendship, is there?

No, Miss, I never went by "Mrs. Hearn."

Mr. Watkin just assumed that I did.

For the day-to-day, I was Alethea Foley. Cincinnati is a big city, but the boardinghouses and their owners all know one another, so do their cooks and their washerwomen, and everyone else who makes their living in those hives. I didn't want it to get back to Mrs. Haslam that I'd left her kitchen to marry one of her boarders. If I had to return to someone else's kitchen one day, I wanted to make sure that I could.

It was a good thing I had that thought—Aunt Sweetie would have been proud—because that was where I ended up, right back at Mrs. Haslam's. A paying job was a paying job. I knew Mrs. Haslam's ways, and she knew mine. I'd heard that she had a string of gals working for her since I'd left and that her cook was about to leave because she was in the family way, unmarried, and can't hide her condition for much longer. When I took over Mrs. Haslam's kitchen again, it was as if I'd never left. I was glad to be paid to cook again.

After Mr. Watkin left that night, I asked Bill to write a letter to Pat for me. There were things that I couldn't say to my husband in front of the boy, so I kept those to myself.

Dear Pat, the letter began, I'm sending you five dollars. I wish that I'd more. I hope you will get well. I hope you still have your hat. Cincinnati isn't the same without you, nor is Mrs. Haslam's. You can write to me there from now on. Miss Caroline isn't in good health, and she went back to Boston. She left me all of her snowflakes—

Yes, it's true, Miss.

Why would I make up a story about *that*? Between you and me, I'm wearing two of the snowflakes right now.

Before Miss Caroline left for Boston, she'd asked me to help her pack up her books. She told me that she was dying. Boston was the right place for such a boring act, she quipped. She and Miss Beryl have cemetery plots there, side by side. We bought them when Beryl came into her inheritance, Miss Caroline said. We were young then, but we wanted to make sure that we would never be apart. Beryl has already been in hers for almost a decade now. It does not seem possible, Alethea, that time can continue to pass when those you love most depart from this life. Is your heart broken, Alethea? Do you remember when I asked you that? What was your answer then? Some bivalve or crustacean? You looked so forlorn in those days. But then, when Patrick Hearn came to stay, I thought for sure that you and he were lovebirds. I have a sense for hidden affairs of the heart. I think I still do, Alethea. No one was prouder than I was when he started writing for the *Commercial*. The *Enquirer* is a rag. Their editors are under the mistaken impression that scandals and the news are one and the same. I read that feature that he wrote about you in the *Commercial*, Alethea. I recognized you immediately, and the boardinghouse setting confirmed it. Our Mr. Bean too. When the *Commercial* began to publish those letters from New Orleans—from "Lafcadio Hearn, our Southern correspondent"—I thought that you had gone down there with him. Clearly, you did not, Alethea. I am very glad to see you again before I go, but you returning to Mrs. Haslam's was not what I had hoped for you. I wish I had something of value to offer you, Alethea, but these books and whatever else I can sell will only get me back to Boston and into a pine coffin, with Godspeed, I hope. But I want you to take those four packages over there on the bed. Have you ever seen such a shade of pink? Chinamen launderers have such peculiar taste in paper, but who better to handle silk than they, I thought. The items inside, I know, are the queerest of gifts, but I hope you will accept them in the spirit that they are being given, Alethea. May they bring you as much joy as they have brought me. If Mrs. Haslam questions you about the packages, you tell her to speak to me, and you let Patrick Hearn know about them when you have the chance. You tell him to come back to Cincinnati to see them for himself. There is nothing in New Orleans except mosquitoes and Rebs.

First time all morning I've seen a smile on your face, Miss. Didn't I tell you from the start that Miss Caroline's story was worth knowing?

Pat never acknowledged my letter, the five dollars, or the snowflakes. He's a writer, so again I thought that he would write to me. Instead, it was Mr. Watkin who stopped by the house to tell me that the danger had passed. Mr. Watkin had not been able to travel to New Orleans himself, but he had asked a printer there to look in on Lafcadio for him. Every time Mr. Watkin said "Lafcadio," I would have a firefly moment when I would forget whom he was talking about. It was easier to hear him spoken about as Lafcadio. I didn't know *that* man. I couldn't see him in my mind. I had no memories of him. My heart stayed in its place. My throat was empty of songs.

I'd invited Mr. Watkin inside the house that time, and he looked around at the shelves and saw the one book that was still there. I followed his eyes, and I said that Bill had read it from cover to cover and started right over again. Mr. Watkin said that, if it was all right with me, he would stop by again and bring Bill a couple more books. He did. That was how the two of them became acquainted, one book after the other. Later, their visits were at Mr. Watkin's shop, where the two of them would pass the time talking about what Bill had read and what he had understood. Bill called him "Mr. Henry." When Bill's schooling came to an end, Mr. Henry offered him an apprenticeship in his shop.

Bill is doing just fine these days, Miss.

Yes, that's right, he's a printer by trade.

Yes, he's married now.

Yes, he's still living in Cincinnati.

Yes, I do see him every day, Miss.

Listen, Bill is a private man with a business and a family of his own now, and he hasn't decided yet whether he wants his name and his story in the newspaper alongside mine. I'm sure he'll let you know when he makes up his mind, Miss.

About two or so years after Mr. Watkin first came into our

lives, he knocked on the kitchen door at Mrs. Haslam's as I was cleaning up after breakfast.

Mrs. Hearn, one day I will show up unannounced with good news again, but this is not the day, he began. Lafcadio has passed away in Baton Rouge. Marsh fever was what I heard, he said, his eyes darting around the kitchen as if it were on fire. I didn't want you to hear about it from a stranger while I'm away. The wife's health is poorly, Mrs. Hearn, and we're leaving the city so that she can be with her people in Virginia. I don't know when I'll be back, but I will be.

I said a prayer aloud for Pat that night.

Dear Lord, Pat was a man with a list of flaws, but he cared for Bill and me, when he was here with us and even after he left us. He cared for Mr. Watkin too, who would do anything for him.

I'd felt a cold hand on my shoulder.

I asked God to forgive Pat for being an unbeliever and to admit him into the Kingdom of Heaven. I prayed that in Heaven there were many books and that when Pat tired of reading them he could look through the clouds down to the blue of the Ionian Sea. May you allow Pat to rest in peace. Amen.

It didn't occur to me that I should have said a prayer for "Lafcadio." If I'd said that name aloud, there would have been a feather along the length of my spine, because that man was alive and breathing.

No, I don't know why Mr. Watkin would tell a falsehood, Miss.

Maybe Mr. Watkin didn't know that it was a lie when he said it. Or, more likely, Pat had asked him to say it. Maybe Pat wanted to go on with the rest of his days freed of his thoughts of me, and he wished the same for me.

With Pat's passing, it was understandable that Mr. Watkin's and my friendship would fade, I thought. Once his wife passed and he returned to Cincinnati, he saw more of Bill than me. Mr. Watkin and Bill still had books to bring them together, and soon they would have the same trade. Mr. Watkin and I, we had nothing in common but one man, whom we knew by different names, whom we'd never even seen in each other's company.

No, I don't know why Pat had kept Mr. Watkin and me from meeting, Miss.

Pat could have, with little fuss, invited Mr. Watkin home for supper. We had a chair waiting for him. We had a dish and a bowl, a matching cup and saucer too. I didn't like the first answer that came into my head—Pat was ashamed of me—or the second—Pat was ashamed of himself. So I'll share with you the third.

Mr. Watkin and I, we didn't know the same man. Pat and Lafcadio were twins who looked the same, but they told different stories, used different words, ate different foods, knew different streets, found companionship in different people, and forgot each other's lies.

Lafcadio had asked Mr. Watkin to fib about his death. Years later, in a moment of longing, maybe with a whiskey or two in him, he forgot and wrote me a letter.

The letter was sent to Mrs. Haslam's, as the letter writer knew that I couldn't have kept up with the rent on the house on my wages alone. He was right. Mr. Cleneay had helped Bill and me out when he could, but his and Charlotte's family continued to grow and he needed to care for them first. The butcher still set aside what he could for Bill and me from his shops—he and his brothers had two by then, and now they have three. I'd kept the yellow-and-white gingham curtains from the kitchen and sold or pawned the rest, except for Bill's books, which had grown in numbers thanks to Mr. Watkin. By the time Bill was ten and eight, he owned more books than most men in Cincinnati have read. He has even more these days.

When Mrs. Haslam showed me the envelope, she gave me a sideway look. I took it from her hand, and I recognized the pie wedge of the "A" and the sideway tines of the "F" of my name. Instead of running off—she still lived in fear that the odors of the kitchen would seep into the fabric of her dresses—she stood there and stared at me some more. I placed the envelope in my apron pocket and returned my attention to that day's pot of soup.

Don't you want to know whom it's from? Mrs. Haslam asked, her head a child's balloon bouncing up and down on its string. She, assuming that I would want to know, said the letter was from Mr. Hearn, that Irishman boarder who became a newspaperman. You remember him, Alethea.

It wasn't a question, and the tone of her voice—as if I'd stolen sugar from her pantry—made me think that she knew more about the goings-on in her kitchen than she had ever let on.

Mr. Hearn sent it to you from somewhere foreign. The name looks French to me, she added, sniffing the kitchen air.

I made certain that my face gave her nothing. I'd watched Molly do it, but it was Aunt Sweetie who taught me how and why. Aunt Sweetie called it putting on your mask. When you wear one, they can't see you or what's in you, she told me. Hers was a smile. Molly's was made up of straight lines, her eyebrows flat, her lips pulled thinner than they already were. Mine was a child's wide-opened eyes, as if the whole world was new to me, as if all that was being said to me was new as well.

Alethea, you don't have anything to say about any of this? Mrs. Haslam asked.

I made sure that my words gave her even less. I said not a one of them, shaking my head from side to side instead.

After Mrs. Haslam left the kitchen, I took the envelope out of my apron to see if she'd opened it. The seal was intact. She must be regretting that decision, I thought. I put the envelope with my coat and purse and went back to my work.

Yes, I was surprised, Miss.

But supper for eight boarders and one Mrs. Haslam didn't care if a Mr. Hearn, dead for how many years, had sent me a letter. Also, there wasn't a thing that I could do about it until I gave that letter to Bill to read. It wasn't going to say a thing to me until his eyes saw it.

If Miss Caroline were still at Mrs. Haslam's, I might have asked her to read the letter to me, but she, Mr. Bean, and even Mr. Wheeler were all gone. Her two rooms were now occupied by two women again, a set of second cousins, a department store clerk and a typist at one of the railroad companies. In the early mornings when the heavy curtains were still closed, I would see Miss Caroline sitting at the breakfast table, but it couldn't have been her because she was with Miss Beryl. Ghost-people, if beloved, were conjured by the living, Aunt Sweetie had taught me. If despised, they conjured themselves to ask the living why.

The return address says Martinique; it's an island in the West Indies, Bill told me later that night.

The letter writer must have been Lafcadio, as his words were nearly foreign to me. Even Bill struggled with a few, as he read the letter aloud to me.

Mr. Pat was writing as if he were someone living in the past, Bill said.

No, I don't have that letter, Miss.

When Bill saw that I was feeding its pages to the coal stove, he had the same face that you have on now. The same sound came from his throat that just came from yours, Miss.

I'll tell you the same thing I told Bill. I don't know *that* letter writer. Why would I keep something sent from a stranger?

Yes, I can recall some of it, Miss.

The letter writer, I believed, was drunk. There were long descriptions of the island and its plants and flowers and its sunrises and sunsets. Bill blushed as he read what then followed about the writer's lonesomeness and regrets. Bill's voice rose with excitement when the writer then boasted that he had five books to his name and aimed to publish more. The writer even claimed that one of them was a cookbook.

Yes, *that* was the title, Miss.

I couldn't believe that the letter writer wasn't telling a lie. Bill, worldly at ten and eight, told me that the title was French, the language spoken on the island of Martinique and in Louisiana, the state where we both had thought that Mr. Pat had lived and died. I recognized "Cuisine" as a fancy word for cooking but not "Creole." Bill said that the word meant white people descended from the French or the Spanish or it could mean colored folks descended from the same. Down in Louisiana, if they were light-complected enough, then they called themselves "Creoles of color," he said. The white in them had to come from France or Spain though, he repeated.

"Not Ireland or Scotland?" I asked, and he replied no.

Bill has tried to find that cookbook, but over the years he hasn't been able to locate a single copy. He even wrote to some of the secondhand bookshops in New Orleans. One wrote back to say that they knew of it, but that there were very few copies in the city because few had been printed in the first place.

No, I'm not curious to see it, Miss.

Truth be told, I'm taken aback that someone would trust Pat or Lafcadio—or whoever he was at the time—to know enough about the kitchen to write an entire book about it. I don't know what Creole cooking is, but if these are colored folks, then I think I know a thing or two about what's on their tables. What I want to know is whether these were the dishes that they cooked in their own kitchens or in the kitchens of others. The two aren't the same. The first is what they hunger for, and the second is what their hunger will make them do.

You don't understand the fullness of my meaning, do you, Miss?

Listen, take pork neck bones, for instance. Long-simmered and served with pan gravy, it's humble fare that we in the kitchen eat. I would never prepare it for Mrs. Haslam and her boarders, and they are poorer for never having tasted it. Like an oyster stew, I can make this dish in my sleep, not because my hands remember it but because my heart remembers it. I ask you how could a white man, Pat or Lafcadio, know how to cook something like that?

Do you know that he'd owned a restaurant, Miss?

Bill doesn't remember reading it in the letter from Martinique, but I remember hearing it. The letter writer claimed that he'd been part owner of a restaurant that served cheap but wholesome fare.

Yes, in New Orleans, Miss.

He thought about calling it The 5-Cent Restaurant, the letter writer began.

How many ways can a cook prepare a five-cent piece, I'd thought, laughing to myself. Roasted, boiled, fried, stewed, souped, pickled, jellied? What's the proper garnish for a five-cent piece, Pat or Lafcadio, a lemon slice or a sprig of parsley?

A nickel, the letter writer explained, was to be the price of every dish on the menu. But before the doors opened, the place was renamed The Hard Times, which to my mind was an even worse name. No one wants to be reminded of their sad lot when they're having a meal, even if it was cheap but wholesome.

I'm not surprised that you hadn't heard of the place, Miss. I don't know who came up with the scheme, but I'm guessing it was Pat, who came to Cincinnati with nothing, who shoveled dirt and dung for his suppers, and who never forgot how much he had to pay for so little on his plate.

Yes, he did send me another letter, Miss.

Its pages also went into the stove. I didn't even show them to Bill first.

When Mrs. Haslam handed me this second envelope, she said that Mr. Hearn of yours wasn't in France anymore.

I was tempted to correct her, but then I thought why.

He's somewhere called Cuba now, she said.

Yes, I burned those letters for a reason, Miss.

They were proof that I had married a man who was alive and well. When their pages reached my hands, I, at two tens and six, was also another man's wife.

I knew what needed to be done, but I needed time. I didn't want those letters, their pages sitting in some pocket or tin, to take that time away from me. That second envelope looked as if it had been opened and resealed. If by Mrs. Haslam, then she knew me, as most people did then, as Mrs. Kleintank.

His full name is John Kleintank, Miss, and yes, he's a Negro. If he were living in Louisiana and if his father were not German, I suppose you could call him a Creole of color.

Mr. Anderson says that it's iconic that my marriage to Mr. Kleintank is the one that I've the license and the certificate for. No, that wasn't his word. Mr. Anderson says that it's ironic that the marriage, for which I've paper proof, was never legal in the eyes of the law.

Because Pat and I had never divorced, Miss.

Patrick Hearn was my lawful husband until the day that he passed, and I, Alethea Foley, was his wife.

Let me stop so that you can write *that* down, Miss.

I want the *Enquirer*'s readers to know that I left Mr. Kleintank. I couldn't be his wife if I was still Pat's. It wasn't the law that I feared, but the Almighty. I'm not a sinner. I can't be, though the Devil knows that he has tempted me to be. I need to get into the Kingdom of Heaven. I've got kin up there. When you believe in God, your path in life isn't simple, but it's clear. You can see the North Star in the darkest sky. You can see Freedom across the Ohio. You can see your mother waiting for you in the Hereafter. No man—John Kleintank or Lafcadio Hearn or Patrick Hearn—was going to keep me from getting There.

The proof that I'd feared then is the proof that I need now. Mr. Anderson would call that ironic. I call it a slap in the face. I call it Pat still having a say, though his body is cold in the ground.

As I've said, Miss, about a month ago I'd received a letter from a publisher. It was addressed to "Mrs. Lafcadio Patrick Hearn." Do you know where it was sent? To Mrs. Haslam's. I suppose Pat must have carried that address with him all the way to Japan. Mrs. Haslam's youngest sister, a widow herself, is now in charge of the boardinghouse, and she got word to me through her cook. That Mrs. Haslam's sister knew that the letter was meant for me, well, that told me that Mrs. Haslam, may she rest in peace, knew about Pat and me all along.

I gave the letter to Bill to read. That was how we learned that Pat had passed, for the second time. There were tears in Bill's eyes. I would rather that he not miss Mr. Pat, as I'd told him years ago. Miss his books, I'd told him. The books you can replace.

I asked Bill if he had known. He said that he must have missed the death notice in the newspapers, same with the observatory—

Yes, yes, the obituary. I know the word, Miss.

I get the beginnings and the ends of them right, don't I? It's the middle that I tend to forget. So many of them are like an overstuffed chicken. Bread crumbs, chestnuts, onions, and oysters. The bird alone is enough, I always say.

The letter might as well have said *Pat left you nothing* because after Mr. Anderson wrote back on my behalf—the publisher had wanted permission to include my name in a book about Lafcadio Hearn—I received a telegram, informing me that Mr. Hearn had a wife and four children in Japan. They are his rightful heirs, and no royalties or remittance of any kind would be due to me. Also, my permission is no longer required as my name will not be appearing in the forthcoming book.

"What does 'forthcoming' mean?" I'd asked Mr. Anderson.

"It means soon, and it also can mean truthful," he'd replied. "They can't just write you out of Mr. Pat's life," he'd fumed.

There was more than one way to arrive at the truth, Mr. Anderson and I agreed.

"There's the court of law and the court of public opinion, and we'll prevail in both," vowed the optimist.

Now, isn't that right, Miss?

ELIZABETH BISLAND

(1861–1929)

. . . .

NEW YORK, 1906

[E]arly in 1874 . . . [Lafcadio Hearn] was working as a general re-porter on the Cincinnati Enquirer. *His work was of a kind that gave him at first no scope for his talents and must have been peculiarly unsympathetic, consisting of daily market reports, until chance opened the eyes of his employers to his capacity for better things. A peculiarly atrocious crime, still known in Cincinnati annals as the "Tan-yard Murder," had been communicated to the office of the* En-quirer *at a moment when all the members of the staff, usually de-tailed to cover such assignments, were absent. The editor . . . was surprised by a timid request from the shy cub-reporter who turned in daily market "stuff," to be allowed to deal with this tragedy. . . . The "copy" submitted some hours later caused astonished eyebrows, was considered worthy of "scare-heads," and for the nine succeeding days of the life of the wonder, Cincinnati sought ardently the Hoffmannesque story whose poignantly chosen phrases set before them a grim picture that caused the flesh to crawl upon their bones.*

. . . .

[I]n the latter part of [1876] . . . [Hearn] was a regular reporter for the Commercial. . . .

    One of Hearn's associates of this period, Joseph Tunison, says of his work:— . . .

"Had he been then on a New York daily his articles would have attracted bidding from rival managements, but in Cincinnati there was little, if any, encouragement for such brilliant powers as his. The Commercial took him on at twenty dollars a week. . . . [ellipsis in the original] Though he worked hard for a pittance he never slighted anything he had to do. . . . [ellipsis in the original] He was never known to shirk hardship or danger in filling an assignment. . . . [ellipsis in the original] His employers kept him at the most arduous work of a daily morning paper—the night stations—for in that field developed the most sensational events, and he was strongest in the unusual and the startling."

For two years more this was the routine of his daily life. He formed, in spite of his shyness, some ties of intimacy; especially with Joseph Tunison, a man of unusual classical learning, with H. F. Farny, the artist, and with the now well-known musical critic and lecturer, H. E. Krehbiel. Into these companionships he threw all the ardour of a very young man; an ardour increased beyond even the usual intensity of young friendships, by the natural warmth of his feelings and the loneliness of his life, bereft of all those ties of family common to happier fates. . . .

One of the charges frequently brought against Lafcadio Hearn by his critics in after years was that he was inconstant in his relations with his friends. . . .

The charge of inconstancy is, to those who knew Lafcadio Hearn well, of a sufficiently serious nature to warrant some analysis. . . . [U]p to this period he appears to have had no ties other than those, so bitterly ruptured, with the people of his own blood, or the mere passing amities of school-boy life. That many of his closest friendships were either broken abruptly or sank into abeyance is quite true, but the reason for this was explicable in several ways. The first and most comprehensible cause was his inherent shyness of nature and an abnormal sensitiveness, which his early experiences intensified to a point not easily understood by those of a naturally self-confident temperament unqualified by blighting childish impressions. A look, a word, which to the ordinary robust nature would have had no meaning of importance, touched the quivering sensibilities of the man like a searing acid, and stung him to an anguish of resentment and bitterness which nearly always seemed fantastically out of proportion to the offender, and this bitterness was usually misjudged and resented. Only those cursed with similar sensibilities——"as tender as the horns of cockled snails"—— could understand and forgive such an idiosyncrasy. . . .

To put the matter in its simplest form, he loved with a completeness and tenderness extremely rare among human beings. When he discovered——as all who love in this fashion eventually do——that the objects of his affection had no such tenderness to give in return, he felt himself both deceived and betrayed and allowed the relation to pass into the silence of oblivion.

. . . .

[Hearn's] . . . years in Cincinnati were at times marred by experiments and outbursts, undertaken with bitter enthusiasm for fantastic ethical codes, and finally caused severance of his ties with his employers and the town itself. The tendency of his tastes toward the study of strange peoples and civilizations made him find much that was attractive in "the indolent, sensuous life of the negro race, and led him to steep them in a sense of romance that he alone could extract from the study,"——says Joseph Tunison,——"things that were common to these people in their every-day life his vivid imagination transformed into romance."

This led him eventually into impossible experiments, and brought upon him the resentment of his friends.

. . . .

Sick, unhappy, and unpopular, flight to other scenes naturally suggested itself. Mr. Tunison thus describes the influences determining the move to New Orleans, which occurred in 1877:——

"As Hearn advanced in his power to write, the sense of the discomforts of his situation in Cincinnati grew upon him. His body and mind longed for Southern air and scenes. One morning, after the usual hard work of an unusually nasty winter night in Cincinnati, in a leisure hour of conversation he heard an associate on the paper describe a scene in the Gulf State. It was something about an old mansion of an ante-bellum cotton prince, with its white columns, its beautiful avenue of trees; the whitewashed negro quarters stretching away in the background; the cypress and live-oaks hung with moss, the odours from the blossoming magnolias, the songs of the mocking-birds in the early sunlight."

Hearn took in every word of this with great keenness of interest. . . . It was as though he could see, and hear, and smell the delights of the scene. Not long after on leaving for New Orleans he remarked:——

"I had to go, sooner or later, but it was your description . . . and all the delights with which the South appeals to the senses that determined me. I shall feel better in the South, and I believe I shall do better."

. . . .

The first work he secured in New Orleans was on the staff of the Daily Item, one of the minor journals, where he read proof, clipped exchanges, wrote editorials, and occasionally contributed a translation, or some bit of original work. . . . Meanwhile he was rejoicing in the change of residence, for the old, dusty, unpaved squalid New Orleans of the '70's—the city crushed into inanition by war, poverty, pestilence, and the frenzy of carpet-bagger misrule—was far more sympathetic to his tastes than the prosperous growing town he had abandoned.

The gaunt, melancholy great houses where he lodged in abandoned, crumbling apartments,—still decorated with the tattered splendours of a prosperous past . . . ; the dim flower-hung courts behind the blank, mouldering walls; the street-cries; the night-songs of wanderers—all the colourful, polyglot, half-tropical life of the town was a constant appeal to the romantic side of the young man's nature. Of disease and danger—arising out of the conditions of the unhappy city—he took no thought till after the great epidemic of yellow fever which desolated New Orleans the following summer, during which he suffered severely from dengue [italics in the original]. . . .

Always pursued by a desire to free himself of the harness of daily journalism, he plunged into experiments in economy, reducing at one time his expenses for food to but two dollars a week; trusting his hardly gathered savings to a sharper who owned a restaurant, and who ran away when the enterprise proved a failure. . . .

Meanwhile his gluttony for rare books on recondite matters kept him constantly poor, but proved a far better investment, as tools of trade, than his other and more speculative expenditures. Eventually he gathered a library of several hundred volumes and of considerable value, together with an interesting series of scrapbooks containing his earlier essays in literary journalism, and other clippings showing characteristic flair [emphasis in the original] for the exotic and the strange.

In 1881 he, by great good fortune, was brought into contact with the newly consolidated Times-Democrat, a journal whose birth marked one of the earliest impulses towards the regeneration of the long depressed community, and whose staff included men . . . who represented . . . both the American and Creole members of the city's population. . . .

His first work consisted of a weekly translation from some French writer—Théophile Gautier, Guy de Maupassant, or Pierre Loti, whose books he was one of the first to introduce to English readers, and for whose beautiful literary manner he always retained the most enthusiastic admiration. . . . These translations were usually accompanied—in another part of the paper—by an editorial, elucidatory of either the character and method of the author, or the subject of the paper itself, and these editorials were often vehicles of much curious research on a multitude of odd subjects, such as the famous swordsmen of history, Oriental dances and songs, muezzin calls, African music, historic lovers, Talmudic legends, monstrous literary exploits, and the like. . . .

. . . .

It was to my juvenile admiration . . . that I owed the privilege of meeting Lafcadio Hearn, in the winter of 1882, and of laying the foundation of a close friendship which lasted without break until the day of his death.

He was at this time a most unusual and memorable person. About five feet three inches in height, with unusually broad and powerful shoulders for such a stature, there was an almost feminine grace and lightness in his step and movements. His feet were small and well shaped, but he wore invariably the most clumsy and neglected shoes, and his whole dress was peculiar. His favourite coat, both winter and summer, was a heavy double-breasted "reefer," while the size of his wide-brimmed, soft-crowned hat was a standing joke among his friends. The rest of his garments were apparently purchased for the sake of durability rather than beauty, with the exception of his linen, which, even in days of the direst poverty, was always fresh and good. Indeed a *peculiar physical cleanliness was characteristic of him—that cleanliness of uncontaminated savages and wild animals, which has the air of being so essential and innate as to make the best-groomed men and domesticated beasts seem almost frowzy by contrast. His hands were very delicate and supple, with quick timid movements that were yet full of charm, and his voice was musical and very soft. He spoke always in short sentences, and the manner of his speech was very modest and deferential. His head was quite remarkably beautiful; the profile both bold and delicate, with admirable modelling of the nose, lips and chin. The brow was square, and full above the eyes, and the complexion a clear smooth olive. The enormous work which he demanded of his vision had enlarged beyond its natural size the eye upon which he depended for sight, but originally, before the accident,—whose disfiguring effect he magnified and was exaggeratedly sensitive about,—his eyes must have been handsome, for they were large, of a dark liquid brown, and heavily lashed. In conversation he frequently, almost instinctively, placed his hand over the injured eye to conceal it from his companion.*

Though he was abnormally shy, particularly with strangers and women, this was not obvious in any awkwardness of manner; he was composed and dignified, though extremely silent and reserved until his confidence was obtained. With those whom he loved and trusted his voice and mental attitude were caressing, affectionate, and confiding, though with even these some chance look or tone or gesture would alarm him into sudden and silent flight, after which he might be invisible for days or weeks, appearing again as silently and suddenly, with no explanation of his having so abruptly taken wing. In spite of his limited sight he appeared to have the power to divine by some extra sense the slightest change of expression in the faces of those with whom he talked, and no object or tint escaped his observation. One of his habits while talking was to walk about, touching softly the furnishings of the room, or the flowers of the garden, picking up small objects for study with his pocket-glass, and meantime pouring out a stream of brilliant talk in a soft, half-apologetic tone, with constant deference to the opinions of his companions. Any idea advanced he received with respect, however much he might differ, and if a phrase or suggestion appealed to him his face lit with a most delightful irradiation of pleasure, and he never forgot it.

A more delightful or—at times—more fantastically witty companion it would be impossible to imagine, but it is equally impossible to attempt to convey his astounding sensitiveness. To remain on good terms with him it was necessary to be as patient and wary as one who stalks the hermit thrush to its nest. Any expression of anger or harshness to any one drove him to flight, any story of moral or physical pain sent him quivering away, and a look of ennui or resentment, even if but a passing emotion, and indulged in while his back was turned, was immediately conveyed to his consciousness in some occult fashion and he was off in an instant. Any attempt to detain or explain only increased the length of his absence. A description of his eccentricities of manner would be misleading if the result were to convey an impression of neurotic debility, for with this extreme sensitiveness was combined vigour of mind and body to an unusual degree—the delicacy was only of the spirit. . . .

[O]ne of his intimate friends at this time, in an article written after his death, speaks of his friendship with the children of her family, with whom he was an affectionate playfellow, and with whom he was entirely confident and at his ease. An equally friendly and confident relation existed between himself and the old negro woman who cared for his rooms (as clean and plain as a soldier's), and indeed all his life he was happiest with the young and the simple, who never

perplexed or disturbed him by the complexities of modern civilization,
which all his life he distrusted and feared.

. . . .

[Hearn's first book, One of Cleopatra's Nights and Other Fantastic
Romances, *a translation of six stories by Théophile Gautier] . . . trav-
elled far before finding a publisher [in 1882], and then only at the
cost of the author bearing half the expense of publication. . . .*

[N]otices had been less kind. The Observer *. . . had declared that
it was a collection of "stories of unbridled lust without the apology of
natural passion," and that "the translation reeked with the miasma of
the brothel." The* Critic *had wasted no time upon the translator, con-
fining itself to depreciation of Gautier, and this Hearn resented more
than severity to himself. . . .*

*"Stray Leaves from Strange Literature" [retold legends and fables,
including those from Finland, Egypt, Polynesia, India, et al.]—
published by James R. Osgood and Company of Boston—followed in
1884 and was more kindly treated by the critics . . . [but] was not very
profitable—save to his reputation. In 1885 a tiny volume was issued
under the title of "Gombo Zhêbes," [sic], being a collection of 350
Creole proverbs which he had made while studying the patois of the
Louisiana negro—a patois of which the local name is "Gombo." These
laborious studies of the grammar and oral literature of a tongue spoken only by and to negro servants in Louisiana seemed rather a work
of supererogation at the time, but later during his life in the West
Indies they proved of incalculable value to him in his intercourse with
the inhabitants. . . .*

*"Some Chinese Ghosts" [retold Chinese ghost stories] had set out on
its travels in search of a publisher sometime earlier, and after several*

rejections was finally, in the following year, accepted by Roberts Brothers.

. . . .

[A] great change . . . had come upon . . . [Hearn's] mental attitude. The strong breath of the great thinker [Herbert Spencer] had blown from off his mind the froth and ferment of youth, leaving the wine clear and strong beneath. From this time becomes evident a new seriousness in his manner, and beauty became to him not only the mere grace of form but the meaning and truth which that form was to embody.

The next book bearing his name shows the effect of this change, and the immediate success of the book demonstrated that, while his love for the exotic was to remain ingrained, he had learned to bring the exotic into vital touch with the normal.

"Chita: A Story of Last Island" [a novella] had its origin in a visit paid in the summer of 1884 to Grande Isle, one of the islands lying in the Gulf of Mexico, near the mouth of the Mississippi River in the Bay of Barataria. . . .

Some distance to the westward of Grande Isle lies L'Isle Dernière, or—as it is now commonly called—Last Island, then a mere sandbank, awash in high tides, but thirty years before that an island of the same character as Grande Isle, and for half a century a popular summer resort for the people of New Orleans and the planters of the coast. On the 10th of August, 1856, a frightful storm swept it bare and annihilated the numerous summer visitors, only a handful among the hundreds escaping. The story of the tragedy remained a vivid tradition along the coast, where hardly a family escaped without the loss of some relation or friend, and on Hearn's return to New Orleans he embodied a brief story of the famous storm, with his impressions of the splendours of the Gulf, under the title of "Torn Letters," purporting to be the fragments of an old correspondence by one of the survivors. This story—published in the Times-Democrat—was so favourably received that he was later encouraged to enlarge it into a book, and the Harpers, who had already published some articles from his pen, issued it as a serial in their magazine, where it won instant recognition from a large public that had heretofore been ignorant of, or indifferent to, his work. . . .

It was because of the success of "Chita" [the serial] that Hearn was enabled to realize his long-nourished dream of penetrating farther into the tropics, and with a vague commission from the Harpers he left New Orleans, in 1887, and sailed for the Windward Islands. The journey took him as far south as British Guiana, the fruit of which was a series of travel-sketches printed in Harper's Magazine. So infatuated with the Southern world of colour, light, and warmth had he become that . . . two months after his return from this journey, and without any definite resources, he cast himself back into the arms of the tropics, for which he suffered a life-long and unappeasable nostalgia.

It was to St. Pierre in the island of Martinique . . . that he returned. . . . Here, under the shadow of Mt. Pelée . . . he remained for two years, and from his experiences there created his next book. "Two Years in the French West Indies" made a minute and astonishing record of the town and the population, now as deeply buried and as utterly obliterated as was Pompeii by the lava and ashes of Vesuvius.

. . . .

[Hearn] was again in New York in 1889, occupied with the final proofs of "Chita" before its appearance in book form, preparing the West Indian book for the press, but in sore distress for money, and making a translation of Anatole France's "Le Crime de Sylvestre

Bonnard" in a few weeks by Herculean labour, in order to exist until he could earn something by his original work. . . . [A]n arrangement was entered into with Harper and Brothers to go to Japan for the purpose of writing articles from there . . . later to be made into a book. . . . [In] 1890, he left for the East—never again to return.

~Elizabeth Bisland's *The Life and Letters of Lafcadio Hearn*,
Volumes 1 and 2 (1906)

KOIZUMI SETSU

(1868–1932)

· · · ·

TOKYO, 1909

Yakumo, the children miss you.

They bid, "Pleasant dreams, Papa," to your photograph every night. They say it first in Japanese and then in English, even little Suzuko. I insist upon it.

The butsudan resides in your writing room now. The scent of your pipe tobacco is no longer here, departing after the second autumn without you. It is the fifth autumn now, and as the days grow cooler the bush clovers in the garden are beginning to show their white petals or, as you would say, they are snowing.

I know you think it inappropriate for a family altar, but I have placed the photographs here, yours at the center and foster Grandfather's and foster Father's to the left and to the right. In front of foster Father is his preferred wagashi, the small crab-apple-shaped one that you were also partial to when we were all in Matsue. It breaks with tradition to offer him a confection every day, but that was his preference in life. But, Yakumo, what is tradition in this novel house of Koizumi? Foster Grandfather has his daily bowl of rice and you your daily bread.

I still order a loaf twice weekly from Takoya, the Occidental restaurant at Shimbashi Station, for Kazuo, Iwao, and Kiyoshi. Unlike her elder brothers, Suzuko has not developed a taste for toasts and soft eggs in the mornings. The two younger boys follow Kazuo's lead in every respect, and he at fifteen now has an appetite that astonishes me. Iwao at twelve is growing taller by the day. Kiyoshi at nine remains my dear one, a tender shoot. Suzuko is six and remembers you only as her "photograph Papa." I tell her that for the first year of her life you called her "Aba, Aba," followed by kisses on both cheeks. She looks very much like me these days, Yakumo, except that she has your nose. The boys all wear theirs well, and perhaps Suzuko will grow into hers. "If your husband's nose was good enough for him," foster Mother reminds me, "then it is good enough for the children." She misses you too, Yakumo.

I hesitate each time. I know that you disapprove.

Too Western, I can hear you objecting. Too bare on the tongue, as you would say. You prefer that I call you "Husband" or "Papa," not "Yakumo," your Japanese true name that took the place of "Lafcadio."

But Koizumi Yakumo, you are Western, and I, Koizumi Setsu, am Japanese. The children are the sweetest fruits of a grafted tree.

I know you are aware of the occurrences, minor and momentous, that take place underneath the eaves of this house, more so now as your work here is done. It is a great comfort to me all the same to share the household matters with you. I hope that it gives you solace as well.

Tonight, I stand before you, not to confess—because one cannot confess to something that is known—but to ask that you understand why I have been remiss of late. The reason for my nighttime absences, Yakumo, is a story. The story is about Lafcadio Hearn and how he became Koizumi Yakumo. You already know of its first telling, incomplete and rushed, that I sent to your Elizabeth for the pages of her book.

Tonight, these pages that I share with you are the second telling of that story. Their facts you will recognize but, perhaps, not their stings. Before I lock them away, you should know what they have revealed.

Rest assured, Yakumo, there will be a third telling, redacted and final, to take their place. That story will go into the world where it will stand sentry, as I do now, to your memory.

I have missed—What was the French that you used to say? Was it *tête-à-tête?*—yes, I have missed the ritual of our nightly *tête-à-tête*, Yakumo.

Once the children are asleep, I light the lamp in your writing room and we begin. These lips do not move, nor do yours. We hear each other's voices all the same. The language that we use—understood nowhere else but within this house of Koizumi—was devised in Matsue, during a winter so cold that it was said that Matsue Castle itself shivered underneath its heavy cloaks of snow.

The frigid winds had blown in from the Sea of Japan, entered the Nakaumi Lagoon, and met there the Ōhashi River and the wide expanse of Lake Shinji, leaving in their wake sheets of ice, glistening pieces of paper floated by the gods. On the first day of the first month of the 24th year of Meiji, I had looked out at the city of my birth, more water than land, and I saw what the poets of long ago had called "a silver world." On that same day of the first month of 1891, you had looked out at the same city, and you saw a new world, which you insisted was still an old one. How unchanged could Matsue have been, if you were already among us, Yakumo?

Within weeks, I was introduced to you in your "birdcage," as you so often called it in jest. In that two-story pavilion tucked into the merchant Orihara's vast gardens so that he could drink in the views of the river and the lake along with sips of tea, saké, and the light of the moon, you were its curiously plumed tenant.

If that moment could be lived again—if you and I could have another lifetime together that begins tonight—I would introduce myself to you in this way:

I was born in the 4th and final year of Keiō, which was not even a full year.

On the opposite coast, Edo was reborn as Tokyo, and that autumn the 1st year of Meiji began. The eastern capital would soon send more changes, insistent and unrelenting as the sea, across the island of Honshū.

In the 6th year of Meiji, another new calendar arrived, this one from the Far West.

Thus, on the first day of school, I learned that I was born in the year 1868 on the sixth day of February.

I learned that mere weeks after my birth the samurai of Izumo Province flanked the snowy road leading up to Matsue Castle, without their swords and upon their knees. Their surrender to Emperor Meiji's army was lit by paper lanterns, the teacher stated. It was a detail that stayed with me because the lanterns were not important to the event or to the lesson at hand. That was the impression of an eight-year-old girl. But with the passing of years, I have come to understand why the teacher had lingered on those flickering sources of light.

I have never dared to ask within my own families whether Father or foster Father were among those who had knelt. Was it daytime but the sun's rays were dampened by cloud cover or was it sundown or a moonless night? No matter the answer, I could see the paper lanterns with their everyday glow. I could see the lights and the long shadows. How fragile those lanterns must have looked in the hands of the battle-worn men. I could see their faces, straight lines, their backs, straighter still. In the days that followed, these men would cut off their topknots and no longer wear their swords in public, as both would be forbidden as remnants of the old way.

I learned that two years after their surrender, the city of Matsue by Imperial edict garrisoned a modern army, whose recruits carried rifles upon their shoulders and marched under the overseeing eyes of a Frenchman on horseback.

I learned that the word "modern" meant improved, from the Far West, and over the seas.

I learned that modern streetlights, with flames fed by coal gas, were installed on the streets between the Ōhashi Bridge and the Tenjin Bridge to encourage the to-and-fro of a modern workday, extended now into the Matsue night.

I learned that modern buildings were constructed of bricks, red as camellia blossoms, with windows paned with clear glass. I learned that these structures housed institutions of progress and change, the new public schools, the new public hospital, and the new post office, among them.

I learned that all children, boys and girls, were required to attend four years of school, which were now public and free. I learned that many never did, as their labor was needed at home, in the back of shops, on fishing boats, and in the nearby fields of rice and barley. For those children who could be spared, we read in the modern textbooks the names of Plato, Cicero, and Franklin, a man who, same as my brothers, liked to fly a kite.

When my classmates and I were eight years old, we were learning these facts and more. We had been born at the borders between two eras, and we saw with our own eyes what it meant to be a part of the old one.

The Ōhashi Bridge was where the worst-offs found themselves. Many of the men who had knelt were now seated on the bridge with their swords, their armors, and their formal haori and hakama spread before them. Silent in their dignity, they were selling without offering. When no items of worth remained, these men sat, silent in their hunger. They were begging without asking. Some chose an honorable death and left wives and daughters on the Ōhashi Bridge to beg and sell their own honor for a handful of rice. Unlike Father, these men could not set aside their code of conduct. They saw only grubbiness and humiliation when they had to feign parity with the lesser men of the mercantile class.

Foster Grandfather and foster Father would have been on the Ōhashi Bridge but for foster Mother. She sewed for the wives and daughters of those lesser men, like the merchant Orihara's, who paid a premium to have their kimono and yukata cut and pieced by a member of the house of Inagaki. Foster Mother sewed until her fingers stiffened with repetition or cold. *Each pull of the thread was another grain of rice, each pull of the thread was another grain of rice,* she mouthed to herself as she worked, her lips parting to reveal her blackened teeth, a vanity of the married women of her former class that she had refused to forfeit, a vestige of the old way forbidden since the 3rd year of Meiji. To open her mouth was to risk punishment, foster Mother understood. A woman's fate remained unchanged, she knew.

Foster Mother pulled and pulled while foster Father planned

for business venture after business venture that would fail, and foster Grandfather reread the works of the poets of yore. His most favored poem was the very first tanka, whose subject was Izumo, the Province of the Gods, the Province of his beloved Matsue. The tanka began with what you would choose as your Japanese true name. I remember you repeating its meaning aloud. "Yakumo" is a poem in and of itself, you marveled, your eye shining, lit by its own sun.

Mother would have been on the Ōhashi Bridge but for me.

Born into the house of Shiomi, Mother came of age attended to by thirty servants. Sixty hands and sixty feet labored in her stead. By the 3rd year of Meiji when she was without them, she at the age of thirty-three was a body without limbs.

Before my birth, it was agreed that if I were a female, I would live in the house of Inagaki, as these distant relatives had no child of their own, and Father and Mother already had two sons and one daughter. The house of Koizumi could spare a daughter to a lower-ranked samurai house, it was thought. Within a decade of my birth, Father and Mother would have two more sons. The house of Koizumi is rich in sons, it was said. But upon Father's passing, these sons did not become Mother's limbs. I did.

In 1879, the 12th year of Meiji, the life of the mind for me came to an end. Upon completing the seventh grade at the age of eleven, I received from the prefectural government fifty needles and thirty skeins of silk threads. As I had completed the seventh grade two years ahead of the other girls, I was also awarded another thirty skeins of silk threads. Altogether, they were weightless in these hands.

Foster Father or—if I am to speak only the truth tonight— foster Mother, as she was the sole earner then, could not afford for me to remain in primary school for the final three years, which would have required the payment of fees. For the girls whose families could indulge them, they would have the newly opened Normal School for the young ladies of Matsue to look forward to upon their graduation.

Setsu, you can use the needles and threads to sew your lips shut, your eyelids closed, a dark hood for your empty head.

Setsu, you can use the needles and threads to sew your blood into the fabric of other people's garments.

Setsu, you can use the needles and threads to sew for every single grain of rice that you will swallow.

I wept when I heard this fate. Disappointment sounded like the voice of a bitter old woman. I feared that a fox spirit or a jealous ghost had entered this body. I feared that the voice was, in truth, my own. I wept until I remembered that the voice belonged to foster Grandmother, who three years ago had departed this world. The ghost was not jealous but stubborn and blind. In life, foster Grandmother never acknowledged the demise of her class, that the men had been defeated, that the women were degraded, that the seat of power in Matsue was no longer in the fortified castle but in the modern bank. She had berated the house of Inagaki for allowing me to attend public school, bemoaning my lowered marriage prospects because I, a highborn girl, would be exposed to the eyes of commoners on the city streets, like a lowly maid. In death, foster Grandmother remained unwavering in her assessment. The future she saw for me was bleak with blood and cloth.

If I had continued my schooling and been among the first female graduates of the Normal School, I would have not met you, Yakumo. Or I would have but as a novice teacher at the

Middle School or, perhaps, the governess to the daughter of the prefectural Governor, introducing my young charge to the fundamentals of the English language.

I had no foreknowledge of my life or the existence of yours, so I could not soothe Setsu at eleven. Even if I had known, she would have not believed me or she would have only wept more.

Setsu at twelve wiped away the tears. She was no longer a child. She was a wage earner in Father's textile mill, a rare business started by a former samurai who had not failed. I can still see her seated at the handloom. There were rows of them, each with a highborn girl, pumping the pedals with her feet and legs, sending the flying shuttles back and forth with hands and arms that Mother soon would not recognize. The repetitive movements would make these limbs thick, branches that could hold the weight of a man, not sprigs bending to the weight of their few blossoms.

At eighteen, Setsu understood that it was not public school that had hindered the prospects of marriage. It was a body that resembled that of a young man's, arms and legs muscled, shoulders strong and straight with not a hint of the elegant slope that had conveyed the leisure and languor of the women of her former class. Unlike Mother, she had not been betrothed at the age of twelve. She, instead, had been weaving a kimono's worth of cloth per day.

Setsu at twenty-two stood before you on a late January morning in 1891, the 24th year of Meiji, because Father had passed away, five years ago. The textile mill departed with him, leaving unpaid debtors behind to mourn. A year before Father's death, First Brother had abandoned the physical house of Koizumi, and Second Brother left it for the family tomb. Third

Brother now spent his days catching and releasing birds, keeping the favored ones in cages not nearly as well crafted as your "birdcage," Yakumo. Youngest Brother at fourteen was still a boy because Mother doted on him, an overgrown songbird. Married long ago, Elder Sister was a member of another house, as was a daughter's fate. Mother would rather waste away than beg on the Ōhashi Bridge, its iron pillars reaching up from the river's depth, its wooden span painted a bright coat of white, the modern incarnation of a previous bridge that had served Matsue well for three hundred years.

Do you remember why the former bridge had endured, Yakumo, despite the strong currents and the frequent storms? It was the first story of old Matsue that I would tell you. Your fellow teachers were too ashamed to share such lore with you. Too Japanese, they thought.

A young man was buried alive in one of the bridge's middle pillars. He had disobeyed an edict from the daimyō about the proper attire required of all men who wanted to cross the bridge on its opening day. A single human sacrifice, Yakumo, had kept the whole structure strong.

It was for the best, I know.

If I had recited that litany of misfortune, you would have placed some coins into the hands of Tsune and waved us both away.

Prior to the introduction, Tsune had explained to me what to expect. She called you the "New Foreign Teacher," as if I did not know your name from the newspapers. She said that you had stayed at the Tomitaya, her family's inn, upon your arrival in Matsue. You were very content there, she boasted. You moved into the merchant Orihara's garden pavilion two months ago, but you kept an arrangement with her that brought two of the inn's young maids, Onobu and Oman, to the pavilion four times a day. They delivered your meals, heated the water for your morning and nightly use, and performed all the household chores. The tip of Tsune's tongue touched the corners of her mouth, as if she had eaten something salty, which told me that she was profiting handsomely from the arrangement. How much will she receive for this one, I wanted to know.

Tsune said a storm cloud was inside your left eye, but your right one was clear. Your nose was typical of Westerners, large and high, and yours ended in a particularly sharp point. Your hair was not the color of straw or, worse, of a sea urchin's inside. Charcoal black with the beginnings of gray, she said. Your facial hair was confined to your upper lip, which she admitted was difficult for her to look at, as it reminded her of a dusky caterpillar. Tsune glanced at this face, which as you know, Yakumo, never gave away my thoughts, and she must have decided that she was not presenting the New Foreign Teacher in the best light. So she added that you towered over the men in Matsue, but not all. Nishida Sentarō, the head teacher of the Middle School, for instance, was of equal height. Tsune's comment was meant as a compliment to you both: Nishida Sentarō is as tall as a foreigner, and the New Foreign Teacher resembles, at least in stature, Matsue's most esteemed young teacher and bachelor. The two are close friends, she whispered, as if it were a confidence that she alone knew.

I had read the articles in the *San'in Shimbun* and the city's other newspapers announcing your arrival and the details of your life to date in Matsue. The city and I knew that you were brought there by the prefectural government to teach the English language to the boys at the Middle School and to the young men at the Normal School. Their previous teacher was a Christian missionary, whose years in Matsue did not generate nearly as much interest as yours would. We read that you arrived in Japan on the *Abyssinia*, which had docked at the eastern port of Yokohama on the fourth day of April, 1890, the 23rd year of Meiji, in time to celebrate the Sakura Matsuri. You traveled then to Tokyo to meet with other Western academics of renown at the Imperial University, according to the papers.

The cherry blossoms had opened for you.

I mouthed this to you as you departed on your final journey, Yakumo.

Late September at the outset of a Tokyo autumn, and yet the old cherry tree outside your writing room had burst into bloom. I have been called a woman with an oak heart, but even I knew that the sakura had shown themselves to you one last time. A fitting farewell, Yakumo. The poets of long ago would have been pleased by their gesture.

According to the *San'in Shimbun*, at the tail end of August you began your four-day journey westward via train, jinrikisha, and then on foot once the mountain paths narrowed. Your traveling companion to Matsue was a graduate from the illustrious Imperial University in Tokyo, a young man identified as Manabe Akira, whose English-language skills, it was reported, rivaled Matsue's own Nishida Sentarō's. You arrived in the city on August 30, and you began teaching on September 2. The city and I read that your teaching days were five hours long and that you taught twenty-four hours per week. One newspaper even reported that your salary was second only to the prefectural Governor's. We were assured that your fellow teachers and students thought very highly of you. "Lafcadio Hearn is too good a man to be in so isolated a place," I remember reading. I had not thought of my hometown as an "isolated place" before you, Yakumo. At school, I had learned that we were a city of forty thousand, a number equal to the fish in the whole of the Sea of Japan, I had imagined.

The *San'in Shimbun* reported that the prefectural Governor honored you with invitations to view the horse races, the competitions of weaponry, the sumo tournaments, the Noh performances, and many of the formal gatherings at the Governor's official residence. Nishida Sentarō was identified as your interpreter and your peer at these events, though illness had prevented the head teacher from being present on several recent occasions, it was noted.

Some in Matsue were more impressed by the accounts of your visit to the Izumo Shrine in Kitzuki. The ancient pine trees of Kitzuki must have shuddered in unison at the sight of the unfamiliar race, it was written. You were the first Westerner, according to the papers, to be granted admittance into the sanctuary of this Shintō shrine. Nishida Sentarō was credited with writing the letter of introduction to the shrine's high priest, which had gained you access. It was Manabe Akira who had accompanied you there because the head teacher was once again too ill to travel.

The women and girls on my lane fussed over that detail when I read the article aloud to them. "Herun-san" and "Nishida-san," the newspapers had dubbed the two of you, forgoing the honorific "sensei," which otherwise would have followed the names of teachers, to suggest the modern nature of the friendship, perhaps. Foster Mother, in particular, was concerned about the frequent mentions of illness in connection with the head teacher. "Twenty-seven is young," she said, as she threaded the eye of a needle. Foster Mother meant that men, unlike women, do not age at the same headlong pace, and that I at twenty-two was fast approaching the end of youth.

None of us on that lane had seen Nishida Sentarō in person, except for Oman, the maid at the Tomitaya. "Nishida-san attends the monthly poetry evenings at the inn, and now he is there several times a week to drink and dine with Herun-san," she told us.

When you, Yakumo, came into contact with Oman at the inn and then at your birdcage, she was fifteen years old. I do not have to remind you that she saw the world through much older eyes. This happens to girls of beauty. They flower early.

"Nishida-san is very handsome," Oman often said, with not a hint of color in her cheeks. She complimented his smooth pale skin and his high cheekbones, touching her own by way of example. She praised his deep voice. "Commanding but not harsh," she said. "The maids would all listen at the edge of the room dividers whenever it is Nishida-san's turn to recite his poems. He rarely stays afterward for the entertainment, the real reason for those poetry nights," she added. "He rarely partakes unless his favorite maiko is there, and she is never there these days because she has a new patron. The postmaster, the other maids say." As usual, Oman's cheeks were the color of fresh snow. Modesty did not show itself upon them.

Oman would have been the New Foreign Teacher's rashamen, but for me.

There is no need to feign ignorance, Yakumo. We are past the time when such truths can wound.

I knew the word for the mistress of a Westerner long before we met. Their stories, from the open port cities of Yokohama, Tokyo, Ōsaka, Kōbe, Nagasaki, Niigata, Hakodate, and Kanagawa, had reached us even here in "isolated" Matsue.

I also had eyes older than my years, though beauty was not the cause, and I saw Oman's glow when she told us stories about Nishida-san. But when she spoke about Herun-san, she touched the neckline of her kimono, at the point where the left side of the garment crossed the right. When she shared with us that Herun-san had rented the merchant Orihara's garden pavilion, foster Mother and I exchanged glances. Would it be a dwelling for one or two? we wondered. Upon describing to us the arrangement that Herun-san had made with the inn, Oman was proud to note the additional pay that she was now taking home to her household of seven.

Oman's Father and Mother were said to be poor in girls, in that there were five daughters and no son. Oman, the youngest, was the last of the sisters to work outside of the house. She never attended a day of school nor did any of her sisters. Foster Grandmother, when she was still with us, used to remind me that Oman's Father belonged to the foot-soldier class. "Their kind lived south of the Ōhashi River," foster Grandmother said. "Only the true samurai houses, the Shiomi, Koizumi, Inagaki among them, were allowed to live within the shadows of Matsue Castle," she declared.

We all live on the same lane now.

I never disrespected foster Grandmother by stating this truth aloud, for it should have been evident to her when she was alive.

Oman, catching the look between foster Mother and me, added that Onobu, another of the inn's maids, shared the workload with her at the garden pavilion. "Herun-san feels sorry for Onobu because of her own bad eye," Oman explained, as she again touched her kimono. "He even gave the landlady Tsune money to take Onobu to a modern doctor, but the landlady kept it instead. When Onobu's eye showed no improvement, Nishida-san asked the landlady what had happened to Herun-san's money, and she lied to the head teacher's face."

"The modern doctor could do nothing for Onobu, as her eye is a curse, the landlady Tsune told Nishida-san," Oman said. "The following week the head teacher informed the Tomitaya that Herun-san would be leaving," she added.

Oman was usually more discreet about the topic, referring to the blind eye only as Herun-san's "condition." The newspapers had written about it but only in passing. An article had noted that Herun-san's students thought him a heroic figure because he sometimes wore an eye patch when teaching. He must have lost the eye in a battle or a duel, these students speculated.

I was grateful to Tsune for speaking so bluntly about your left eye, Yakumo. As with the paper lanterns at Matsue Castle, I could imagine the storm cloud. When I saw it in person, I thought of the moment before the summer rains, a natural occurrence, and that thought kept me calm as I stood before you, as your right eye appraised me, as the thick disk of glass that you held up to it magnified the unblinking orb.

We all live on the same lane now?

Foster Grandmother's voice echoed in these ears.

We all live on the same lane now?

She meant to mock me.

We all live on the same lane now?

I would be twenty-three years old within days.

We all live on the same lane now?

I have two households to help feed.

We all live on the same lane now?

Dignity and honor, foster Grandmother, do not fill empty bowls.

We all live on the same lane now.

I lowered the eyes. I willed the shoulders to slope. I whittled away the thickness of the arms and legs, thankful for the three layers of silk brocade that hid them. Foster Mother had lent me her formal kimono, the only one that she had not sold, for the introduction.

The face refused to change. It remained, as it is today, plain.

When Tsune and I entered the garden pavilion, I had swept its interior with the eyes. The tatami was new and green, its rice-straw-and-sunlight scent floating above the smell of pipe tobacco, which also inhabited the room. The kotatsu at the room's center must have been burning charcoals all night, as the room felt as temperate as a spring day. Around the hem of the kotatsu's thick quilt covering were untidy stacks of newspapers and books. I saw only one zabuton there. Where does a visitor sit or kneel in this dwelling? I wondered. A large hibachi sat nearby. Two heating sources for one modest room, I noted, and began out of habit to calculate the cost of the charcoals needed to keep them both warm.

Poverty reduced everything to a number. I have been reminded of this of late, Yakumo.

I have not had to deprive the children of heat or other comforts. That is not what I mean to suggest. Foster Mother and I have had to reduce the household expenses but in ways that the children have hardly noticed. Foster Mother sews all of their clothes now, except for the boys' private school uniforms, which must be purchased as they are imported from England. Rest assured that their education will always be the first priority within this house of Koizumi. Foster Mother also prepares all their meals, making certain that once a month they enjoy a Sunday supper of beefsteaks, buttered English peas, and steamed carrots, sliced crosswise like coins. Kazuo, same as you, compliments foster Mother's beefsteaks and says that they are even better than those at the restaurant Takoya. We do not dine there as often these days. Kazuo claims not to miss the Occidental dishes there in the least. Iwao and Kiyoshi chime in to say the same, though Iwao was seven and Kiyoshi was only four the last time we all dined there as a family. Suzuko was not even one then, yet she nods her head now in agreement.

Suzuko is not like her brothers, Yakumo. Remember how she would babble when she was in your arms? She is less of a mountain brook now. The high fever that almost took her from me three years ago took some of her away with it. Foster Mother tells me that I have raised only boys and assures me that girls can grow up more quietly. There are days when Suzuko does not say a word. There are days when she does not even look up when I say her name. I remind myself that you were like this as well, that you were often elsewhere. Suzuko is often elsewhere too. I hope that she is not lonesome there, Yakumo.

This house of Koizumi is not the same without you. To deny these changes is to deny that you are the heart of this house.

We have tenants now, Yakumo.

The small house at the edge of the property where the

household's handyman had lived is now rented to a young couple, a department store deliveryman and his wife. The income it brings in is not much, but it does pay for the school supplies for the boys. The royalties from the book by your Elizabeth pays for their private school tuition. The royalties from all of your books, Yakumo, take care of their other needs. Mr. McDonald—Kazuo and the boys call him by his full naval rank "Paymaster Mitchell McDonald, U.S.N.," after which they always add "Papa's American friend in Yokohama"—makes certain that the payments are received here in Tokyo, and he does not hesitate to cablegram your publishers in America and in England whenever they are delinquent, which is often the case these days.

We have only one maid for all the household chores now, Yakumo.

Though the same as before, I am the only one who dusts and cleans your writing room. No one is allowed to touch your books, your papers, or your high desk and chair. The oil lamp, the lotus-leaf-shaped dish for your worn pen nibs, the small tabletop hibachi for lighting your pipes, the conch shell are all where you left them. How the maids used to jump whenever you blew on that shell—Pa-wo! Pa-wo!—two extended blasts, as if a steamship were departing from the other end of the house. The student houseboys would laugh and tease them for never anticipating your call. How cross you were with me, Yakumo, whenever I would dispatch a maid to your writing room before you had the chance to Pa-wo! Pa-wo!

I was that maid once.

Of course, I knew when that hibachi had grown cold.

What I did not know was when that seaside memento would cease to fill the rooms of this house.

Almost fourteen years we had together, Yakumo.

Less than one in Matsue, three in Kumamoto City, less than two in Kōbe, and eight here in Tokyo. A garden pavilion and then a house in the shadows of Matsue Castle, two houses in Kumamoto, three in Kōbe, and two in Tokyo. The only one that you owned is this one, and you left it just two and a half years after entering its garden gate. Tallied, these numbers suggest a brief, nomadic life, sheltering under rented eaves, lacking in land, weak in roots.

Numbers are poor storytellers.

Every city and every house was a home, Yakumo, because we were each other's country. You thought it was called "Japan," but that was the country outside. The country inside was founded by two unlikely travelers. In Kumamoto City, that country added to its populace, sending for foster Grandfather, foster Father, and foster Mother. Then Kazuo arrived to become its first native-born. The other three children claimed their citizenships in Tokyo. When you departed, I was left an exile in the country outside. I miss what was once under the eaves of this house, Yakumo.

At first, the garden pavilion was the foreign land, as far from Matsue as I had ever been. I, as novice travelers tend to do, located and clung to what was familiar there. On the morning of the introduction, I was consoled by a bush warbler in a large hinoki cage. A gift from the daughter of the prefectural Governor, Tsune had told me. The bush warbler was singing a mating song because the little fellow had been duped by the warmth of the pavilion into believing that spring was already here.

I knew what I would do first, if I were to stay. I would slide open a shōji window, the one nearest to the little fellow's cage, and allow in a thread of cold so that he would know that winter was still in Matsue.

Yakumo, you needed no reminder. You had on an overcoat, a "seaman's" because of its double row of buttons as I would later learn. Underneath it, you wore a padded kimono, a pair of Western suit trousers, white tabi on your feet, leather gloves on your hands, a knitted scarf around your neck, and on your head a hat—national origin indeterminate—with a wide soft brim the color of a maitake. I would have thought you addled if I had not known of your sensitivity to the cold.

"The New Foreign Teacher," Tsune had told me, "has been flat on his back for weeks with a fever and a rasping cough. He complained that the pavilion was drafty and that Oman's and Onobu's visits were not frequent enough to keep the kotatsu, the hibachi, and him warm. He asked for a live-in maid, but Oman cannot be spared at the inn," Tsune claimed. "Also, he wanted someone older. Someone who can read and write, he specified. Both are unusual requests for a foreigner," Tsune said.

"There has been a misunderstanding," I informed Tsune. "I do not know the English language."

"Read and write Japanese," she said.

"Yes, Japanese. How unthinking of me," I replied. "May I ask you a question?"

This was the moment when Tsune volunteered the storm cloud, Yakumo, though your left eye was not my question or my concern.

"Do you have some English?" I asked her.

"Of course. I know how to say 'thank you, please, sorry, yes, no, good, bad, eat, drink, hello, goodbye, man, woman, big, small, and the bill,'" Tsune rattled off.

"And the New Foreign Teacher, he has some Japanese?" I asked.

"He knows how to say thank you, please, sorry, yes, no, good, bad, eat, drink, hello, goodbye, man, woman, big, small, and shrine," Tsune replied. "He has been in Japan for about five months, so the New Foreign Teacher is not a quick learner," she said, laughing.

"Shrine?"

"Yes. He enjoys visiting them, even more than most Westerners. The jinrikisha men who wait outside the inn all know this about him. He waves his favorite one over and says 'Miya!' and expects that the man will take him to a new one each time. The New Foreign Teacher will expect the same of you."

"Expect what of me?" I asked.

"You will be his live-in maid. You and he will negotiate any additional tasks that he will require of you. Do you understand the arrangement?"

"I understand the arrangement," I replied.

"He is eager to meet the daughter of a *great* samurai," Tsune added. "Samurai are *still* important to foreigners," she said, unable to hide her contempt.

"I see. I will try my best then."

"You will have to! There are many who would want this position. If I had more time, I would offer the New Foreign Teacher a choice. But he wanted someone immediately, so I could find only you."

"How do you speak with him?" I asked, ignoring yet another of her insults.

"We point. We draw pictures. We playact," Tsune answered. "It was easier when the Imperial University man was still staying at the inn. Now, if it is a small matter, then one of the students from the Normal School will drop by with a message or a request. For matters of importance, the New Foreign Teacher sends Nishida-san over. For this arrangement, Nishida-san has not been involved. The New Foreign Teacher knows he can trust me. This is a small matter, anyhow."

Tsune was an arrogant woman.

I was an observant one.

I knew immediately that you did not trust Tsune. I did not trust her either. We were in agreement from the beginning, Yakumo.

"Koizumi?" you asked.

I nodded, confirming Father's house.

"Shiomi?"

I nodded again to confirm Mother's house. I raised for a moment the downcast eyes.

Behind the handheld glass, your magnified right eye was gentle but dull as rusted cast iron. I knew that look well. I had seen a man's disappointment before.

You picked up a book from atop one of the stacks. You opened it and ran a finger down its Japanese title. On the facing page was its title in the English language, I presumed. You wanted me to read the former aloud to you, to test Tsune's veracity and mine.

"*A Japanese-English and English-Japanese Dictionary*, fourth edition," I complied. "By Ja Se . . . He . . . bun," I continued, hesitating over the author's foreign name, transcribed there in katakana characters.

"J. C. Hepburn," you corrected, as you raised the glass up to your right eye again.

I noted a change. Flecks of gold were now floating inside a ring of moss, at its center a chestnut freed from its burr.

We stood this way for what must have been a long while, as the bush warbler sang in his cage.

Tsune became impatient and began to point at you and pull at a sleeve of the formal kimono.

When foster Mother offered to lend it to me, I had hesitated.

"He is expecting a samurai's daughter," foster Mother insisted.

"He will notice the shorter sleeves," I objected, pulling at their fabric, wanting them to stretch to a maiden kimono's more generous length.

"He is not looking for a bride," foster Mother said.

"He will know."

"That woman from the inn already knows," foster Mother said.

"Tsune knows?"

"Yes, she knows. Oman must have told her," foster Mother replied. "That woman summoned me to the inn to inquire about the circumstances. I told her the truth."

"What is the truth?"

"Foster Father regrets his decision," foster Mother answered. "Foster Grandfather did not approve from the start. We should have listened. Inaba Province people are untrustworthy, he had warned us about Maeda Tameji."

"Please do not say his name."

"The second son of the former samurai house of Maeda, from Inaba Province, the letter from the go-between had stated; is willing to be adopted into the house of Inagaki, upon marriage."

"I remember the letter, foster Mother."

"We thought that our prayers had been answered," she said. "A male heir, the continuity of the house of Inagaki, and you as our daughter in name as well as in heart. Also, you were already nineteen then," she added, making a case for the bridegroom all over again.

"I remember the prayers, foster Mother."

"The go-between's letter confirmed the hopeful outcome of your visit to the Yaegaki Shrine," she continued.

"I remember the prophecy, foster Mother."

"Your paper and coin had floated to the farthest end of the shrine's Mirror Pond. A newt had touched it, nudging it along. Marriage, we rejoiced, though it would be to someone from afar, we knew."

"The prophecy came true," I said.

"The Mirror Pond never lies," foster Mother agreed.

"It omits though."

"Yes," she acknowledged.

"Less than a year."

"Less than a year," foster Mother repeated.

"Tsune knows about the dissolution?" I asked.

"I informed her that your name was removed from the Inagaki family registry and returned to the house of Koizumi, once your husband had disappeared," she replied.

"He did not disappear, foster Mother. He went to Ōsaka."

"May he die in Ōsaka then."

"Koizumi Setsu?" you asked, ignoring Tsune's flailing gestures and sleeve tugging.

"Koizumi Setsu," I confirmed.

You lowered the handheld glass.

Tsune continued to point and jab, but you turned your attention to the *Dictionary* again. You sat down on the zabuton and leafed through its pages. Then you pointed to an entry, reading the English word aloud to me, "agree."

I kneeled beside you on the tatami, and I read the Japanese that followed aloud to you, "agree."

You located two more entries, "begin" and "today." I echoed their counterparts to you, first as a question and then as a statement.

By now, even Tsune understood that an arrangement was being reached between Lafcadio Hearn and Koizumi Setsu.

Wanting to ensure her finder's fee, Tsune intervened. She again pointed at you and then at me. She moved her legs up and down, as if she were walking. She turned her back to you, as if she were departing. She turned toward you again and showed you the cupped palms of her hands, two empty bowls. "The bill," she said, first in Japanese and then what must have been its English twin.

Yakumo, you placed in her hands two banknotes.

Tsune closed her fingers around them, the claws of a crab snapping.

You shook your head.

She shook her head, feigning forgetfulness, and then handed one of the banknotes to me.

The weight of a month of rice was in those hands, Yakumo.

"Already know what to do, I see," Tsune spat out, before she departed.

You returned to the kotatsu and lost your legs underneath its quilt covering. You returned to the pages of the *Dictionary*, compiling a list of words. The task absorbed your attention.

The bush warbler was no longer singing. The warmth of the pavilion had lulled him to sleep. His bamboo perch swung slowly back and forth.

I searched the room again for a zabuton, where I could kneel until your attention turned my way again.

You are not a guest here, Setsu, I reminded myself.

I begged your pardon.

You did not look up from your writing.

I climbed the polished wooden steps that led to the second floor of the pavilion, and I found there a room stale with sleep and unwashed clothing. I slid open a shōji window and the wooden shutters, and I looked out at Lake Shinji and the Ōhashi River, as if for the first time. Snowflakes were descending in large unfamiliar shapes, the feathers of some lost bird. The hills and the mountains bordering the lake had receded into the clouds. The Ōhashi Bridge was barely visible in the mid-distance. The winds of Matsue were the only familiar presence, as they picked up and rushed into the room, shaking the wood and rattling the paper.

I closed the shōji window and looked behind me.

A hibachi, its maw filled with ash, sat cold in the center of the room. I could see my breath when I exhaled, same as within the house of Inagaki all winter long. In a corner alcove, the bedding quilts were folded up for the day, along with three zabuton stacked one on top of the other.

I could place those zabuton together and sleep on them tonight, I told myself. I could bring the bush warbler's cage here to keep me company. Herun-san should not be sleeping up here. No wonder he has been ill for so long. How could Oman and Onobu have been so careless? I will need assistance bringing his bedding quilts downstairs tonight. I will find "carry" in that *Dictionary*. "Help" will be needed as well.

I too was making a list, Yakumo. My words were utilitarian. Yours had other aims.

At the noon hour, Onobu and Yao, another of the inn's young maids who from this day forward came in lieu of Oman, arrived at the garden pavilion with the lacquered boxes containing your midday meal along with a parcel of clothing and foodstuff that foster Mother had gathered for me. Yakumo, as you had already paid Tsune until the end of the month, she saw no need to change the maids' routine or to reimburse you, which confirmed for me that she profited handsomely from the New Foreign Teacher.

While Onobu set up the trays and brewed the tea, I returned to the second floor, and with Yao's help I took off foster Mother's formal kimono, exchanging it for an everyday one, tying up its sleeves in preparation for the day's chores.

Foster Mother included in the parcel a mirror and an ivory comb, which Father and Mother had given to me long ago. On the seventh day after my birth, these items had accompanied me to the house of Inagaki along with a wet nurse, whose feet did not touch the snowy ground because she and I were carried there in a covered palanquin. In the lean years that would follow, I had offered to sell the comb and the mirror, but foster Mother had refused. I knew, eventually, that she and I would have to sell whatever was of worth that remained.

I sent the formal kimono back to foster Mother along with the banknote tucked inside one of the sleeves. More I hoped would soon follow.

That was the beginning of the story, Yakumo.

It was not the one that I had sent to your Elizabeth for her book.

You and I both know that the beginning is not the pearl. It is the grain of sand.

I would have never presumed, Yakumo, to tell your story to her or to any other stranger, but for Mr. McDonald.

Within days of your departure, he had cablegrammed your publishers asking for a full accounting of your royalties and copyrights. He reviewed your bank accounts here in Tokyo on my behalf. He made the train trip between Yokohama and Tokyo several times in the course of the following month, bringing with him toys and imported sweets for the children every time. His assessment at the end was clear. New sources of income have to be found for the house of Koizumi.

Mr. McDonald was firm in his resolve and urgency. He said that I was "only" thirty-six years old. "Not an old woman," he insisted, in his decorous Japanese. The Koizumi children will require financial support for years to come, he said.

Mr. McDonald devised a plan, and a biography would be one of these new income sources. He said that interest in your life and your books was high, as your obituary had appeared in newspapers throughout America and England. A "Mrs. Wetmore" would write the biography, but she would need my recollections of your years in Japan. "Mrs. Wetmore is a woman of means now and does not need or want the royalties," Mr. McDonald said. "They will be assigned to you, Mrs. Koizumi." The proceeds, he assured me, would allow the family to remain in this house.

When Mrs. Wetmore was first named, I did not know that she was a woman of means now. I did not know anything about her, until I remembered that three years before your passing, Yakumo, you had dedicated a book to a "Mrs. Elizabeth Bisland Wetmore." When I learned that she would publish your biography under her maiden name, "Elizabeth Bisland," I understood that I had known of her all along.

Elizabeth is hungry.

Elizabeth is angry.

Elizabeth has my hat.

Kazuo's notebooks were full of Elizabeths. You used her name in the daily English-language lessons that you gave to your eldest son. How I envied him for these lessons with Papa. You had stopped teaching me the English language before he came into the world. Herun-san's language, as you called it, served us well enough, you thought.

The Japanese words that you acquired never found their rightful order. They were, as you had been on that winter morning in Matsue, addled seeming. Often, they were unrecognizable because you had disguised them with your own meanings, obscure and strange.

"Herun-san speaks Japanese like a poet," foster Grandfather used to say to me. "A drunk one," he would add. If foster Grandfather had too much sake, he would be even more descriptive. "A drunk lady poet," he would say, mimicking your words in a high voice, as they, admittedly, were echoes of my own.

There are Japanese words that only women say, Yakumo. Your fellow teachers must have informed you of this when you were in the company of the geisha and maiko who entertained after the monthly poetry gatherings at the Tomitaya. Nishida-san must have shared with you the origin and function of this women's speech, but, perhaps, the nuances of vocabulary became lost in the affairs of men and forgotten in the acts that followed.

Foster Mother knew that foster Grandfather was fond of you, but her lips pulled into a taut line whenever she heard him joking at your expense. "Herun-san can speak Japanese any way he pleases," she would say to me in private. "A man who feeds *both* of your families can speak any way he pleases," she reminded me, as though I could forget.

When we were no longer in Matsue, I understood that this poet whom you had become had yet another distinguishing trait. "A drunk lady poet from Izumo Province," foster Grandfather could have said, though he never did because he was very proud of his Izumo dialect. I was not proud or partial to the speech of my region, but it was all that I knew, Yakumo.

A drunkard, a poet, a female, a rustic.

I was aware of what you became in Herun-san's language. You never spoke it in front of your fellow teachers and students— Why forfeit the English language when you were the one who wielded it best?—but you freely bandied it in front of shopkeepers, jinrikisha men, steamship passengers, fishermen, farmers, and anyone else whose path crossed yours. You were as proud of Herun-san's language as foster Grandfather was of his Izumo speech.

I would stand aside while you attempted to converse. Then, when all had failed, I would ask the question that you had intended but as if I were asking it of you. The listener would overhear, understand then the nature of your inquiry, and a conversation would begin anew with me as the interpreter.

Women's speech, Yakumo, coming from this mouth was

expected and could be understood. An Izumo dialect also could be understood and easily dismissed, especially once we were among the learned men in Tokyo, as a woman's lack of education or, if the listener were feeling generous, as a regional charm.

The children, one by one, learned Herun-san's language. I worried that they would speak it outside of the house, but the children understood, without being told, that it was a family language with no currency beyond the garden gate.

Yakumo, you will be pleased to know that the boys have taught Suzuko the meaning of "Tani-no-oto," the earliest of entries in Herun-san's language. She says it now whenever she sees the neighbor's rotund cat squeezing through the bamboo grove.

I had accompanied you to a sumo tournament in Matsue, and the grand champion that season was named Tani-no-oto. You delighted in him and in the sound of his name. Days later, when you said his name to me, I corrected you, thinking that you were reaching for the Japanese word for azaleas, lotus flower, toad, or whatever else you were finding noteworthy in the gardens of the merchant Orihara that morning. You shook your head and repeated "Tani-no-oto!" as you gestured toward the edge of the koi pond. Then you mimicked a sumo's wide-legged stance.

"Ah, that toad is Tani-no-oto! Yes, so are you," I teased, which made you laugh out loud like a boy, not a man of forty years.

I could not deny that Herun-san's language has its usefulness and its appeal, but later on, whenever I would look through Kazuo's English-language notebooks—his handwriting more steady with each passing year—I wanted *that* language as well. Over time, I would learn to identify the individual letters but not their meanings once they were grouped. Within Kazuo's notebooks—these letters joined as if they were formed by one length of thread—the "E," a curving corseted thing raising itself high above the rest, was an oft-repeated sight.

Elizabeth is hungry?

Elizabeth is angry?

Elizabeth has your hat?

I know the answers now, Yakumo. There is no need to claim otherwise. "Elizabeth Bisland" was the name that was always on the tip of your tongue.

I remind myself that we are all capable of having two hearts. Even me, Yakumo. Perhaps you had even more. Late at night when the world is hushed, these hearts murmur in languages foreign and familiar. In the light of day, it is the heart nearest to yours that prevails. This is not a wife's solace speaking. It is what keeps her upright and unbroken. Proximity, she knows, is her advantage.

A month after your departure, your Elizabeth in the guise of "Mrs. Wetmore" requested, via a cablegram from America, that I send her "Lafcadio's Japanese years as soon as possible. By mid 1905 at latest. Biography must publish 1906. To ensure continued interest."

Mr. McDonald, seeing my distress as he translated her words, assured me that Mrs. Wetmore would only include brief excerpts by me, which she would choose with the utmost care and discretion, in her account of your life. "The weight of this project would be on her shoulders," he said.

Americans mourn differently, I told myself. They send disjointed missives, the speed of their arrival taking precedence over their content. They plan for a future without the deceased. They bustle with the deeds of the living.

I am Japanese.

I held on to your story, Yakumo, until I could take a breath again for the both of us. To tell another's story is to bring him to life, and you, Husband, are still here. Every day, you and grief rise in me with the sun:

I see you in the garden of this house, greeting the vein-blue morning glories. When the autumn without you arrives, these stalwarts are still clinging to the garden fence, their leaves yellowing, their flowers growing smaller with each cool day. You prefer them best at this time of the year. Strong, you call them. Brave, you name the last of their blooms.

When the toasts and eggs are set out for the boys, I see you at the table, half in a dream, adding salt to your coffee, laughing aloud at yourself when the children laugh.

The household's jinrikisha man, older than you but not by many years, departed the same day you did, as if fulfilling a feudal pact between retainer and master, and yet the two of you still leave from the garden gate on your teaching days, you in a Western suit and your mushroom hat, your books and papers wrapped by these hands in a blue-and-white furoshiki, your midday meal wrapped by the maid's. You despise the formal costume of your country and your discomfort when wearing it shows. The university faculty and students have expectations, I remind you, as I button the white shirt's stiff, binding collar. They want a Western professor, not a Tani-no-oto Japanese, I tease, as I tie the laces of the leather shoes that, you complain, confine and pinch your feet.

Lafcadio Hearn, reporting for duty! is your usual rejoinder, as you salute me as if I were an admiral issuing commands.

When the sounds of the jinrikisha's wheels and its runner's sandaled feet return in the late afternoon, I greet you at the front door, and the maid out of habit begins to heat the water for your bath. You smile, kiss me on both cheeks, and ask whether any letters or packages have arrived that day from America.

Yakumo, is this your way of asking for your Elizabeth?

Her correspondence, wearing their "Mrs. Wetmore" disguise, waits for you in your writing room, where you sit at your high desk, the right side of your face bent toward its surface, your eye nearly touching the paper and ink, until the light of the day begins to fade. I light the oil lamp. The tabletop hibachi for your pipe I leave cold because I long to hear the Pa-wo! Pa-wo! of the shell.

When the family gathers at the table for the evening meal, I see you walking into the room last. I still wait for you to begin. There are nights, though, when you forget about your hunger and your family's, and I do not catch sight of you again until the moment before I turn down the light.

Pardon me for being the first to sleep, your drowsy voice tickles the ear.

I hear you, Yakumo.

Every night.

"Pardon me for being the first to sleep" were my words. I had spoken them to you since the birdcage in Matsue, since before you understood their meaning, since before I meant them.

You never were the first, Yakumo.

Until now.

I close these eyes and I join you in the dream world where grief slips below the horizon, replaced by the rising moon of memory, and we are in Matsue again with the bush warbler and his song.

That little fellow and Yao were such a source of comfort to me during those early days. We three took to one another immediately, but the bush warbler had fallen truly for the maid Yao. He sang to her and only her whenever she was in his line of sight. Despite your distaste for Tsune, you were tempted to keep the arrangement with the inn so that Yao could keep the bush warbler and me company.

I showed you in one hand the amount that you paid to Tsune and in the other what you could pay directly to Yao. It was easy to see who was overpaid and who did the bulk of the work.

When you agreed with my judgment, I knew that you intended it as a gesture of affection, Yakumo. With Yao as your new live-in maid, there would be, between us, a different arrangement in place. I took your decision, however, as the beginning of trust. Trust and affection were of unequal weight, and I preferred trust, as it had to be earned. Affection could be pity or a purchaser's remorse in disguise.

Within the close quarters of your birdcage, I could not hide these hands, coarsened by their years at the loom. Were you sparing them household work because you were sparing yourself? Did you think that the hands of a common laborer would disappear and those of a highborn woman would take their place again? Affection would have only compounded such doubts. Trust did not have to ask such questions of shame.

I knew that Tsune would attempt to make a fuss or pretend that she did not understand, if one of your students was tasked with letting her know. As for Nishida-san's assistance with a household matter, I was not yet trustworthy in the eyes of the head teacher, and therefore he was not yet trustworthy in mine. The New Foreign Teacher's change of heart, coming from this mouth, left Tsune with little recourse except to gossip about it to the innkeepers, shop owners, jinrikisha men, and maids of Matsue, who together did a better job disseminating information than the city's newspapers.

That rashamen is already making changes!

That rashamen swooped in like a bird of prey, and the rest of us lost our shares!

That rashamen is Matsue's shame!

"Rashamen" soon followed me like a hungry dog whenever I left the birdcage to visit with foster Mother, leaving banknotes for her and for Mother tucked inside her sleeve each time.

At least I am not a hungry dog! declared the straight back.

Foster Mother is not a hungry dog! added the silk of another new kimono.

Nor is Mother! affirmed the freshly dressed oval of hair.

After Yao, the next to join the birdcage was Hinoko, the first of the felines to belong to the house of Koizumi. With spring still days away, the pavilion's veranda was a chilly place to take in the sunset, but the panels of persimmon- and wisteria-colored silks that draped the river and the lake at that brief moment of the day soothed and solaced me. As the sun began its descent, the winds carried with them the sounds of whimpering and crying. A baby, I thought. Then the winds brought shouts of "Throw it in! Throw it in!" that grew into a determined chant. I ran toward those voices and down to the nearby shores of the river, where I saw one of the gardener's sons holding a kitten, squirming and drenched, by its long tail. The boy was dipping the little creature into the Ōhashi and pulling it out again. I had seen this boy, no more than eight years of age, working alongside his Father in the merchant Orihara's gardens. The boy's face—his lips now pulled back to show his teeth and his brows pushed together into one—made him unrecognizable as a human child. I shouted at him to give me the animal. The others ran off, and the gardener's son did as he was told.

When you returned to the pavilion that evening, you found a ball of black fluff, sleeping near the bush warbler's cage. The story of Hinoko—I had named her for the gold sparks in her eyes—then began. I was the storyteller and you the listener, as were our roles in the years to come.

Our cohabitation, three months by then, had resulted in a short list of words that could be exchanged without having to consult the pages of the *Dictionary*. These words suggested an air of having grown old together, a vocabulary winnowed by the passage of years. They also lent a sense of amity. I was loath to disturb that fiction with the introduction of words such as "anger" and "fear" or "helpless" and "weak," but those were precisely the ones that I would need in order to tell you the story of Hinoko.

Your eye opened wide, your face went pale, and you paced back and forth, uttering exhortations that I had not heard from you before. Your anger at the gardener's son and his cohorts was clear. So was the pity that you felt for the defenseless Hinoko. I would see that outrage and injury emerge from you again. The plight of weaker beings, animal or human, always wounded you so, Yakumo.

Once the story was finished, you went to Hinoko and cradled her in the crook of your arm, and you wept.

Yakumo, I had never seen a man cry.

Hinoko began to wake, and she licked your hands with her sleepy tongue. Her long tail, the reason for her torment as it was thought to bring with it misfortune, caressed your shirt-front and sleeves.

Yao had asked in the merchant Orihara's kitchen for an abalone shell to use as a feeding bowl for Hinoko. When you placed her onto the tatami again, she headed toward the shell and its slick of rice porridge. Hinoko was a smudge of ink as she lapped up the remainder of her meal. You returned to the storyteller's side, and you reached for her hands and held them.

We stood that way until Hinoko was sated.

Yakumo, I was beginning to understand that the hands—with kisses as if they were lips, with caresses as if they were cheeks, with intertwined fingers, as if they were limbs—were where you displayed the intentions of your body and then your heart. I did not pull the storyteller's hands away from yours. That night was the beginning of trust but not the beginning of affection, as you would have preferred.

I took care of your needs then, Yakumo, but I could not in truth claim to care. I do not mean to wound you, but we must see the past for what it was, a clear cold night.

Once the matter of the sleeping arrangements was agreed

to, I ordered new bedding quilts and four padded kimonos for you. It was much too cold to wash and properly dry the ones that I had found moldering on the second floor of the birdcage. Foster Mother oversaw the work with the assistance of five other seamstresses. The new items were finished in a week's time, allowing me to leave more banknotes inside of her sleeve.

Soon I made another change to the household. Herun-san was hungry. The Japanese meals that Tsune sent from the inn did not seem to fill you. You drank many cups of tea-colored liquid from a glass bottle, which I later learned was whiskey, in order to make up for the lack. I had heard about Kamata Saiji's Occidental restaurant and that his kitchen was one of the few in Matsue that boasted an "oven." The prefectural Governor's kitchen was said to have one as well. "Required for the baking of breads and for the roasting of beef and other meats," Kamata would tell me.

The first time I went to Kamata's restaurant, it was not yet opened for the day, but after I told him my employer's name he allowed me inside and directed me into the kitchen, where he was chopping onions.

"Herun-san's stomach sent you?" Kamata asked me, acknowledging his odd turn of phrase with a low laugh.

"It did not send me," I replied, "nor did Herun san."

"Apologies. I heard that he had been ill. I thought he would want some Occidental fare to get him well again."

"Do you think it will help?" I asked, relieved to hear my own thoughts coming from the cook's mouth.

"Of course, of course!" Kamata replied. "Herun-san is always happiest dining here."

"He dines here often?"

"Even *you* are surprised? I would have thought . . ."

"I have only started to work for him," I said.

"Right, yes," he said. "Well, we all have secret things that we like to eat, yes?"

"Is your food a secret?"

"You did not know. The landlady at the Tomitaya does not know. If I were a betting man, I would say that even that head teacher friend of his does not know that Herun-san eats here regularly."

"But he prefers Japanese fare," I insisted.

"Yes, yes, but that is all research and study to him," Kamata explained, "and after the newspapers made such a fuss over his 'commendable preference' for Japanese food, he had to maintain the appearance of eating it."

When I heard that Kamata was a man from Ōsaka, I was not inclined to trust him, but in that open port city he said that he had learned how to cook in the British style. "From men who were not born in Britain but in a country called India," Kamata said. "Those men," he assured me, "were the very best cooks of British fare."

"You cook only in the British style?" I asked.

"Yes."

"Herun-san is from America. The newspapers wrote that his rail journey to the *Abyssinia* began there," I said, certain that I had caught Kamata in a lie.

"Herun-san is a British national. His Father is from Ireland, you know."

"No, I do not know."

"Ah, well, you can tell by the way that he speaks the English language. It sounds like he is singing, yes?"

"No."

"Then you will have to take my word for it."

"I will," I replied.

"Roast fowls, roast beefs, beefsteaks, meat pies, Lincolnshire or Manchester sausages, breads—Herun-san almost wept when he saw the cottage loaves that I bake—and, of course, those 'puddings' that the British end their meals with, not to be confused with the savory 'puddings' made with blood that begin their mornings," Kamata said, listing his menu for me.

"Could you send a selection over to the Orihara's garden pavilion this evening?" I asked, as I had no knowledge of which items to choose.

"Of course, of course. Let me save you a walk over here tomorrow. The order will continue for the rest of the week, unless I hear from you otherwise," Kamata said, as he showed me out of his kitchen.

"I have not paid you," I said.

"I will get it from Herun-san the next time I see him," Kamata replied. "I know he will back here soon."

When you saw the lacquer boxes from Kamata, along with the three glass bottles of "Bass ales," suggested by the cook as the usual accompaniment of the British table, you behaved as if they did not appeal. You ate with your usual briskness the evening meal from the Tomitaya, and then you looked up at me and smiled, like a child asking for more. You nodded toward the offerings from Kamata, which I then served to you. He had the foresight to include Western utensils for your use and a set for me as well, which was unnecessary, as you finished everything on your own, except for a thick slice of bread that you set aside for your morning tea, which told me that Kamata should supplement that meal as well.

Months later when we, along with Yao, the bush warbler, and Hinoko, moved into the house in the shadows of Matsue Castle, which had a proper kitchen, separate and away from the main house, I sent Yao to Kamata to learn some of the basic preparations, which she in turn shared with foster Mother. He taught Yao how to brew your morning coffee and the British way of tea, how to prepare soft eggs and toasts, and how to pan-fry beefsteaks. Everything else, Kamata's oven would continue to provide. He was right about your fondness for those cottage loaves, Yakumo. You would close your eye when you bit into a thick slice of that bread, as if otherwise tears would fall.

"Herun-san has put on weight?" Kamata asked me, about a month into his arrangement with the household. He then laughed low as if he already knew.

"How would I know?" I asked.

"I mean on his face. You can see weight gain on a man's face, yes?"

"Yes."

"Well?"

"Yes, he has," I replied. "A lot of weight," I admitted, turning my back to him.

Kamata must have known many rashamen in Ōsaka. His manners toward me were informal from the beginning, speaking to me as if I were a younger sister or a longtime friend. This immediate familiarity only deepened my disgrace, Yakumo.

Mother had heard about my changed circumstances, and when she saw them for herself, she had no words for me. Her silence told me what I needed to know. Upon the dissolution of the marriage, my name had been returned to the Koizumi family registry. She regretted that now.

The story of Mother took many nights to tell you, Yakumo.

June had just begun, and the hydrangeas in the gardens of the house in the shadows of Matsue Castle were weeks away from their full-clustered blooms. The house's owner had been among the last of the former samurai in the city to occupy his own estate. I had been inquiring about its availability through foster Mother for months. My watch over the house was, perhaps, indecent. When would the animal, weakened by hunger, abandon its lair? Eventually, they all did, and then other animals found their way in. The fourteen ample rooms, the three gardens, and the adjacent wooded hills full of birdsongs, I knew, would please you.

I was planning ahead, Yakumo, knowing that you could not endure another winter by the river and the lake. I did not know that we would not have another winter in Matsue.

Seated on the veranda, deep underneath the eaves of that house, the gardens before us lit by fireflies and the full moon, I began.

Say it plain, you requested. The *Dictionary* did not allow for subtlety was what you meant.

After the story of Hinoko, there had been a string of others. At first, repetition was a necessity because the *Dictionary*, its entries each requiring pause and consideration, impeded and halted the telling. By the time I reached the end of a story, you had forgotten the beginning. Then repetition became a desired unfolding, as you slowed and directed the telling to suit your needs: "Tell me again what the samurai said to the blind musician. Tell me again what the grandmother said when she saw the blood." The key, I had learned, was to tell you the same story upon each repetition but to use fewer and fewer words. Implied, redundant, irrelevant—whatever the reason may be—there was always a word that could be thrown back into the sea. To say it plain was to find a pearl within that sea.

The pearl, that night, was Mother. I needed you to see her, Yakumo.

You had heard from your fellow teachers of the brave deeds of the men of the house of Shiomi, but none of them had told you about Shiomi Chie. A woman's story, they dismissed. Gossip not worth their breath, they thought.

Mother survived two husbands, I began.

On the cusp of thirteen, she was betrothed to the first son of a samurai house whose family name was no longer said aloud now. When her husband failed to appear in their sleeping chamber on their first night of matrimony, she fell asleep waiting for him. She awoke to the muffled sounds of her new husband and a young maid, who had only hours before swept clean the very courtyard where they now both lay, publicly declaring their love. The blood was fresh and bright red, pouring from her neck and his stomach. Shiomi Chie looked down at her husband's face and then at the maid's. So this is love, she thought. She then alerted the guards at the front gate that they had slept through a murder-suicide, and she returned to the sleeping chamber to await her widow's fate.

Soon the samurai house was a river of tears, mostly shed by the maids who had long known of the love affair between the young Master and Yuki. Shiomi Chie shed no tears. She showed humility and deference toward her deceased husband's family, careful never to utter his name or his deeds in the days to come.

The maid's own name was erased from the story even before her body grew cold. By morning, the news of the lovers' deaths had swept through Matsue, and Shiomi Chie was being praised in the houses in the shadows of Matsue Castle as a female worthy of the Shiomi name. Among the maids in these same houses, Shiomi Chie became known as the "Ice Bride." Among the maids in the house of her deceased husband, she was known as the "Blood Bride."

You gasped when you heard these words, Yakumo.

You asked me to say them again. Then you asked if they were *all* true.

"No," I admitted.

"Ah, even better!" you declared, slapping your knees.

The story of Hinoko had brought you to tears, Yakumo, but the story of Mother made your eye shine, brighter than the moon that night.

At the end of that June, an article appeared in the *San'in Shimbun* that detailed how the goodhearted and generous Lafcadio Hearn had rescued the birth mother of his rashamen from imminent eviction. The paper claimed that Mother received a monthly allowance from Herun-san when, in fact, it was more. It noted her hunger but not Third Brother's and Youngest Brother's, which also had to be fed. Ensconced with her sons in a newly rented house, modest but furnished once again with all the household items that Third Brother had sold off over the years, Mother refused my visits.

Upon seeing the house of Koizumi identified in the newspaper as the birth family of a rashamen, Setsu at twenty-three left her body in a long curl of smoke, pulled up and into the sky. The Setsu who remained was unrooted and thus light on her feet. She had the sudden urge to travel. Like many travelers before her, she had lost a home and was in search of another.

I followed you, Yakumo.

First, I ventured only as far as Kitzuki. To escape the mid-July heat in Matsue, you and Nishida-san had secured rooms at Inaba-ya, a seaside inn facing the Inasa bay. You longed to see the Izumo Shrine again and looked forward to beginning and ending your days with a swim in the Sea of Japan.

"I am half fish," you declared, as I packed your traveling bag.

"Your people were fishermen?" I asked.

"No, military and medical."

"Your Mother was a healer?"

"No, my Father was in the army and a doctor. My Mother was a 'Shiomi Chie.'"

You would later shorten this entry into Herun-san's language to "Chie" to mean a woman of noble birth, beautiful, and brave. Her tragic end was implied.

That was the course of the conversations back then. As with the paths in the merchant Orihara's formal gardens, they were rarely in a straight line. You went in one direction, and I went in the other. Somewhere in between, we met.

Mother survived you, Yakumo, by two years.

She died in Ōsaka, the city of those who disappear. In her last month of life, she sent a letter in which she declared that she would leave this world with regrets and that I was one of them.

Her regret, more precisely, was the life that I had with you, which began not in the birdcage in Matsue but in Kitzuki by the sea.

A day after your arrival there, you had asked Nishida-san to write a letter to me. It requested that I travel to the inn as soon as possible. I recognized the head teacher's handwriting, and for a brief moment I thought the letter was from him. His hand must have trembled, when you began, "One day without you and already it is too long."

I left for Kitzuki, catching the small steamship that had taken you and Nishida-san along the length of Lake Shinji. Disembarking at the village of Shōbara, I hired a jinrikisha, and I traced your steps. For hours, the long narrow path took me through rice paddies and frog songs. As the sun was poised to set, a torii appeared in the distance, and the jinrikisha man announced that we had reached Kitzuki. At the inn, the maid who answered the front door informed me that the foreigner was still in the sea. The maid was expecting me and without hesitation showed me upstairs to your room, informing me that the adjoining one was also for my use. I wondered what Nishida-san had said to prepare her. I had not asked about his whereabouts, as I had no expectation that he would want to greet me.

Your clothes were in a wrinkled heap, Yakumo. Your money had spilled from its carrying pouch. There were handfuls of seashells gathered on the tenugui that I had given to you as a going-away gift. You had tucked that cotton cloth into your traveling bag without a word about how fitting its seigaiha pattern was for a seaside holiday. I had chosen those blue-and-white waves with some care, Yakumo. A sigh welled up inside of me. He is elsewhere already, I thought.

From the windows of your room, I saw you walking toward the inn, lit by the lanterns lining its front path. I hurried downstairs to greet you. By the front door, the maid was already waiting with a yukata neatly folded in her hands. A routine is in place, I noted. Her skin is pale for someone living so near to the sea. Her body is no more than fifteen. She could be Oman's twin, I thought, as this heart became a moth beating its drab, futile wings.

When you caught sight of me, Yakumo, there was not a breath between your recognition and your elation. You sprinted toward me with the legs of a youth, not a man of forty-one. Your black hair was damp, and the cloth of your gray yukata stuck to the seawater on your body. You wrapped your arms around me and lifted me off the ground, as if offering me to the sky.

I heard the maid sucking in the salt air, astonished by the open show of your affection.

The moth flew away.

The following week we became man and wife at the Izumo Shrine. Ōkuninushi, the Shintō god of marriage, was a witness. Nishida-san was the other.

We had been together as man and woman, months before. A cloth had covered the bush warbler's cage.

The commitment to each other came later, its rites completed by the Kitzuki letter.

The marriage ceremony came last.

For your Elizabeth's book, I had to reverse the order of those three acts. I did it for the dead and for the living, Yakumo. What good is the truth to your legacy, the children's future, and for the present that I must now live without you?

When the one-year anniversary of your passing had neared, the cablegrams began arriving again, breathless as before: "Mrs. Hearn, your contribution completed, I trust. Translation under way, I presume. Manuscript sent to my summer address posthaste." Kazuo translated the words for me, his eleven-year-old's voice reminding me that your biographer was impatient and waiting.

Elizabeth is hungry!

Elizabeth is angry!

Elizabeth has my hat!

I was determined to hold on to what was mine. I had no intention of sending anything to your Elizabeth. Foster Mother must have known, as she took me aside that night and showed me the household accounts, which she had been managing on her own. Almost a full year without your university professor salary, Yakumo, and there was not much left that this house could trim, except for the house itself.

I resolved not to be a Chie, wasting away, taking the sons of Koizumi with me. And little Suzuko, how could I ever allow her to become me?

But I still could not breathe for the two of us, Yakumo. Thus, when I began that first telling of your story, the ghost of you was here by my side, holding me by the hand.

Minari Shigeyuki was the scribe. My handwriting has always been poor, and the thought of showing it to the translator would have added to my discomfort. Also, storytelling was what I knew; story writing was your domain. It soothed me to have a listener as attentive as you had been, Yakumo. Do you remember what you had said about this distant relative of mine when you first met him? You declared in feigned exasperation that I was related to everyone in Japan. Then you noted with admiration that Shigeyuki had the face of a Tokugawa samurai. That stern elongated face hid a nimble, refined intellect that surprised even you, Yakumo. You were pleased to offer the young scholar a room within this house, and he repaid you in kind with the research that he would conduct on your behalf. Fireflies in the poems of yore, you first requested of him. He found them everywhere in the ancient texts, yet he had never seen them before you. "Herun-sensei is a conjurer," he had confided in me.

Shigeyuki is still employed by the Institute for the Compilation of Historical Materials, Yakumo. He remains unmarried. He and I both know that he will remain so. A remnant of the old way, deviant and degenerate are what some of the Tokyo newspapers write about the practice of nanshoku these days. So many of the modern men of this city seem to agree. No wonder Shigeyuki prefers the archives.

A man who must hide his heart can be trusted with your own, I told myself.

Ochiai Teizaburō, your former student from Tokyo Imperial University, was the translator. He asked nothing by way of compensation. He vowed, Yakumo, that he too would do anything for Herun-sensei. He repeatedly apologized to me for any mistakes that he might have made, as he had completed the translation in such haste. I repeatedly apologized to him, as I was the sole cause of that haste. I had given him the pages of your story with only a month remaining before their English counterpart had to be in your Elizabeth's hands.

I had wanted to begin that first telling with the day of your final departure, but then I heard your advice, Yakumo—*Leave the end for the end, Sweet Wife!*—and I began with the introduction in Matsue instead. But soon I became lost in its timeline, revealing and indiscreet.

Shigeyuki, who had been transcribing silently up until then, asked if he could interrupt the recitation of events. "Facts are akin to fish bones," he said. "If what you want is to serve the flesh, then the bones can be discarded," he suggested.

A man who must hide his heart is also a skilled storyteller, Yakumo.

I discarded the bones and served forth the following to your Elizabeth:

In early January, 1891, the 24th year of Meiji, Lafcadio Hearn and Koizumi Setsu married in Matsue. Tsune had no role to play in the introduction and was made to disappear. Nishida Sentarō gallantly stepped in. I raised the house of Nishida from foot-soldier class to samurai, and I bestowed upon the head teacher a familial connection to the house of Shiomi, which facilitated the plausibility of his performance as a trusted go-between. The early days of silence within the birdcage and the *Dictionary*, our unsteady bridge, I mentioned only in passing. Instead, there was always Nishida-san, a friend to us both, to serve as interpreter. He was present for you, Yakumo, so this characterization was only half untrue.

Elizabeth Bisland was no *San'in Shimbun*, and for this I was grateful. She had asked for my age at the time of the marriage, but she sought no explanation as to why I had been without a husband at the age of twenty-two. Thus, the first marriage was allowed to disappear entirely—it went to Ōsaka, as it were— from that first telling and then from the pages of your Elizabeth's book. The *San'in Shimbun* would have asked more questions, Yakumo. They would have been wary of a fish with no bones.

Elizabeth is American, I reminded myself, as I wrapped those pages—your story, translated, was already unrecognizable to me, Yakumo—for their journey overseas, backed by a thin piece of wood to keep them neat and crisp upon their arrival, as you had so often done.

Yakumo, I know you are smiling. *Sweet Wife!* is what you are thinking. Is "sweet" the same as "simple" in Herun-san's language, Yakumo?

I know more about your Elizabeth now. The *San' in Shimbun* would have been honored to have her, a journalist of renown in the city of New York before she became Mrs. Wetmore. Like you, Elizabeth was a well-documented traveler.

Kazuo, curious in recent years about his Father's biographer, has read the book that Elizabeth Bisland wrote about her famed race around the world. He told me that she was twenty-eight years old at the time. Unmarried, I presumed. Though she lost the race—Is travel often a competition for Americans, Yakumo?—to another reporter named Nellie Bly, your Elizabeth beat you to these shores. Upon arriving in Yokohama in December of 1889, the 22nd year of Meiji, Elizabeth Bisland met there Paymaster Mitchell McDonald, U.S.N., who became her American friend in Yokohama before he was yours, Yakumo.

How small this world is. How like a grain of sand you can become when the stories of that small world are kept from you. When they are eventually told, they are waves, Yakumo, sweeping your legs from under you.

Mr. McDonald gifts the house of Koizumi a considerable sum of money every Christmas, Yakumo.

Last year, it meant the difference between taking in boarders and not. The thought of dividing up this house keeps these eyes from closing at night. Mr. McDonald has a family of his own to care for, and I ask myself—and now I ask it of you—whether these gifts are, in truth, from Mrs. Wetmore, a woman of means now?

The royalties from her biography had ebbed, and Mr. Mc-Donald had suggested that it was my turn now. He said that a book published under my name would attract great interest with readers abroad and here. He proposed that I expand upon what I had already recounted for Mrs. Wetmore. Mr. McDonald already had a title in mind, Yakumo. He suggested the English word "reminiscences," which Kazuo said was akin to "memories."

"What is the difference?" I asked Kazuo, and his reply showed him at fifteen to be very much your son.

"Poets have reminiscences. Mothers have memories," Kazuo declared.

So, I began again, Yakumo, but this time without you.

If your Elizabeth at twenty-eight could travel the world on her own, then Setsu at forty-one could tell a story without you, Husband. To equate the two acts may not be entirely sound, but so be it. That is what happens when you are the first to sleep. Those who remain awake are free to act and to act singly.

Setsu is hungry.

Setsu is angry.

Setsu has your hat.

With Shigeyuki again as my scribe, I returned to Matsue for the last days in the house in the shadows of the Castle:

As the winds whipped through those rooms of wood and paper, rattling them like dried seedpods, you looked around you, shivered, and declared that you were happy to be departing for southern climes. I had never imagined a life on the island of Kyūshū and in the city of Kumamoto, as I had never imagined a husband named Lafcadio Hearn, but your destinations were now also mine.

"Double the salary, Sweet Wife," you had said. "Teaching hours will be longer but not by much."

"I see," I replied.

"You *see*? You mean 'Good news!'" you corrected me.

"Good news!" I echoed.

"We will send for the house of Inagaki. You will not be lonely in Kumamoto City for long, Sweet Wife."

Yakumo, you did not offer to bring with us the three members of the house of Koizumi. Perhaps Nishida-san had spoken to you about the *San'in Shimbun* article and the disgrace that it had brought to my birth family's name. Nishida-san might have advised you that while marriage between a British national and a Japanese national was not binding under the laws of either country, a wife in name would be better than a rashamen in public, given your position as a teacher and your reputation as a scholar and writer. That conversation might have prompted you both to depart for Kitzuki to consider your next steps, Yakumo. That conversation might have prompted you then to send for me.

Do you remember, Yakumo, how Nishida-san had reddened when you asked him to interpret the word "honeymoon" for me? I thought he would run out of the inn and into the sea, when you insisted on explaining to me—which meant Nishida-san explaining to me—what the Western ritual of "honeymooning" entailed. By the end of that night, when even I drank sake, I laughed out loud when you raised your cup "To our honeymoon!" and we three said, "Kampai!"

In Kitzuki at the shores of Inasa bay, Setsu at twenty-three heard, for the first time, the language of her birth offering the words of a man in love with her. When Nishida-san interpreted for you, it was his voice that I heard and his language that I understood.

Maeda Tameji had spoken to Setsu at nineteen of hunger and other bodily needs. He forgot those words along with "family" and "honor" when he abandoned her and his other burdens for the city of Ōsaka. At night when sleep was absent, Setsu then counted the years still before her. White hair and silence were what she thought they would bring by way of companionship. In the dark, she resolved to accept that this body would never carry within it a second beating heart. Without husband and without children, a woman's life was as quiet as a snowfall, she had been told. In the dark, she knew that the snow had begun. She lay there and knew that the snow would cover her in the end.

When Setsu at twenty-two found herself in your birdcage and she understood there only the bush warbler's song, she thought of it as the opposite of silence. She did not think of it as the start of a new life though. She thought of it as what came after the end of one.

Yakumo, with Nishida-san by your side, you were no longer a drunken poet, though sake had flowed freely into cup after cup. In Kitzuki, you were a poet whose recited words made the evening sky a swirl of starlight and the moon a flutter of wings.

That night you and Nishida-san had argued briefly about a writer, a Frenchman whose books you admired and he did not. I asked what he had written, and you gave me a long explanation that Nishida-san then condensed into "a novel about a French naval officer and a Japanese woman named Chrysanthemum."

You were taken aback, Yakumo. You took your friend's refusal to interpret every word of what you had said as a betrayal. I could see it on your face, first as a small collapse of your brow and then as a twitch at the corner of your right eye. In later years, the person seated before you would have been shown to the door, followed by instructions to me to never allow them back inside of the garden gate.

You and Nishida-san stared at each other, daring the other to speak first, while the waves crashing outside took over the conversation. You both wore your hair longer during those summer days, the ends grazing the shoulders, the thick locks swept to one side and tucked behind an ear so they would not curtain the forehead and the lashes. In that moment when you were both bound in place by pride, Nishida-san's hair fell over his eyes and then yours followed. Out of habit, I reached over and tucked back your hair. Then I did the same for Nishida-san. When the hand returned to the lap, I realized what it had done. A sharp intake of air replaced the sounds of the sea.

Yakumo, you began to laugh and slap your knees. Nishida-san caught my eyes briefly, as if he were seeking my permission, and then he joined you.

Setsu dropped her head into her hands. Into her palms, she vowed to keep a stronger hold on her limbs, her heart, her body as a whole.

The conversation between you and Nishida-san resumed, while the sea breezes kept the mosquitoes at bay.

I awoke at dawn to seabirds squawking for their first meal of the day. As I finished dressing, I heard footsteps in the inn's passageway. I slid open the door, hoping to see a maid, as I wanted my morning tea served earlier than usual. Instead, I saw

Nishida-san's back. He turned around and nodded. I followed him down the stairs, where he bid me good morning, formal as if I were his own Mother. Then he offered his apologies.

"An unexpected business matter awaits my attention in Ōsaka," he claimed. "A change in travel plans is unavoidable," he said and handed to me a list of the villages and inns where he had intended to travel with you—but not with me—in the weeks to come. "You may find this helpful," he added.

I nodded but could not think of anything appropriate to say. Nishida-san did. "A honeymoon is a ritual for two," he said, his eyes cast downward, as though he were reading an inscription on the tatami.

Habit took over once again, and I said, formal as if he were Father, "I see. I will try my best."

Nishida-san could not hide his smile. The vision of me "trying my best" during a honeymoon was embarrassing to us both. Upon exchanging a deep bow to hide the color of our cheeks, he departed for Ōsaka, and I returned to your room.

To travel with you, Yakumo, was to be always by your side.

Nishida-san had taken care of every detail during our stay in Kitzuki and our day trips thereabouts, from hiring the small boat that took us from Inasa bay to Hinomisaki—where you were pleased to learn yet again that you were the first Westerner to visit a remote village and its Shintō shrine—to interpreting every question that you had for the two fishermen who rowed that boat.

"Is there a name for these rock formations?" you had asked Nishida-san, and he had asked the fishermen. "Why do the people call them 'tortoise-shell stones'?" you wanted to know, and Nishida-san asked on your behalf. After some back-and-forth between the two fishermen, one of them offered Nishida-san a story, and he offered it to you. I was left to enjoy the passing seascape with its huddles and crags jutting from the depth.

But once the travels without Nishida-san began, I was the one who had to connect you to the land and to the sea. I learned that the border between the two was where you preferred to travel, the villages that clung to a sea cliff or clustered around a protected bay or, better still, on the islands that barely rose from the Sea of Japan and appeared to sink back into it at dusk. You said the shoreline was what a traveler to an island touches first, and what the traveler touches last. Sacred, you named it.

I tried my best, Yakumo.

In Matsue, I knew the shop owners, the bathhouse attendants, the peddlers, the purveyors of foodstuffs, or I knew of someone who did. The destinations that Nishida-san had chosen were all in neighboring Hoki Province. He had intended to travel with you to the villages along its coast and then eastward and inland toward Lake Togo. I knew no one in Hoki Province, Yakumo.

Early in the journey, you and I had arrived at an inn, spacious and lively with prosperous, merrymaking guests. The innkeeper greeted us, and after a cursory look around, you greeted him with a lone English word. Then in Herun-san's language, you said "Hell!" shaking your head. "Hell!" you repeated, but this time directed toward me. You went out to the awaiting jinrikisha, leaving me to apologize to the innkeeper for your offense.

After a long, silent ride to another inn—a very small one run by an ancient-looking husband and wife, who gasped when she saw your face—you explained with the assistance of the *Dictionary*, a constant traveling companion but a poor stand-in for Nishida-san, that "Hell!" in both languages meant that the first inn was too smoky, too loud, and the men drinking there were all too Tani-no-oto from their new wealth, and if you had wanted that, you would have stayed in Matsue and gone to the merchant Orihara's.

I did not err again, Yakumo.

For the duration of the journey, I made certain to ask the jinrikisha men, before I hired them, whether they knew of inns at the intended destinations that were built long ago, very clean, provided excellent food, and yet had the fewest number of guests. "Haunted ones?" they joked with me.

At the seaside village of Hamamura, we were lodging at a small inn that met with all of your requirements, plus another that you said was somewhat elusive but was best described by the English word "cozy." How the body feels when you drink a cup of hot tea on a very cold night, I remember, was your definition. We had timed our arrival in Hamamura for the Obon, as Nishida-san had thought that its Bon-odori, the annual dance to welcome back the spirits of the ancestors, would intrigue you. He had heard that the dance was different from village to village along the Hoki coast. What Nishida-san had not anticipated was that the people of Hamamura and the nearby villages did not want a foreigner to frighten their ancestors upon their yearly return. The villagers refused to perform their Bon-odori in front of you, Yakumo. The innkeeper, her face wrinkled as a dried, salted plum, was the one who informed me. Once the people of Hamamura had made up their minds, the other villages followed suit, dispatching representatives to the inn to warn the innkeeper not to send the foreigner and his rashamen their way.

"The foreigner is harmless," I heard myself saying to the old woman. "In his yukata and straw hat worn low, none of the returning spirits will even know."

Her eyes—their lids pried wide open by unseen fingers—informed me that I had overstepped the bounds of honor. To deceive the ancestors on the one night of their return from the unseen world, I could see on her ashen face, was an unforgivable offense.

"Cholera," I said to you instead. "All large gatherings are forbidden. No Bon-odori this year. A shame," I added.

Husband, you believed me.

Even when the villagers of Hamamura threw fistfuls of sand at us as we departed, you believed me. Forgive me, Yakumo, but even you were not blind to their bodies, their arms tensing and uncoiling.

What I feared more was their silence. The villagers thought that you would not understand if they jeered or shouted, so they did not waste their words.

We were seen but unseen. We were the returning spirits but with no families there to greet us. We had died among strangers. A curse, Yakumo.

"Gentle and silent" was what you would say to Nishida-san, upon our return to Matsue.

"The villagers on the Hoki coast were gentle and silent?" Nishida-san asked me if those words were true. Friends of his, passing through Hamamura, had heard the villagers tell a very different story.

My face burned with the shame that I had felt in Hamamura and that I could not show there.

Nishida-san quickly apologized for having made such an error in judgment. "I should not have sent Herun-san to the Hoki coast," he said. "But he takes such pleasure from being the first, as you know," he explained.

"I know."

"I should have thought about you, Setsu," he said. It was the first and only time that Nishida-san would call me by my true name.

Upon hearing "Setsu" released from his lips—an intimacy implied, an affection kindled, a heart so near to mine—I heard my true name for what it had been until then, an afterthought in the lives of men.

"I know," I repeated with a sharpness in tone that took him by surprise.

You continued to believe, Yakumo.

We would again find ourselves in remote villages where your Western face was the first. At each location, you professed—and I voiced for you—a keen interest in Shintō shrines, Buddhist temples, and the local folklore, superstitions, and beliefs, but the faith that you harbored within you was the one that you wanted most to find. You looked at the bodies around you, and you deemed them gentle. You wanted to see in those bodies something distant and apart from the brutal ones that you had known.

A body is a body, Yakumo, gentle and brutal. Nothing, in truth, separated yours from theirs.

I know you remember the heat and the odors rising from the bodies that surrounded us in Mitsu-ura. Two and a half hours from Matsue by jinrikisha and then the remainder of the journey on foot—a steep climb followed by a slippery descent via a narrow, crumbling path—before we reached the tiny fishing village of Mitsu-ura, and it was not even the final destination of the day. Someone in Matsue—may he make that journey for an eternity—had told you about a sea cave that was said to be visited every night by the spirits of young children, who leave behind their footprints on a sandbank where there is a statue of Jizō, the Buddhist god who protects their spirits and eases their loneliness in the unseen world. Mitsu-ura was where we could hire a boat to take us to that sea cave.

While the jinrikisha man went to find someone to row us to the cave, we waited inside the dwelling of a fisherman to whom I had paid a considerable sum because it was there or under the hot sun. The village was too small to have an inn, and no one was able to name even a teahouse. Soon the narrow alleys separating the fisherman's house from his neighbors were swarming with villagers. I asked the fisherman to slide close the walls of his house. He was reluctant because of the summer heat and because he was now a part of an entertaining show.

In Mitsu-ura there was also silence, Yakumo.

You nodded and offered your greetings in Herun-san's language to the assembled villagers. They came closer each time, as if you had invited them to take a better look. The fisherman soon had no choice but to close up his house as I had asked, but its shōji walls were torn in so many places that the sight of the foreigner and his rashamen simply became smaller and more haphazardly framed. The viewing continued, and the fisherman demanded loudly from within his dwelling that his neighbors pay due respect to his "foreign visitor." It took all of my will not to inform the fisherman that you were not there to visit with him. As sweat beads ran down your face, Yakumo, a shadow or a memory darkened your eye.

When the jinrikisha man returned, he wove his way through the dense crowd, and together we headed for the boat and its two rowers, a husband and wife. The villagers parted to allow us a clear path, but they followed closely behind and stood at the shoreline until we were a dot in the offing. They were not there to bid us farewell or safe passage. They were waiting, same as children watching a fish on a hook take its last open-mouthed breath.

As the boat left the bay of Mitsu-ura, you jumped into the water. I assured the husband and wife that you had not changed your mind. I asked them to continue rowing, as I knew that you would swim behind the boat until you needed a rest. The boat-woman stared at me, as if she were unsure how I could be speaking the same language as she. *He is the foreigner, not me!* I wanted to say to her but did not because it was, perhaps, no longer true. Instead, I kept quiet and kept watch for your arms, slicing up and through the water's surface, and for your familiar face.

The questions began as soon as you climbed aboard the boat, refreshed and cleansed. To the rowers, Herun-san's language was entirely foreign, and I was its interpreter, unreliable at best. The boatman refused to address me directly. He answered my questions, which were your questions, as if his wife had been the one to ask and thus the appropriate recipient of his answers. As the boat glided into the entrance of the caves—it was not one, as you had been told, but a series of caves connected by a sunlit pool of water, all hidden from view behind the cliff face—the boatwoman picked up a rock by her bare feet and tapped the side of the boat. The echoes grew so loud that you covered your ears. I did the same. Then you wanted to know why she had behaved so, and I asked her. The boatwoman replied that all who came into these caves announced themselves in this way. To whom, you wanted to know and I asked. The boatwoman did not answer right away and seemed to be searching her memory for the correct reply. But before she could offer one, you swung a leg over the side of the boat and were about to slip into the water for another swim. The boatwoman grabbed the interpreter's arm—the strength of her grip made me grab on to yours. The boat swayed from side to side, and the boatman watched without saying a word, as the three lurching bodies stilled themselves and eased back into place.

"It is forbidden!" the boatwoman warned me.

"It is forbidden!" I warned you.

"A quick swim," you assured me.

"A quick swim," I assured her.

Her response was to pick up the rock again and tap the side of the boat, harder and louder than before. The echoes felt like strong, unseen waves that could tip the boat over at any moment. When we could hear one another again, the boatman grunted a warning, and I said to you, "Shark!"

You believed me, Yakumo.

Once we were back in Matsue though, you, like the boatman, would not speak to me. We had had disagreements, minor and stemming from the day-to-day nature of living under the same roof, but never a raised word and never a raised hand. I did not even recognize your silence as anger, at first. I thought you were writing about the caves and thus cocooned in the elsewhere of your thoughts. The caves, I must admit, had been worth the difficulties of the journey. The tiny footprints in the sand were exactly as you had been promised. The heap of straw sandals left for the spirits of those children, by the pilgrims who had preceded us, haunted us more. The world of the living and the world of the unseen overlapped in those caves, and as the boat made its way out again we thought about all the tiny ones who would not.

When you awoke, still silent, four mornings in a row, I apologized for your disappointment. I thought that your ire toward me had to do with the missed opportunity to swim in that hidden, sun-dappled pool.

"You lied," you said.

"Yes," I admitted.

"I know the Japanese word for 'ghost,' Sweet Wife. The boatman said it, yes?"

"Yes."

"Then why did you say 'shark' to me?" you asked.

I lowered my eyes.

"You know me, Sweet Wife," you continued.

"Yes."

"I want a ghost more than I want a swim."

"Yes, Husband."

"It is a shame not to hear a story, Sweet Wife."

"It is, Husband."

I would see the shadow in your eye again, Yakumo, in the village of Kaka-ura, and a year later in the town of Uragō on one of the Oki islands. You continued to believe, even when the crowd there became a mob and a policeman had to be summoned to keep the peace.

A body is a body, gentle and brutal, Yakumo.

With time, your anger toward me departed, and I welcomed the words of Herun-san's language back to the house in the shadows of Matsue Castle, where it had kept that newly formed, sparsely populated country running smoothly. Yao, the maid, was soon to bid it farewell though, as she did not wish to move with the household to Kumamoto City. We left the bush warbler with her, as he would have died brokenhearted without her. Hinoko had found a feral mate and departed with him months ago.

On the fifteenth day of November, 1891, the 24th year of Meiji, your students, more than two hundred of them, escorted us to the wharf in Matsue, where your fellow teachers were among those who had gathered to bid us safe passage to Kumamoto City. Foster Grandfather, foster Father, and foster Mother were there too, but soon they would embark on the same journey in order to be with us again. Yao was there. Kamata was there. The jinrikisha men who waited in front of the Tomitaya were there. Tsune, Onobu, and even Oman were there. I searched the faces for Nishida-san's. Only illness would have prevented him from saying his farewells. Even on his better days, his fits of coughing brought with them droplets of blood. I saw them when we three were in Kitzuki that summer.

Nishida-san's absence at the wharf and then the shores of Matsue receding became one moment of loss for me, Yakumo. I could never think of Matsue without thinking of Nishida-san. I could never long for Matsue without longing for Nishida-san. When he passed from this world too soon, Matsue did as well. It was as if that city had only one inhabitant, thirty-four years of age, and when he departed for the unseen world, the city faded from all of memory's maps. In the years since, I have asked myself, *How can one man have carried within him an entire city?*

A wife cannot say such words to a husband. A husband cannot hear such words from a wife without demanding, *Why am I not the man married with Matsue?*

Please believe me, Husband. I did not know that the second telling of your story would unearth Nishida-san's and mine. Brief and barely begun, it is a story that I have carried within me, written and rewritten many times in the language that he and I share, but there was no place for it to go after Kitzuki, no words to continue it after "Setsu" and "I know." His was my second heart, Yakumo. Yours was the one that was near.

It is better that you hear this now, Husband. When I join you in the unseen world, the wound of it will have healed.

Before we leave Matsue behind us, Yakumo, this was the ghost story that you had been so sore to miss:

The boatman, as you heard, had said "Ghost!"—and not "Shark!" as I had claimed—but he was not warning you. He was warning the ghost. Same as their fellow villagers, this man and woman of Mitsu-ura saw you, Yakumo, as a body that did not belong there. Same as the villagers on the Hoki coast, their allegiances were not with the foreigner and his rashamen but with the dead among them. In the hands of this man and woman, I had entrusted your life. On their boat, your body and mine had been taken behind the face of a sea cliff so remote that, if we were to scream when the boatman brained us with a rock or a hardwood oar, no one would have heard, and the echoes of our cries, like us, would have died.

I yelled "Shark!" because I needed you to comply, Yakumo. The boatwoman did not want you to sully the sacred waters of the sea caves. Her husband was of the same clear opinion. I needed you to stay with me. I did not want us to perish there. No one would have looked for us until it was too late. The villagers of Mitsu-ura would have claimed that they never saw us depart from their bay. Fearful of being falsely blamed, the jinrikisha man who had taken us there from Matsue would have denied any receipt of the fare.

I will not ask for forgiveness, Yakumo, for these untruths. If I were given a second life with you, I would say and behave the same. There are fewer ways to save a life than you would think. There are even fewer ways to live a life, given the circumstances that we cannot change.

You have told untruths about me, Yakumo. They sting us like nettles, I know.

Kazuo at fifteen is reading your *Glimpses of Unfamiliar Japan*. He tells me that he is practicing his English, but I believe that he is reading your first book about the country outside because he is missing you. He recognizes the stories of ghosts and other wandering spirits as the ones that foster Grandmother had told to keep him tucked in for the night. He identifies others as the oft-repeated family stories of Papa and Mama's travels in Izumo Province and the surrounds. Kazuo has finished the first volume and is now reaching the end of the second. He has asked me questions, Yakumo, and there is one that I cannot answer.

"Papa wrote about you, Mama," Kazuo began.

"Did he?"

"No," he answered. "I misspoke. He only wrote about your true name. He explained to his readers that there are two kanji, both pronounced 'setsu,' one meaning the node of the bamboo and the other 'virtue, fidelity, and constancy.'"

"Which one did Papa say I was?"

"He did not."

"I see."

"The passage was actually about the bamboo, and why the people of Matsue display it during the New Year Matsuri."

"I see."

Yakumo, as I grow older, this face reveals more of this heart. Kazuo must have caught a glimpse of both because he offered that "a lady of Matsue" in volume two was certainly a reference to Mama. The story that *she* told to Papa, Kazuo said, reminded him of one that I had often told him and his siblings about my youth:

I was two—but, perhaps, that is far too young to have a memory, so the memory may be a story that was told to me—and I had been taken to the open fields near Matsue Castle to see the modern army marching and performing precision drills, dressed in their new trim uniforms, their rifles gleaming. Their commander was a Westerner who rode on a horse, chestnut brown. This man's face was the color of a freshly caught tai fish. He wore a full beard, which made his ruddy face appear small and half the size of a Japanese man's. I remember him descending from his horse and leading this animal over to where we children had gathered. Some immediately ran off, and the ones who stayed began to cry.

I did not run nor did I cry. The Westerner knelt in front of me—"his beard a small furry animal on his face," I often said at this point in the story, which always made the children laugh out loud and you too, Yakumo. The Westerner asked for my age. He unfurled his fingers, first one then two. I mimicked him. His beard moved, lifting slightly upward, and his eyes shone, and I took that to mean that he was pleased. He reached into a pocket of his uniform—I remember him wearing an overcoat with many polished buttons—and he took out a small object with a thin reed-like handle, which was no longer small once he had placed it in the recipient's hands. He then led his horse away from the crying children whose distress had been greatly increased by the recognition that I alone had received a gift. What it was none of us knew, but the gift was gilded in parts and clear in others, and the whole of it caught the early afternoon Matsue light.

I showed the object to foster Father, and he showed me how to hold the small oval of glass by its handle. He hovered the glass over an ant crawling toward a clump of flowering thistle, and I looked down to find that the ant had grown greatly in size. Foster Father warned me never to hold the glass over an insect for too long, especially when the sun was bright and high in the sky, as the small creature would die. I did not want the gift after hearing of its power to kill, and I gave it to foster Father. He said that the gift was mine alone to keep. You were brave to stand your ground, he declared.

Years later, when I was in school, I learned that the man was named Frédéric Valette from the country of France, and he was one of the first Westerners to come to Matsue in 1870, the 3rd year of Meiji.

Yakumo, remember how Kazuo would ask—and then Iwao and Kiyoshi would as well—to see the Frenchman's glass? I instead would show them the one that you kept on your desk and tell them that Papa's magnifier was many times stronger than that little old thing that Mama has kept with her all these years. I liked very much how the boys would look at your glass and then back up at you, Yakumo. Their Papa was, in their eyes, the stronger of the two.

Kazuo told me how your "lady of Matsue" recounted my story on the pages of your book, and how *her* details were not the same as mine: a daimyō, not an Imperial edict, had brought the Frenchman to Matsue; Mother, not foster Father, was with her that day; the insect magnified was a fly, not an ant. Kazuo, like his Papa, reveled in the minute. He was thorough in his assessment and cataloging of the discrepancies between her story and mine.

He doubted me, Yakumo.

Kazuo then wanted to know why I was nowhere else in your book. He asked this of me as if it were proof that I did not exist, that this body was not of bones, of flesh, and of his same blood. He pointed to the pages where you wrote about the sea caves, a locale that he and his siblings knew well from the stories that I also had told them, particularly when they had misbehaved or been ungrateful for the blessings of their lives. When Kazuo was very young, he had wept inconsolably over the tiny straw sandals, as you had done when you saw them with your own eye, Yakumo. Kazuo at fifteen now demanded to know why Papa wrote that a jinrikisha man, not Mama, had been Papa's traveling companion on that boat.

"I am the jinrikisha man."

The correction came from these lips before I could stop it, Yakumo.

Kazuo laughed out loud. Then he apologized to Mama for the disrespect.

He took a moment to consider the claim and asked if Mama was Papa's "companion" at the Yaegaki Shrine.

"I am the companion."

"Were you the 'charming Japanese girl' who told Papa about how a doll can acquire a soul?" he asked. "She is in the chapter about Kitzuki, the one that Papa dated the twentieth of July, 1891."

"I am the charming Japanese girl."

Yakumo, you had misremembered. You and Nishida-san arrived in Kitzuki on the twenty-sixth of July. I arrived two days later. "Our honeymoon" was what followed.

Kazuo was not satisfied. He went through the pages of your book again, reading them anew.

"You were Papa's 'attendant' and 'interpreter' at Hamamura?" he asked.

"Yes."

"You were Papa's 'companion' and 'friend' in Uragō?"

"Yes."

"'Akira' who traveled to Matsue with Papa?"

"No."

Yakumo, you included Manabe Akira, the Imperial University man, who had traveled with you to Matsue in the pages of your book? I am certain that he was pleased to be remembered for the companionship that he had provided you. Such courtesy would have pleased me too, Husband.

"'Kinjuro, the ancient gardener' in Matsue?" Kazuo asked.

I smiled upon hearing that long-ago name. "I was not, but I was the interpreter for Papa and him," I answered. "Kinjuro," I said, "was the gardener at the house in the shadows of Matsue Castle, but he was not ancient. He was in the prime of his life, and probably why the maid Yao did not want to leave Matsue behind."

"Why did Papa write that Kinjuro was bald and his head looked like 'a ball of ivory'?"

"Did he?"

"Yes."

"What was Papa writing about, Kazuo?"

"Papa asked Kinjuro about souls and how many of them the gardener believed that he had."

I did not remember that exchange, Yakumo, but I did not want Kazuo to doubt you. A sting worse than nettles, I know.

"Kazuo, on the subject of souls, whom do you believe, an old man at the end of his life or a young man, hale and handsome?"

"A body is a body," Kazuo, an old soul, replied. "It depends more on the man's words."

"Perhaps Papa knew that his readers were not so wise and tended to prefer the ancient over the young."

"Perhaps," Kazuo agreed.

I tried my best, Yakumo.

I thought that Kazuo was done with his questions, but he had saved the impossible one for last.

"Am I a half-caste?" your son asked.

If Kiyoshi at seven had asked this of me, I would have answered, "You are half of Papa and half of Mama," and he would have smiled. Kazuo at fifteen has no taste for such sweet words.

"Yes," I answered, looking him in the eyes to show him that there was no shame in mine.

"Am I better off dead then?"

"Did someone say this to you? One of your classmates?"

"Papa did."

"Kazuo!"

"Mama, he did. He wrote it in his book for all to read."

"Kazuo—"

"Papa wrote that he was in a cemetery in search of the faces of Jizō, and he saw in that city of the dead a half-caste girl with pretty blue eyes. He wrote that she was better off among the dead than the living. He wrote that she was 'the ghost of another race.'"

"Kazuo—"

"Mama," Kazuo again interrupted, this time with the finality of a closing gate.

I could not leave him there, Yakumo. In the hopes of bringing him back to us, back to the country inside, I told him the story of his birth:

You came to us, Kazuo, when Papa and Mama were living in Kumamoto City. The household had grown to ten—the house of Inagaki, the maids, a jinrikisha man, a student houseboy—and we were all waiting for you, the eleventh member of the household, to join us. Papa knelt by my side, holding on to Mama's hands for most of that night. Foster Mother objected to his presence in the room but could not shoo him away.

"Go write, go write," I told him, and reluctantly he listened.

Before he left, he bent down and said to you, a full moon still within me, in Herun-san's language, "Come into this world with good eyes!"

In the first hour of the seventeenth day of November, 1893, the 26th year of Meiji, Lafcadio Hearn—as that was still his name back then—became a new man. Your first cries called him from his writing room, and he came running.

"Papa," I greeted him, as foster Mother lifted the cloth from your old man's face.

"A boy!" she announced.

"A boy," I repeated.

Papa cried.

You cried.

I cried.

Foster Mother laughed at the three of us.

Papa could not stop looking into your eyes, Kazuo, which were a startling blue—seas, Papa called them—which later deepened into your curious grays. Papa thought it fitting that you should have two true names.

Leopoldo, he named you.

Kazuo, I named you.

When the sun rose that morning, Papa was still by your side. "A new day!" he regaled you, kissing you on both cheeks.

Lafcadio Hearn became Koizumi Yakumo for you, Kazuo.

Papa did not know that Iwao, Kiyoshi, and Suzuko would join us in the years to come. He knew only that he had a son now, a continuation of his line, an heir to carry on his name. But if you, Kazuo, became a "Hearn" and a British citizen and Mama along with you, we would no longer be subjects of the country of our births. We would become foreigners within our own land, unable to purchase even the smallest parcel of it or to choose within it where we could call home. We would live only within the open port cities, which Kumamoto City was not. This house of Koizumi, which was then the house of Hearn, was in Kumamoto City because of Papa's position as a teacher within a prefectural-government-run school. Should his services no longer be required, he—and his British son and wife— would no longer have the right to remain there. What would become of that household of eleven, I know, was the question that kept Papa at his desk writing late into the Kumamoto night.

Mama at twenty-five did not know that there was another fear that can take hold of us in the later years of our lives. Papa at forty-three knew that the man he called "Father" had passed from this world at the age of forty-eight. Papa knew that if he, Lafcadio Hearn, were to die without settling this matter of citizenship, his marriage would remain outside the bounds of British and Japanese laws, and thus his estate would pass to his family overseas. The house of Koizumi—the house of his Japanese son and wife—would receive nothing but grief and loss.

It was *your* arrival, Kazuo, that prompted Papa to become a legal subject of Japan. This act spared you, your siblings to come, and Mama of the indignities of renouncing our own citizenships. The process of becoming a citizen, rarely pursued and questioned at every turn, was not completed until the fourteenth day of February, 1896, the 29th year of Meiji, when you were two years old, and Lafcadio Hearn at forty-five was reborn as "Koizumi Yakumo." His new name, a required change, was added to the Koizumi family registry. Papa had followed the only legal path opened to him. He had become an adopted son of a Japanese family in order to become an adopted son of Japan.

This house of Koizumi was in Kōbe by then. We had moved to that open port city when you were almost one year old, so that Papa could write for an English-language newspaper. I had been sending weekly letters to foster Grandfather, who had chosen to return to Matsue to live out his final years, to keep him informed of household matters—though, in truth, it was because he missed Papa, whom he called "the Poet"—and it was foster Grandfather who settled the question of Papa's true name.

I had never considered, Kazuo, how daunting it could be to name oneself until Papa was faced with it. We were all born to a name, our first gift and not our last if we were lucky. Though you did not ask—as Papa never did—I will share with you, Kazuo, that if I were faced with the choice, I would give to myself the "Setsu" of a node of bamboo. The other meanings are heavier stones to carry.

Papa was hesitant to come to a decision, which was a trait that I did not know that he had. Foster Grandfather's "Yakumo," sent from the very province that it honors, was so fitting that Papa could not stop saying it aloud. "Yakumo is a poem in and of itself," Papa marveled. He took you from Mama's arms and paraded you in his own, going through the rooms of the Kōbe house, singing in Herun-san's language and then in English, "Koizumi Kazuo Leopoldo meet Koizumi Yakumo! Koizumi Kazuo Leopoldo meet Koizumi Yakumo!"

Yakumo, your eldest son listened to my story, but I cannot say with certainty that he has forgiven the writer who saw a little girl in a cemetery—Was there even such a being, Yakumo?—and saw for her a fate worse than death. I have done what I can to assure Kazuo that the writer and Papa were no longer the same man.

What I could not tell Kazuo about the story of his birth was that, before his arrival, you had been in misery. When you traveled there, you stayed for days in the nest that your beddings had become. In misery, you refused to allow in sunlight or even a breeze. In misery, you complained of pains in your eye and wore on it, day and night, a cloth soaked in cool water. In misery, you existed on a diet of whiskey, which made you sing to yourself late into the night. What these songs mourned or regretted, I could not tell, because they were in the language of your birth.

Yes, Yakumo, I know. English is not the language of your birth. It is the language of your Father's.

"Mother did not know English," you had told me.

"How did Father and Mother speak?" I asked.

"Father knew some of her languages," you replied, "but it was not enough."

In Herun-san's language, "not enough" and the word "hunger" were one and the same.

As with the lanterns at Matsue Castle and the storm cloud in your left eye, "hunger" made me see them, Yakumo. Your Father and Mother sitting across from each other, their plates half empty, wanting for more.

Perhaps in misery, your songs were in English and other languages as well. They were all foreign to me, Yakumo. When I waited for your return, I slept on the other side of the closed dividers to your room, and there I heard you. "A-e-TE-A" came from your lips most often. When "A-e-TE-A" began your forlorn songs, you could not finish them. Whiskey slurred your words, but "A-e-TE-A" silenced them, Husband.

I have thought about A-e-TE-A in the years since your passing, and I believe it to be a name. I assume that the name belongs to a woman. Alcohol rarely loosens in men the name of an aunt or a grandmother, Yakumo. Was she another Elizabeth? I have looked through Kazuo's English-language notebooks to find an A-e-TE-A. I believe "A" begins the name, but I cannot be sure. I have not found a trace, Yakumo. I have even thought of asking Kazuo to write to your Elizabeth to inquire, but it shames me not to know the letters that form the sounds that form the name that forms the woman whom I believe A-e-TE-A must be. It shames me more that Kazuo would be the first to know, should your Elizabeth send a reply.

I would ask you, Yakumo, but I have no whiskey in this house of Koizumi tonight.

No, Husband, the whiskey would be for me.

Yakumo, during the first and the second tellings of your story, I have found that Kumamoto City and Kōbe have no distinct borders in my memory. Both cities you despised. You accused them of losing themselves to the West. You saw their redbrick buildings as affronts. You disliked the telegraph poles that marred their views. Even the steamboats and the trains that sped us from city to city you found fault in. Too loud, you complained. Too fast, you decried. Your students were dull and sullen. Your fellow teachers preferred beer and cigars to sake and pipes or, worse, were Japanese Christians. You were insulted by the Japanese women in their Western-style dresses and hats. Those horrid heeled boots are ruining their feet, you railed. You cringed when you heard them speaking the English language. You abhorred the modern Japanese, Yakumo, though you were there to educate their sons. You retreated to your Father's language, writing until you fell asleep atop the pages that became your articles and your books.

Yakumo, I could travel with you to Kumamoto City, Kōbe, and soon to Tokyo, but I could not accompany you when you were in misery. It was not language that separated us there, but I did believe that language—the English one—could bring you back when you had been away for too long.

Before Kazuo came to us, I had pleaded with you to teach

me. "English is ugly," you said, "coming from the mouth of a Japanese." You meant the mouth of a Japanese woman, Husband.

Silence was available to us both, Yakumo. At first, you also did not recognize mine as anger. When you did not hear "Pardon me for being the first to sleep" for the first time since the cohabitation, you must have known something was awry. You dismissed it though, as an oversight, an uncharacteristic moment of carelessness that had kept this back turned to yours. Four nights of that back broke yours, Husband. You woke me on the fifth and said, "Sweet Wife, we begin tomorrow."

"Begin what?" I asked, rubbing the eyelids open.

"Begin English," you answered. "Sweet Wife cannot be ugly," you apologized.

I kissed the tops of your hands that night, which made you laugh low, a wiser man of forty-two.

In the months that followed, we sat across from each other for an hour every evening as you said English words aloud to me, repeating them, as I slowly wrote them in my notebook, choosing the katakana and hiragana characters that most closely mimicked their sounds. It was a list of nonsense words to any other Japanese eyes but mine. Setsu's language, you called it. After each entry, I added its meaning in Japanese to remind me what these sounds meant. Before the lesson ended, I would read these "English words" back to you.

We began with the foodstuffs found on the table: "onion, potato, mushroom, bread, salt, sugar."

Then came the objects within the other rooms of the house: "book, paper, hat, dish, saucer, soap, shoe."

Next were the phrases of day-to-day life: "Are you hungry? I have your hat. Have you the paper? I have your sugar. No, I have not. Yes, I have it."

These phrases became less and less useful as the weeks went by: "Have you my old iron gun? No, I have not your old dog. Have you your bad cap? I have the ugly leather shoes."

I repeated them dutifully because I did not want these lessons to stop, which they did once the new moon that would become Kazuo began to wax within me.

When I asked you why you had not taught me the letters of the English alphabet, you explained that first I must learn how to form the sounds of the language with the tongue and mouth before I could learn how to read and write the language, and grammar would come last of all.

When Kazuo was ready to begin his English-language lessons, your teaching practices had thankfully changed. The house of Koizumi was in Tokyo for about a year by then. You, his proud Papa, were the Chair of English Language and Literature at Tokyo Imperial University. "I am a man with no university degree of my own," you had said to me, smiling broadly, before the jinrikisha man took you to the campus for your first lecture, when you were reborn yet again, Yakumo.

Kazuo at four was already speaking like a poet, to borrow the words of foster Grandfather, the three languages of this house of Koizumi: English, Japanese, and Herun-san's. You thought it best that he learn how to read and write English and Japanese at exactly the same time so that one language would not overtake the other or cause undue bias, as he would need both in the years to come. "Kazuo does not look like a Japanese boy," you reminded me, as if I could ever forget his face. "He will be a tall man, the doctor predicts," you said, looking at Kazuo's chubby limbs, imagining them towering over his countrymen one day. "Japanese is his practical language," you declared, "and English is the language of his soul." You would waver on this point in the years to come, assigning to Kazuo's soul a national allegiance that would shift with your own. By the end, you had decided that his soul, like yours, was entirely Japanese.

Either way, you are wrong, Yakumo.

A soul is not limited by language. Language, same as the body, is shed upon our passing. No longer dependent on the vagaries of words—the misplaced, the ill chosen, and the false friends—you are fluent now, Yakumo. I will be as well one day.

No, Yakumo, I did not come to this thought in a book or in an old tale. It is my own, Husband.

Kazuo's daily English-language lessons were in the early mornings before your university classes, which meant that your first pupil of the day was often groggy with sleep and whimpered whenever you lost patience with him. "Lucky boy," I would remind him after you had left. "Papa is a Tokyo Imperial University professor. Only the brightest young men in the country can study with Papa," I told Kazuo.

I needed those lessons to continue, Yakumo, for Kazuo and for me.

Listening at the edge of the room divider, I was teaching myself the alphabet and its sounds. Studying their oversized letters that you wrote on the sheets of old newspapers for Kazuo's benefit, I would teach myself to identify their shapes—"A," the gable roof of a Shintō shrine; "B," a double-lobed gourd;

"C," a comb ornament for the hair—but these letters to my great regret would never join hands and dance for me the way that they would for Kazuo.

Iwao had already joined the house of Koizumi by then but with less fanfare than his elder brother, as the month following Iwao's arrival, the household had been deep in mourning.

Nishida-san at thirty-four had left this world. You were forty-seven, and I was twenty-nine. You wept and berated the gods for being so cruel. You tried to reverse Nishida-san's fate and yours. You pledged aloud to the gods that they could take everything from you, if Nishida-san could live again.

Everything, Yakumo? Even Kazuo and Iwao? I wanted to scream into the Tokyo night.

So this is love, I thought.

I too had felt the loss, Husband. Nishida-san's hand had written the only letter that I had ever received from you. It was a letter of love. Should distance separate the two of us, we were on our own now, no bridge to connect the shores.

I have given thanks and offerings to the gods that they did not hear you, Yakumo, or if they did, they rejected outright your foolish, selfish, sentimental plea.

You resolved to honor Nishida-san by becoming a letter writer yourself. "*I* want to write a letter to you, Sweet Wife," you told me.

"Are you going somewhere?" I asked in jest.

Your reply was a half smile that said "yes" and "no."

You began to sit beside Kazuo when I tutored him in Japanese, determined to learn the fundamentals of hiragana and katakana, which Papa and son both acquired in admirable time. But when Kazuo learned kanji—the first of the thousands of characters with their multiple strokes, each stroke with their prescribed, exact order upon the page—you found them a thick, impenetrable tangle of vines. I assured you that what you had learned was enough, that we would not hunger.

In the remaining years allotted to us, Yakumo, I was grateful for every one of your letters. They did not come from afar or from over the seas, for which I was also grateful. They were only a night train away in Yaizu, the small fishing village that brought you to the shores of the North Pacific Ocean during the month of August when Tokyo steamed, smelled of rotting refuse, and was renamed "Horrid Tokyo" by you. The "summer house of Koizumi," as you often called it, was a set of simple rooms in the house of the fisherman Otokichi. There, Papa, half fish, and Kazuo, one-quarter fish, stayed for a month's worth of daily swims. The summer household grew to include Iwao and even foster Father, before he left for the unseen world. At the tail end of your stay, I arrived with Kiyoshi, once he too joined the house of Koizumi—"We are rich in boys!" you said to me—and, the last August there, I brought Suzuko not even a year old in my arms.

The maids and the student houseboys of the house of Koizumi would come and go with us, in varying combinations, a band of travelers attracting second glances, as the other train passengers attempted to guess our relationships to one another.

In Yaizu, there were no sand-throwing villagers, but there were many who had never seen a cut of beef, a loaf of bread, or a bottle of whiskey. You brought along your own, but you rarely emptied the bottle. "The ocean air, Sweet Wife!" you enthused by way of explanation.

Before your morning meal was when you wrote to me,

Yakumo. Your letters were not the multipage affairs that you penned for America and England, the ones that I, and not Yao or any of the other maids, had delivered to the post offices of Matsue, Kumamoto City, Kōbe, and Tokyo in order to assure you that they would begin their long journey with due care. When this task first became a part of my daily routine, I wondered what had happened that week in Herun-san's life. I looked at those thick envelopes and imagined who had passed away or married or given birth. I could not believe that the matters of your everyday life would require so many pages to document and to relay.

Yakumo, the letters that you wrote to me were less than a page, sometimes as brief as two or three sentences: "Weather is good. Kazuo studies well. No other news."

In Yaizu, your pen found other ways to express itself that made this reader laugh out loud. A sleepy-eyed snail drawn at one corner, a scrawny duck at another, a Tani-no-oto toad, a coiled snake, and a straggly blackbird lived on these pages too. Once, there was even a Jizō statue, weeping pebble tears. These little bodies, offering themselves as comical asides, interrupted your wobbly rows of hiragana and katakana. These letters—their Herun-san's language, their childlike drawings, their keen desires to see this plain face again—could not have been written by any other man, Yakumo.

Your August letters were delivered to the Tomihisachō quarter at the western fringe of Tokyo, where the house of Koizumi, upon its arrival in this city, had been growing in numbers, under the eaves of yet another rented dwelling. How I rejoiced when your letters arrived at *this* house instead, Yakumo.

"According to the maps, the house is in Ōkubo village, just west of Tokyo's city lines," I had told you when I first found this property. "It is small and will need more rooms added, but the gardens are old and established. They have seen life, as you say, Husband. There is a bamboo grove at the back, and, Husband, I heard a bush warbler singing there."

Do you remember your response, Yakumo?

"Do you have money?" you asked, not looking up from the page that you were writing.

"Yes," I replied, hard and sharp, not echoing the playful tone of your question.

You looked up and saw a plain woman's face staring back at you, and you saw in those straight lines a warning that you should put down your pen and listen.

"Good!" you said, "Tell me more, Sweet Wife."

"Husband, all the houses in the village are in the old style. There are no Western buildings there yet," I said.

You nodded your head, and soon the decision to purchase this house was made.

But once the work on this Ōkubo house began, you did not want to hear anything more about it. You claimed that you only knew "a little about writing," and everything else was my domain. Your only two requests were for a writing room where your high desk and chair could face toward the west, your favored direction, and for a heating stove to be installed therein. I made certain that the writing room, to be constructed as part of the new wing, would be situated far from the front door and away from the boys' rooms. I asked the builders to fit your writing room with clear glass, in addition to the shōji, so that the colder months would never again cause you discomfort,

Yakumo. The room, I knew, also had to be "cozy." I suggested that a Western rug, which you said was called an "Oriental" rug, could be placed atop the tatami to achieve the desired effect, but you rejected the idea outright. The rug is here now, Yakumo, and it is cozy as I thought it would be. I inquired about the cost of building more bookshelves, which I told the builders should be confined to the writing room, as the rest of the house would remain in the Japanese style. At first, the builders wanted to hear these instructions from the master of the house. These men were afraid that I had no mind of my own or, if I did, I would change it. You refused to visit this house until the work was completed, Yakumo. "A waste of time," you dismissed, with a wave of your hand and a kiss on both of these cheeks. So, these men, all of them, had to adapt and to obey this woman's every word or not be paid.

On moving day, you left for Tokyo Imperial University from the Tomihisachō house, and the household's jinrikisha man had been instructed by me to take you at the end of your teaching day to this Ōkubo house, where everything was already in its place.

You met for the first time the gardener who had remained with the property, and you gave him two young musa basjoo plants to add to the grounds. They were the only indications that you had been aware that a change of residence was taking place that day. "Wherever there is the most sunlight," you wanted the gardener to know and I told him. "Their glossy leaves bring to mind the plantain trees of the West Indies," you explained and I conveyed. The gardener nodded his head, but did not ask where the West Indies was in the world. His thoughts, as they should have been, were focused on where these plants would grow best in this corner of Ōkubo, Yakumo. The next morning, I asked the gardener whether these plants, once they matured, would bear fruit. "Yes, but they cannot be eaten," he replied. "Bitter and full of tiny seeds."

"Impractical," I said and gave him the permission to find a place for them anyway. In a sunburned corner of the garden, which you would name "the West Indies," the gardener planted the musa basjoo, which have yet to bear their fruits, Yakumo.

Within months, I would find you in the West Indies, weeping.

"All gone," you said. Your words did not seem to believe their own claim.

"What is gone?" I asked, worried that the gardener had taken away one of your beloved plants.

"Saint-Pierre, Sweet Wife. A city of twenty-eight thousand souls."

"An earthquake? A fire?" I asked.

"A volcano," you replied, your legs giving way. You knelt on the pebbled path and continued to weep.

"Husband, the boys will hear. They will be frightened, if Papa cries," I whispered.

The West Indies, you had told me early in the cohabitation, was a grouping of islands on the other side of the world, where you had lived on the island of Martinique, in the city of Saint-Pierre, during the years prior to Japan. You showed me two books that you had written there. You turned their pages slowly, reluctant to leave their words behind. With hand gestures and *Dictionary* words, you told me that the garden snakes in Matsue were not the same as those in the West Indies, where these creatures, convivial and less aloof, would crawl onto your arm and bathe there with you in the heat of the tropical sun. When you saw the sun, setting ablaze the waters of Lake Shinji and the Ōhashi River, you bemoaned that a sunset in Matsue was not the same as those in the West Indies.

I did not believe you, Yakumo.

I, in truth, stopped listening to you when you engaged in these comparisons, so I do not remember now what had separated the two suns. Why does the New Foreign Teacher travel, if what he longs for is a place where he has already been, I asked myself. Sameness is not possible, I remember thinking. So why seek it? I wondered.

Yet for this Ōkubo house, I had instructed the builders that the new and old wings needed to look exactly the same. The halves needed to appear as if they were part of a whole, I told them. The builders questioned why the rashamen did not want an entirely new Western-style house for her foreigner. They never dared to ask this in front of me because I, as far as their wages were concerned, was the master of this Ōkubo house. They nodded their heads and complied when I specified that the eaves of both wings, should be wide and generous. As deep as the eaves of the houses in the shadows of Matsue Castle, I could have said but did not because none of these men had been to isolated Izumo Province. Many of the details that I wanted for this Ōkubo house were taken from those rented in Matsue, Kumamoto City, and Kōbe or from the long list of inns where we had once stayed. This desire—not for sameness but for a reminder of where we had been—was triggered by travel or, rather, from having traveled. I regretted that Setsu at twenty-two had no understanding and little compassion for the New

Foreign Teacher, who at forty had already circumnavigated the globe, his heart an atlas of such longings.

To your West Indies, the gardener later added at your behest a grouping of rare agave plants that you brought back from Yaizu, their long silver-gray leaves—the boys called them "swords"—looking as if they were covered in a fine layer of dust. The agaves, I knew, were your memorial to the lost city, Yakumo. The destruction of Saint-Pierre—I could not have known—was a harbinger of the losses that were to come.

In the months that followed, you were often elsewhere but not in the usual manner. You awoke early and wrote letters, more than you had in recent years. At the morning meal, you regaled Kazuo, eight years of age, about your years at boarding schools, years that you despised, you had told me. Young boys are animals, you had said, pointing at your storm-cloud eye. If Kazuo failed to show interest, you scolded him for his "mosquito" voice. If he listened intently, you slapped him on the back and encouraged him to have seconds of his toasts and soft eggs so that he would grow even taller. If you noticed that Iwao, Kiyoshi, and I were listening to your every word, you switched from Herun-san's language to English. At midday, you whistled in the West Indies. In the late afternoon, you skipped with the boys along the eaves of this Ōkubo house. The hours of sleep you found unnecessary and wrote even longer into the Tokyo night.

You were in this elsewhere, Yakumo, because you had given your last lecture at Tokyo Imperial University.

Teizaburō, the translator, still bristles with anger over your treatment. "How could the most prestigious university in Japan have severed its connection to the most distinguished Western writer of Japan?" your former student posed to Shigeyuki, the scribe, the last time they were both here at this Ōkubo house.

"Money," Shigeyuki replied, his one-word answer uncharacteristically blunt. "The replacement, Sōseki Natsume, was hired as a lecturer for a fraction of Herun-sensei's salary. Even we at the sleepy Institute had heard about the outrage."

"Ah, not for long, not for long," Teizaburō assured him. "The rumor is that Sōseki will ask for a pay raise or leave altogether. Who would have imagined that he would make a name for himself by writing a novel in the voice of a cat? Absurd and a fad is what I say, but he has published five more books since, each better received than the last. I, frankly, am astonished."

"What would Herun-sensei think about this Sōseki?" Shigeyuki asked.

Neither had an answer. I think you would have liked the cat, Yakumo.

Without the university professorship, you no longer had a reason to go beyond the Ōkubo garden gate. Koizumi Yakumo at fifty-three sought refuge in the country inside. From your writing room, you looked westward, back toward the far shores of your youth, exhausted by the waves that had carried you away.

Pride had left your body, Yakumo. As with the men of the house of Koizumi before you, this was the same as your spirit departing. When pride had left Setsu at twenty-three, when it rose up and coiled toward the Matsue sky, the body that remained was no longer tied to the land, a winged maple seed afloat. For you, Yakumo, the body that remained was a husk, separated from the grain, weightless. Your back stooped. Your hair snowed. Your gait slowed. Your eye twitched. Your cheeks hollowed. Your mouth filled with blood. A burst blood vessel, Dr. Kizawa, the family doctor reported. Your voice silenced for months. Your daily walks lost to you as well.

The heart that belongs to Suzuko was already within this body by then, but the roundness of her was not yet visible to your eye, Yakumo. A fourth Koizumi, even if a son, no longer seemed a reason for celebration. But when Suzuko joined the household later that autumn, you held her in your arms and called her "Aba, Aba," kissing her on both cheeks.

Foster Mother and I looked at each other, but we both held our tongues. Later, with Suzuko asleep in her arms, foster Mother worried that the misfortune could not be undone.

"It was Kazuo's first word," I reminded foster Mother.

"Yes, but——" she began.

"Iwao's and Kiyoshi's too," I added.

"It was probably every baby's first word in this country," she said. "You know that is not why I worry."

"Herun-san is only giving Suzuko a suggestion, an early tutorial," I assured her. "He cannot help but to teach——"

"Saying 'Aba' *to* a newborn is not a lesson," she objected.

Foster Mother was right, Yakumo. Saying goodbye, even if it was in the singsong prattle of babies, is a self-inflicted curse.

"Herun-san has no plans to travel," I said to foster Mother, choosing the image for the end of life that seemed most fitting for you, Yakumo.

I doubted foster Mother even more after you made your announcement. She had worried needlessly, I assured myself.

"Waseda University, Sweet Wife!" you declared at the beginning of 1904, the 37th year of Meiji. Your voice was rid of its waver, a moth that had lived inside your throat for months.

"You have good news, Husband?" I asked.

"Yes, good and new!" you answered.

"Tell me, Husband."

"Only four hours a week, two lectures on English literature every Wednesday and Saturday, *and* the Waseda's campus is closer to Ōkubo by jinrikisha."

"It is very good news, Husband!"

"The dean of Waseda looks like Nishida-san. A good omen. I will invite him to the house, and you will see, Sweet Wife!"

Suzuko, babbling in these arms, decided at that moment to offer you her first word, the same one chosen by her three brothers. We both heard her, Yakumo. You rejoiced, repeating "Aba, Aba" back to her, believing your lessons had resulted in an unqualified success. "Little Suzuko knows her name," you cooed.

I was silent as Papa and daughter blithely bid each other, "Goodbye, Goodbye."

When August arrived, you, Kazuo, and Iwao boarded the train to Yaizu. The evening before, you and the boys sang for Kiyoshi, Suzuko, and me a rousing rendition of the national anthem, which you proudly had taught to all of the children when the war had begun earlier that year. Kazuo and Iwao, each with their agave-leaf sword, marched around the room, saluting you in turn. You called them brave and bold like their countrymen who were at war.

"Japan is coming into its own," you said to me. "Neither the West nor the East can threaten our nation," you declared.

Japan was again at war with a foreign enemy. First, China was our enemy. This time it was Russia. As with the Koizumi men before you, you found meaning in war. You looked at the list of battles, the ships lost, and the territory won, and you saw the character of a man, of a nation, and of a generation. I did not, Yakumo. I looked at Kazuo at ten, Iwao at seven, and Kiyoshi at four, and I feared for the wars that would come for them.

I took Kazuo aside that evening and asked him to write to Mama every day. "Do not let Papa see," I began. "Let it be a surprise when I show him at the end of the month how diligent you have been at practicing your Japanese characters, Kazuo. Tell Mama, if Papa is tired or crossed. Tell Mama, if he does not finish his meals. Tell Mama, if he is restless at night or sleeps late into the morning," I instructed. Kazuo nodded his head, his serious face intent on fulfilling what was being asked of him. I looked at him and wished that he were older. Children should not have to care for their parents, I knew.

These worries soon subsided, as every day I received not one but two letters, one from Kazuo and the other from you.

You wrote at sunrise, "I miss you. I wish I could see your face now. Do I still have to wait?"

Nishida-san could not have written a finer letter, Husband.

You had been eager for Yaizu, but you were just as eager to return to Tokyo. You had asked me to order a new haori and hakama for you to wear at your first lecture. The older Waseda professors did not wear Western suits, and this, you felt, gave you permission to discard yours as well. "I am old enough now," you claimed. You meant that you are Japanese enough now, Yakumo.

You would return from that campus with your hands on your chest, tugging at the cloth of your haori. I wanted to send the household's jinrikisha man to Dr. Kizawa's house, but you refused. You insisted that a pour of whiskey would make the pain go away. It did, until a week later when it returned with a force that made you nod your head in agreement when I again insisted on summoning the family doctor to this Ōkubo house.

"A new kind of sickness," you told Dr. Kizawa in Herun-san's language, which I repeated to him in Japanese. You were still seated at your high desk, attempting to write a letter, when he arrived. "Sickness of the heart," you diagnosed, without looking up at the doctor's face. Dr. Kizawa enjoyed your company, in health and in sickness, Yakumo, and did not take offense. He asked about your Waseda students and suggested that *they* were the source of your discomfort. I repeated his joke to you, and you smiled and raised your eye to greet his. He asked you to lie down on the tatami, and he listened to your heart. He listened for a long while. I had the urge to push him aside and listen to it too. Dr. Kizawa looked up at me and said that the cherry tree, outside your writing room, was in full bloom. You heard "sakura" and understood the subject of his remarks. You and I looked out of the windows. We had not even noticed them, Yakumo.

"Snowing," you said.

"Snowing," I repeated.

Dr. Kizawa left instructions for you to rest, eat a light meal of broth and soft tofu, and to halt your teaching for a month or two. To me, he said to send for him immediately once the pain returns.

"Returns?" I asked, as I walked with him to the front door.

"Yes," he replied, his face showing me what he had hidden from you.

Death is the ending to all of our stories, Yakumo, and yet its arrival can still manage to surprise and unsettle, like a child's cry in the forest.

Seven days later, on the twenty-sixth day of September, 1904, the 37th year of Meiji, you awoke at six thirty in the morning, earlier than usual, to birdsongs rising from the bamboo grove. I helped you dress in your yukata and tabi, and you took your morning meal in the writing room. As you sipped your bowl of broth, you told me that last night you had dreamed of a faraway place. It was not a country where you had been before, but it was familiar to you all the same. There were blackbirds there, the sky dotted with them, as if they were gathering. Perhaps you had followed them to that place or they had followed you. You were on a mountainside, green with low trees, the underside of their leaves flickering silver, flowers wild with the color of morning light, nearby an unseen sea. You said that the breezes there carried with them the scent of butter, thyme, and honey. You closed your eye and took in a deep breath, as if these scents were here in Ōkubo.

I breathed in as well. I smelled only bread toasting.

Kazuo and Iwao were at the table for their morning meal, waiting to see whether Papa would join them that day. Foster Mother encouraged them to begin without you, and they did, taking heart in her suggestion that, perhaps, Papa will join them tomorrow. Kazuo then came to the writing room to wish you "Good morning, Papa," before he and Iwao headed to school.

"Pleasant dreams. The same to you," you replied and kissed Kazuo on both cheeks, as if he were Suzuko or me. He pulled away from such an open show of affection, and he looked over at me to explain your words and your action. I had nothing to offer him, except to signal with the eyes that it was time for him to go.

You spent the day in your writing room, looking out at the garden. The cherry blossoms had dropped their petals overnight, transforming a small patch of Ōkubo into a silver world. You asked me to walk with you out to the West Indies.

"Tomorrow, Husband," I replied.

"Yes, tomorrow," you agreed. "It is too cold today, Sweet Wife."

It was not, Yakumo. I shivered all the same.

You joined us at the evening meal, your first with the children since Dr. Kizawa's visit. You pushed away your supper, uneaten, and asked for a small glass of whiskey instead. "With water, if you must, Sweet Wife," you said. You laughed, like a boy of ten and not a man of fifty-four, at Kazuo's stories about his classmates and their efforts to learn the game of cricket. Iwao wanted to entertain you too, but his story got him a mild scolding instead, as it was about his teacher who had mocked a student for stuttering. "A monster!" you cursed Iwao's teacher. Kiyoshi climbed onto your lap, like an overgrown house cat. Suzuko contributed to the conversation by repeating her first and most favored word, until foster Mother hastened her away.

"Pleasant dreams, Papa," the boys said to you, as I helped you to your feet.

You wanted an hour alone in your writing room, before you turned in for the night. "I want to write a letter," you explained.

"But I am right here, Husband," I teased.

"You are, Sweet Wife, you are," you replied, smiling.

Yakumo, when I returned to check on your progress, you were slumped over your high desk. The piece of paper in front of you was blank, not yet touched by the nib of your pen. "The sickness is back," you whispered, your face an apology.

Upon arriving at the house of Koizumi, Dr. Kizawa had nothing to listen to. Your heart had joined your spirit, Yakumo.

Your body became ash and bones, and their destination was Zōshigaya Cemetery, which will be mine as well. We will call that village of the dead the last shared country. We will wait there for many years, if the gods are merciful, before the children will join us, one by one.

Until then, Yakumo, your memory lives with me here in this Ōkubo house.

I have kept all of your letters, even that final pristine sheet. I tell myself that I was its intended recipient, that "Setsu" was the name on the tip of your pen. I will lock the letters away until there is no one left who is fluent in Herun-san's language, until what is lost will render your words and mine immune to judgment and ridicule. How many generations will it take, Yakumo?

The pages of this second telling will keep your letters company. I must learn from your example, Yakumo. What was once fact—because you alone claimed it to be—can lose its lacquer, chip and blister over time. What was once opinion—or the echo of the prevailing winds—can take on the weight of conviction. What was a matter of taste can reveal a lifetime of foibles and faults. What was a term of affection can disclose a failing of character. What was love can be read as mere proximity.

Rest assured, Husband, the third telling of how Lafcadio Hearn became Koizumi Yakumo will withstand Kazuo's scrutiny, Iwao's, Kiyoshi's, Suzuko's, and their children's and their children's children. It will go into the world as the *Reminiscences of Lafcadio Hearn* by Koizumi Setsu and feed the houses of Koizumi and Inagaki, my aim since the age of twelve.

These pages that I have shown you tonight, Yakumo, they are still weak with truths. I will shore them up by removing more bones.

ELIZABETH BISLAND

(1861–1929)

. . . .

NEW YORK, 1906

It was while Lafcadio was living in the house by the Ōhashi bridge that he married, in January, 1891, Setsu Koizumi, a lady of high samurai rank. The revolution in Japan which overthrew the power of the Shōguns and restored the Mikado to temporal power had broken the feudal structure of Japanese society, and with the downfall of the daimyōs . . . fell the lesser nobility, the samurai, or "two-sworded" men. Many of these sank into as great poverty as that which befel [sic] the émigrés after the French Revolution, and among those whose fortunes were entirely ruined were the Koizumis. Sentarō Nishida, who appears to have been a sort of head master of the Jinjō-chūgakkō, in special charge of the English department, was of one of the lesser samurai families, his mother having been an intimate of the Koizumi household before the decline of their fortunes. Because of his fluency in English, as well as because of what seems to have been a peculiar sweetness and dignity of character, he soon became the interpreter and special friend of the new English teacher. It was through his mediation that the marriage was arranged. Under ordinary circumstances a Japanese woman of rank would consider an alliance with a foreigner an inexpugnable disgrace; but the circumstances of the Koizumis were not ordinary, and whatever may have been the secret feelings of the girl of twenty-two, it is certain that she immediately became passionately attached to her husband, and the marriage continued to the end to be a very happy one. It was celebrated by the local rites, as to have married according to English laws, under the then existing treaties, would have deprived her of her Japanese citizenship and obliged them to remove to one of the open ports; but the question of the legality of the marriage and of her future troubled Hearn from the beginning, and finally obliged him to renounce his English allegiance and become a subject of the Mikado in order that she and her children might never suffer from any complications or doubts as to their position. This could only be achieved by his adoption into his wife's family. He took their name, Koizumi, which signifies "Little Spring," and for personal title chose the classical term for Izumo province, Yakumo, meaning "Eight Clouds"—or "the place of the issuing clouds"—and also being the first word of the oldest known Japanese poem.

· · · ·

In . . . [a former samurai's] house, surrounded with beautiful gardens, and lying under the very shadow of the ruined Daimyō castle, Hearn and his wife passed a very happy year. The rent was four dollars a month; his salaries from the middle and normal schools, added to what he earned with his pen, made him for the first time in his life easy about money matters. He was extremely popular with all classes, from the governor to the barber; the charm and wonder of the life about him was still unstaled by usage, and he found himself at last able to achieve some of that beauty and force of style for which he had so long laboured. He even found pleasure in the fact that most of his friends were of no greater stature than himself. It seems to have been in every way the happiest portion of his life.

· · · ·

Unfortunately this idyllic interval was cut short by ill health. The cold Siberian winds that pass across Izumo in winter seriously affected his lungs, and the little hibachi, or box of burning charcoal, which was the only means in use of warming Japanese houses, could not protect sufficiently one who had lived so long in warm climates. Oddly too, cold always affected his eyesight injuriously, and very reluctantly, but under the urgent advice of his doctor, he sought employment in a warmer region and was transferred to . . . the great Government College, at Kumamoto, situated near the southern end of the Inland Sea. . . .

Matsue was old Japan. Kumamoto represented the far less pleasing Japan in the stage of transition. Here Hearn remained for three years, and at the expiration of his engagement abandoned the Government service and returned to journalism for a while. Living was far more expensive, the official and social atmosphere of Kumamoto was repugnant to him, and he fell back into the old solitary, retiring habits of earlier days—finding his friends among children and folk of the humbler classes. . . .

It was in Kumamoto that Hearn first began to perceive the fierceness and sternness of the Japanese character. . . . Such characteristics, however he might respect or understand them, were always antipathetic to his nature, and his relations with the members of the school were for the most part formal. He mentions that the students rarely called upon him, and that he saw his fellow teachers only in school hours. . . .

The constant change in the personnel of the teaching force of the college, and many annoyances to which he was subjected, caused his decision at the end of the three years' term to remove to Kōbe and enter the service of the Kōbe Chronicle. . . .

Kōbe was at that time, 1895, an open port, that is to say, one of the places in which foreigners were allowed to reside without special government permission, and under the extra-territorial rule of their own consuls. Of Hearn's external life here there seems to be scant record. He worked as one of the staff of the Chronicle,—his editorials frequently bringing upon him the wrath of the missionaries,—he contributed some letters to the McClure Syndicate, and there was much talk of a projected expedition, in search of material for such work, to the Philippines or the Loo Choo Island; a project never realized. The journalistic work seriously affected his eyes, and his health seems to have been poor at times. He made few acquaintances and had almost no companions outside of his own household. . . .

. . . .

I think it was at Kōbe he reached his fullest intellectual stature. None of the work that followed in the next eight years surpassed the results he there achieved, and much was of lesser value, despite its beauty. He had attained to complete mastery of his medium, and had moreover learned completely to master his thought before clothing it in words— a far more difficult and more important matter.

. . . .

[I]t was plain that literature and journalism would not suffice to sustain a family of thirteen persons. For Hearn in becoming a Japanese subject had accepted the Japanese duty of maintaining the elder members of the family into which he had been adopted. . . . He referred to the fact occasionally with amused impatience, but seems never to have really resented or rebelled against the filial duties which to the Western point of view might appear excessive. His eyes, too, began to give warnings that could not be ignored, and with reluctance he yielded to the necessity of earning a larger income by reëntering the Government service as a teacher. Professor [Basil Hall] Chamberlain again came to his aid and secured for him the position of Professor of English in the

Imperial University of Tōkyō, where his salary was large compared to anything he had as yet received, and where he was permitted an admirable liberty as to methods of teaching.

. . . .

[Hearn's] life outside of the university and of his own home he narrowed down to a point where the public began to create legends about him, so seldom was he seen. The only person ever able to draw him forth was his friend Mitchell McDonald, whose sympathy and hospitality he constantly fled from and constantly yielded to. . . .

Under the strain of constant work his eyesight again began to fail, and in 1902 he wrote to friends in America asking for aid to find work there, desiring to consult a specialist, and to bring for instruction in English his beloved Kazuo—from whom he would never be parted for a day. He was entitled to his sabbatical year of vacation from the university, and while he took advantage of it he wished to form other connections, as intrigues among those inimical to him made him fear for the tenure of his position. . . . An arrangement was made for him to lecture for a season in Cornell University at a salary of $2500, and these lectures he at once began to prepare. When, however, he applied for leave it was refused him. . . . [C]onvinced that it was intended as a slight by the authorities in their purpose to be rid of him, he resigned. . . .

He plunged more deeply, at once, into the preparation of his work for the American lectures, but shortly before he was to have sailed for America the authorities at Cornell withdrew from their contract on the plea that the epidemic of typhoid at Ithaca the previous summer had depleted the funds at their command.

Vigorous efforts were at once undertaken by his friends in America to repair this breach of contract by finding him employment elsewhere, with but partial success, but all these efforts were rendered useless by a sudden and violent illness, attended by bleeding from the lungs, and brought on by strain and anxiety. After his recovery the lectures prepared for Cornell were recast to form a book, but the work proved a desperate strain upon already weakened forces. . . .

To me he wrote . . . "I don't like the work of writing a serious treatise on sociology. . . . [ellipsis in the original] I ought to keep to the study of birds and cats and insects and flowers, and queer small things—and leave the subject of the destiny of empires to men with brains." Despite which verdict he probably recognized it as the crowning achievement of his long effort to interpret his adopted country to the world.

Shortly after its completion he accepted the offer of the chair of English in the Waseda University. . . . Meantime the University of London had entered into negotiation with him for a series of lectures, and it was suggested that Oxford also wished to hear him. It had always been the warmest of his desires to win recognition from his own country, and these offers were perhaps the greatest satisfaction he had ever known. But his forces were completely exhausted. The desperate hardships of his youth, the immense labours of his manhood, had burned away the sources of vitality.

On the 26th of September, 1904—shortly after completing . . . [a] last letter . . . —while walking on the veranda in the twilight he sank down suddenly as if the whole fabric of life had crumbled within, and after a little space of speechlessness and pain, his long quest was over. . . .

Acknowledgments

This novel was a journey—eight years from start to end—that began with a Sea Change Residency (Provincetown, Rhode Island), a generous gift of the Gaea Foundation that gave me not only a room of my own but an entire house for two precious months in March and April of 2010. There, as the Atlantic Ocean crashed and howled, I heard clearly the first line of this novel. Water and wind, I knew, would be the leitmotifs of the story that I wanted to write.

The following year, a Guggenheim Fellowship afforded me travel to the island of Lefkada, Greece, where I took into my lungs the scent of the Ionian Sea and of ginestra in full bloom, two blessings of Lafcadio Hearn's island of birth that he never experienced as an adult. I thanked him on the slope of Stavrota, the mountain rising from the middle of Lefkada, for taking me there. Hearn said you're welcome and told me that my journey was far from over. He was right.

Along the way and during the years that followed, I found temporary creative homes, each welcoming in their own invaluable way, at the Liguria Study Center for the Arts and Humanities (Bogliasco, Italy); Helsinki Collegium for Advanced Studies (Helsinki, Finland) as a visiting fiction writer; PowderKeg (Brooklyn, New York); Civitella Ranieri Foundation (Umbertide, Italy); Akrai Residency (Palazzolo Acreide, Sicily, Italy); U.S.-Japan Creative Artists Fellowship (Tokyo, Japan); Agnes Scott College (Decatur, Georgia) as the Kirk Writer-in-Residence; Baruch College (New York City) as the Harman Writer-in-Residence; Hedgebrook (Whidbey Island, Washington); Accademia

Acknowledgments

Tedesca Villa Massimo (Rome, Italy); and Djerassi Resident Artists Program (Woodside, California). It was at Djerassi, perched in the Santa Cruz mountainside with the Pacific Ocean a blue fringe on the horizon, that I wrote the last line of the novel in May of 2018. This time I thanked not only Hearn but the women whom he had introduced me to: Rosa Antonia Cassimati, Alethea Foley, Koizumi Setsu, and his first biographer, Elizabeth Bisland. They kept his secrets and theirs so close. They divulged so little. They made me work for every word. It has been an honor to be in their company. I miss them already.

I owe the deepest of thanks to the following for helping me to keep the lights on in my own home as I wandered and wrote: the American Academy of Arts and Letters Rosenthal Family Foundation Award, Janet Silver, Leslie Shipman, Martin Hielscher at Verlag C.H. Beck, and Paul Slovak at Viking Penguin.

The journey was not a straightforward one, and it took me to unexpected, unrelated-to-Hearn locales such as Helsinki, where, for three months in 2012, I learned to breathe deeply again, read for pleasure again, and found the will to write again. I am grateful for the friends in that serene city by the Baltic Sea: Martti-Tapio Kuuskoski, Outi J. Hakola, Laura Lindstedt and the Lindstedt family in Sotkamo, Donna McCormack, Kay Edwards, José Filipe Silva, Simon Rabinovitch, Taavi Sundell, Antti Sadinmaa, Maijastina Kahlos, Jin Haritaworn, Elisabeth L. Engebretsen, Marja Utela (and to Annabel Fan for the e-introduction to Marja), and in particular to Oanh Pham, who gave me a glimpse of life at the far northern end of the Vietnamese diaspora.

I am indebted to Michiko Boyer, who patiently tutored me in Japanese before I left Brooklyn for Tokyo in 2015 (she knew exactly the vocabulary I would need: *daigaku*, *eki*, and *konbini*); Sawako Nakayasu and Manami Maeda at the International House of Japan in Tokyo, who with care and warmth administered the U.S.-Japan Creative Artists Fellowship program; Fukuko Kobayashi and Issei Wake for generously helping me to secure housing at Waseda University; and

Acknowledgments

Kobayashi-sensei for traveling with me to Matsue, where I "met" at the Lafcadio Hearn Memorial Museum a Koizumi Setsu who, at last, made perfect sense to me.

I also raise a glass, again and again, to the following intrepid denizens of Tokyo for the kindness and generosity that they showed to this sojourner who would have been lonely and lost—well, even more lost—during her three months in their beautiful maze of a city without their convivial company: Yoshiko Hayashi (and to Andrea Louie for the e-introduction to Yoshiko); Mariko Nagai; Jon Wu; Jeff Kingston; Machiko Osawa; Leza Lowitz; Roberto Mollá (who was in Valencia, Spain, but in Tokyo in spirit) for the e-introductions to Tomohiko and Tamoko Matsumoto, Francisco Silva, Yumi Uemura, and Makiko Hamabc; my fellow U.S.-Japan Fellow Paul Kikuchi for the face-to-face introductions to Yuki Takabe (now Yuki Ishida), Yukie Higuchi, and Noriko Iwanaga; and Mayumo Inoue, who wonderfully e-introduced himself and introduced me to Kaori Nakasone.

The end of my stay in Japan was made complete by an invitation by professor Kyoko Yoshida to speak at Ritsumeikan University in Kyoto, where I had the honor of meeting Shigemi Nakagawa, Masahiko Nishi, Riyo Niimoto, Yuki Matsumoto, Keiko Shimojo, Hitomi Nakamura, and Raphaël Lambert.

A historical novelist is always time traveling, and her best and truest companions are historians and research librarians. The following have gone above and beyond: Thomas Boardman, the library director of Temple University–Japan Campus; at the Public Library of Cincinnati and Hamilton County's Information and Reference Department: Tom Moosbrugger (reference librarian), Alex Temple (senior library services assistant), Keith Good (senior library services assistant), and Stephen Headley (reference librarian), who found the date of death for Alethea Foley, an important fact that I had not seen in any of the secondary sources that I had consulted; and Yoji Hasegawa, a historian, an author, and a literary translator, whose book *A Walk in Kumamoto: The Life and Times of Setsu Koizumi—Lafcadio Hearn's Japanese Wife*

Acknowledgments

(Global Oriental, 1997), introduced me to a fully documented woman. Within the pages of Hasegawa's book there was another invaluable gift, his English translation of Koizumi Setsu's 1918 memoir, *Reminiscences of Lafcadio Hearn*.

The following dear friends read the various first drafts of this novel, and they deserve not only recognition but a medal because they waded through a morass of typos, misplaced modifiers, and grammatical errors that only an English-as-a-second-language writer could make, not to mention the camouflaged plot lines, character underdevelopments, and a narrative chronology that refused linearity at every turn: Barbara Tran, David L. Eng, Jeff Kingston, Kyoko Yoshida, Alan Brown, Lizzie Skurnick, Shelley Salamensky, and Jeffrey Angles.

Thanks also to illustrator extraordinaire Yuko Shimizu for seeing between the lines of this novel a bird's nest adrift on the sea and bringing that arresting image to the cover design, and to photographer Haruka Sakaguchi, who presented me with a photograph that made me feel truly seen.

I save the very last lines for Damijan Saccio, because without him there would not be a first line. We have been each other's companions at home and abroad for twenty-nine years. Long ago I gave him a postcard of Elliott Erwitt's 1963 black-and-white photograph of three women waiting next to a "Lost Persons Area" sign, and I wrote on the back of the postcard that without him I would be *there*. I meant it. I still do.